STEALING THE ALPHA

THE COMPLETE SERIES

KATE RUDOLPH

COPYRIGHT

THE ALPHA HEIST

1

The job went tits up sometime after Mel grabbed the flash drive from the vault. And vault was a highly overrated term for that sorry excuse for an executive safe. This whole thing should have been much harder. From what she could tell, the company was run by a bunch of scientists without a thought in their heads for real security.

All the better for her.

Even better still, the laughable security made it a one man – or woman – job. More money for her, and fewer people liable to fuck something up. Just as she liked it. While she was sprinting down the final corridor of the building, she didn't let herself think about how Krista and Bob might have made it a bit easier for her. She was perfectly capable of working alone, and had been for a while.

The barking of the dogs preceded the clomping footsteps of the security guards. Mel could outrun the guards, no problem. The dogs were another issue. She hoped they didn't catch up. She had sharper fangs and much nastier claws, but violence against the innocent had never been her go to. She'd do it if necessary, but the animals didn't deserve it.

What the hell had tripped that damn alarm?

She slammed through the double doors, barely feeling the impact before she sprinted through the parking lot, the only light coming from the feeble streetlights. Mel would have been kicking herself if she could spare the energy. Her car was nearly a mile away. There was no reason she should have needed to sprint the distance. She was sure she hadn't tripped any alarms.

And yet here she was, running her ass off to flee the scene.

But, fine, she'd do it. The only other choice was to be captured by idiot humans and their pets. Or to kill them all. Neither option appealed, so the sprint it was. She cleared the parking lot and made it to the grass of the small woodland bordering the office. This park claimed to integrate itself seamlessly into nature to provide a healthier habitat for the employees. Mel had yet to see a corporate building successfully blend in with nature, and this research facility was no different.

Crickets chirped and nocturnal creatures dove for cover as she passed them. They would have done so if she were just a regular person, but adding to their confusion was her scent which must have scared them all the more. The half-moon hung high overhead, giving her more than enough dappled light to navigate through the copse of trees.

While she could see clearly, the security guards couldn't. She could still hear them, but their running had slowed. And so had the dogs. Good.

After she ran a few more yards silence engulfed her. The woods looked the same, but all sound vanished. Mel looked behind her and saw the faintest shimmering of the air. She lifted up her hand slowly and pushed out. The air resisted.

A ward.

She could have pushed all the way through; this wasn't meant to keep her prisoner. But her curiosity got the better of her. "Show yourself, witch." She let the menace lace her voice. It wasn't quite a snarl.

A woman stepped out of the shadows. "Is that really how you're going to address me, Mellie?" She looked somewhere around forty, though Mel had never learned her exact age. Anyone with magic could cast a glamor and appear however old they wanted. Looks meant nothing when a person might be thirty or three hundred. The woman wore black pants and a dark gray top, all the better to fit in so late at night. Her only jewelry was a pair of simple diamond earrings nearly obscured by dark brown hair that hung past her shoulders.

And now some things fell into place. "Hello, Tina. Did you trip the alarm?" She was surprised at her own scorn, she'd long been used to Tina's antics.

Tina laughed, a full-throated affair that would have echoed through the woods if not for the ward. "Perhaps you're just getting sloppy."

Mel bit back the reply she desperately wanted to make. "If I'm sloppy, then why are you offering me a job?"

Tina put a hand to her chest and her mouth dropped open - she looked the picture of innocence. "I'm hurt, my dear. Perhaps I just wanted to talk."

"In the middle of a forest with guards chasing me?" Mel leaned back against one of the sturdy oaks, acquiescing. "Fine Let's talk."

Tina tossed her hair back behind her shoulders and planted her hands on her waist. "The Scarlet Emerald."

If Mel had been holding anything she would have

dropped it. As it was, she barely kept her expression neutral. "What makes you think I'm not insulted by that suggestion?" The Scarlet Emerald was legendary among shapeshifters.

Tina scoffed. "Please, you'd do anything if the price is right."

That little remark made Mel want to turn this whole thing down flat. Who the hell did Tina think she was? Some two-bit thief who couldn't cut it as a witch. Not a powerful one, anyway. But Mel wasn't ready to burn that bridge. Not now. "There are maybe – *maybe* – three people who could pull it off. And this is all off the top of my head." She held up a finger, "Cyn got nicked by vampires two years ago, she's out for the count. Ice Queen wouldn't even try it. That leaves me. And once I'm discovered, there will be a bounty on my head big enough to buy Kansas. Not interested."

"Are you afraid of that kitty cat?" Disdain dripped from the older woman's voice. "Torres, despite his castle, couldn't keep you out if he tried."

Lucio Torres, alpha of a small clan of cats, was the current owner of the Scarlet Emerald. Everyone knew that. Without research, Mel didn't know much more. Obviously he could take anything in a fight, and his security had to be top notch. But she could beat it.

Though she wasn't going to. That mark had a death sentence attached.

"You don't even want to know the price?" Tina quirked a brow. With a flash of her hands, she dangled a pure diamond suspended on a platinum pendent. "For your trouble."

Unconsciously Mel reached for it, heart pounding. But Tina snatched it away again. "Is that Ava's?" Mel asked. Hate bubbled in her throat and she could feel her claws tear beneath her skin, ready to rip out at the right moment.

Tina smiled, "Yes. Scry worthy."

Taking the job would be suicide. She'd get herself, and probably her team, killed. "What's the timeline?" She was just getting the facts, no obligation.

"Three weeks."

Double suicide. She'd have no time to prepare before she had to pull it off. "Just let me hold the gem for a minute."

Tina tossed it, and Mel easily plucked it from the air. It was a long slender diamond, set in platinum that twisted around the top. The chain was long enough to wear between a woman's breasts and the gem was nearly clear. Mel curled her hand around it. She could picture Ava wearing it, a drop of blood clinging to the tip.

The diamond gave her hand a little resistance. Mel let it go and watched it zoom back to Tina, who said "tell Krista I said hi." She smiled and left, not waiting for Mel to confirm that she'd take the job.

They'd both known she would the minute she touched the stone.

There were worse ways to die.

2

Eagle Creek, Colorado had two dingy motels and one restaurant that Mel felt safe enough eating at. It wasn't the clientele she was concerned about - it was the food. And she'd been known to eat her kills bloody when she ran as a cat. But a woman in human skin had to have some standards. Krista and Bob were already at their table. It was the one in the furthest corner, on the opposite side of the room from both the bar and the bathroom.

The Eagle Creek Bar and Grille – the second E, of course, made the place classy – was a small affair. Perhaps twenty tables and a sturdy bar fitted with a dozen stools. It could accommodate the residents of the town just fine, but the campers who tromped through on their way up into the mountains would probably not see the charm. Mel didn't see it herself either, but it was better than microwaved ramen from the gas station.

At seven on a Tuesday night the place was crowded. All but one table was full and the waitresses all bustled around, serving drinks and slinging food like nobody's business. From the back and forth with the customers, all of those waitresses had worked here for some time and many of the customers were regulars. In a town this size, they'd have to be.

The gruff man behind the bar was a shapeshifter, probably a cat. And if Mel had to guess, so was the family of four at the table closest to the window. But both children were pre-shift. Almost no shapeshifters were hit by the change until they were well into their teens. But the parents weren't mates. Not if the father's eyes glued to her own chest were any indication.

Everyone else was human. She could tell by looking. With the perfume she wore, it was impossible to distinguish by scent. A handicap, but worth it since it would make it difficult for the pack here to tell that she was a shapeshifter. Cash register at the front, safe probably kept in back, maybe bolted to the floor if they were smart. She could clear them out of a few grand in minutes, but it wasn't worth it. Not when they'd be in town for weeks and had plenty of cash to burn.

She saw Krista huff impatiently, her arms crossing in front of her. The woman embodied the word pixie. Barely five feet tall with short, spiky brown hair and skin that practically glowed bronze, she looked like some sort of punk forest nymph. And knowing exactly how hard she could punch, Mel knew she'd never tell the woman that.

Bob, on the other hand, was… Bob. They'd worked a couple of jobs together before she went on her own, and he was the first call she made once she needed a team for herself. But if someone asked her to describe him, even while she was looking straight at him, she couldn't. He was a man, with brown, or was it black, maybe blond hair, and eyes… the eyes were where they belonged, along with a nose and mouth. She thought his skin was dark, but couldn't quite describe the tone. It had to be a perception spell, but she never felt that pinprick of magic that any normal witch gave off. But when it came down to it, she always knew he was Bob and that he was there for her. Nothing else needed in her book.

She slid into the booth opposite her partners. At her nod, Krista activated a sound deflecting ward. It would distort everything they said so that no one around them could understand the substance of their conversation, but they'd still hear the murmur of their voices. No one ever questioned it and the magic was so subtle that not even Mel, with her highly attuned senses, could get a fix on it.

"So, why did you want us here?" Krista asked. "I thought teamwork wasn't your game anymore." There was an edge to her voice, and Mel knew it was warranted.

"Tina brought me the job." Krista's eyebrows shot up even as her lip curled, so Mel continued. "And there's no way in hell I can do it alone. I don't trust anyone more than the two of you to help me get this done."

"The Scarlet Emerald?" Bob asked, his voice as even as ever. "Do you think I have a death wish, Kitty?"

Mel's hand fisted at the nickname. He must have been really pissed off. "Yes. And in payment you can have any item from my collection you want. One each." She'd split her stash in half and give it all away for a shot at Ava. But it didn't need to come to that.

"And you had to bring us into shifter territory to make the offer?" Krista didn't look satisfied. "The two of us probably broke three treaties just flying here, let alone sitting in a bar thirteen miles from King Cat's castle!" If it weren't for the need for discretion the younger woman would have smacked her fist against the table. "This is manipulative bullshit, Mellie, don't pull it on me. If you want me for a job, just ask."

Bob didn't say anything, but he nodded in agreement.

Mel took a moment, and tried to let the tension out of her shoulders. "Will you help me steal the Scarlet Emerald? I can't do it without you." It didn't even hurt to say it, not to Bob and Krista. That was a surprise.

Her partners shared a smirk. "And that diamond as big as Bob's fist?"

Mel knew exactly what she was talking about. It had taken six months of planning to boost it. "It's yours." She looked at Bob.

He shrugged, "I'm sure I'll think of something." He would, he always did.

She leaned forward, elbows on the table. She could almost hear her mother's voice yelling at her to move them. "It's going to be tricky. No blueprints on record, no details of the security system. And they're shapeshifters, which means they're about twenty times harder to steal from than anyone else, except maybe a coven-protected compound."

Krista bristled at the assessment. "Try stealing from a coven without someone to break wards."

"There's nothing on file with the county?" Bob asked.

Mel smiled, "According to the records, Mr. Torres lives in a 1,400 square foot, two-story house with three bedrooms and two bathrooms." She pulled a folder from her bag and set out the photos on the table in front of them.

Castle wasn't quite the correct term for Torres' compound. It was far too modern. Everything was straight lines and cement, the windows small on the ground level and slightly larger beginning at the fourth story. The entire thing rose as high as the trees around it, and luckily the trees came nearly all the way to the actual building. From a defensive perspective it was a stupid decision, but a cat couldn't resist the call of the woods.

"Clearly the county has falsified records." She looked at Krista. "How can you get me in?"

While Krista would punch anyone who looked at her wrong, her true talent was reconnaissance and tactical magic. "I've got something. I'll need two hours, should be able to get a passable interior."

Perfect. "When can you get started?"

Krista smiled. "Tonight. I've been wanting to use this baby for months." Krista loved to create magical devices that could infiltrate even the most secure locations.

Mel shivered and looked around. A man in a leather

jacket had just walked through the door. It felt like a live wire touched right to her chest, among other places, when she looked at him. Just the force of him was primal. She wrenched her head back. "Looks like the big guy's here. Can you move now? I'll buy you some time to get set up." With the alpha gone, the danger of casing the place would be minimal. If anyone could do it, Krista and Bob could.

Her co-conspirators shared a glance and had a silent conversation, expressions flashing so quickly that Mel couldn't determine their meaning. It wasn't telepathic, they'd simply worked together for so long that some conversations didn't need to happen out loud. Bob finally nodded. Krista said, "Give us as much time as you can, but keep him here for at least twenty minutes. We'll rendezvous at the cabin in three hours." Mel nodded. She'd rented out a nice vacation cabin for the month in the outskirts of town, just over the county line from Luke Torres' territory. If he asked the right people about the heist he'd eventually figure out who did it, but she didn't want to make it as easy as checking the ledger of the two motels in town.

Krista brought down the ward and the scent of the cats who'd just entered nearly overwhelmed her, but she kept her expression neutral. Bob and Krista slipped out and Mel didn't watch them go. Her eyes turned to the alpha.

She had work to do.

Something was wrong in ECs. Luke felt it the moment he walked through the door. Upon first glance, everything seemed normal. Nearly everyone in the place lived in town, though he spotted the small family who were staying at Sid's Motel on their way through the mountains. But they were fine, completely human and unaware that there were any people who weren't.

He hit up the bar where Sinclair was wiping off the shiny surface. "Any news?"

The man's beard covered half of his face and hung down several inches. It hid a nasty mess of scars and obscured his jawline enough to hide the fact that his face had once been beaten in. It also made him look closer to sixty than thirty, but that was his own business. "Vince and the others are out back taking a smoke. They've got a table. Haven't started nothing since they got here."

Just the group he needed to see. Vince Hardy and company were exactly the kind of little shits he didn't need to be dealing with right now. "And our guests?"

Sinclair's beard shifted as he grinned, "Which ones?"

That gave Luke pause. Someone must have rolled into town after he got his update. As crazy as it sounded, with the summit coming up in two weeks he needed security on lockdown. No strangers in town that he didn't know about, no surprises. "I know about the family."

Sinclair nodded to the booth in the far back of the room. "Three folks. Think they're human but couldn't get a clear read. Must just be passing through. No room rented."

Luke looked over to where his man pointed. A tiny woman sat beside a towering man, and both sat across from a red head. The only thing he could see were her full, curly locks. Even then, just seeing them was a punch to the gut. He tightened his fist and took a deep breath. Sure, it had been awhile, but the sight of her hair shouldn't have put him on edge.

Her friends got up and left before he could even could even consider listening in to what they were saying. She stayed behind. He watched the other two leave out the main exit, and it seemed like the red head didn't plan to follow. He turned back to Sinclair. "When did they come in?"

The bartender shrugged, "Half hour, hour ago

maybe? Ordered drinks but no meal. Just been talking. I got Lucy on their table but she said they weren't saying anything fishy. I'll keep an eye out."

"You do that."

Vince and his friends came back in and Luke nearly gagged from the smell of tobacco. How any werecat could smoke cigarettes confounded him. The tiniest whiff and it felt like his nostrils were burning. But idiot kids would always be idiot kids. Vince Hardy was one of those lowlife kids who'd been given everything and chose to do nothing with it. He pissed away his trust fund on booze and fancy shit and couldn't hammer a box together to save his life. But Luke didn't get to kick him out of the pack for being a stupid kid. Though he did take a bit more satisfaction in his punishment than he should have.

He stood at the bar and waited for Vince to see him. The kid was taking up as much space as he could. He nearly leaned into the red head's booth to look down her shirt. His lime green polo shirt offended Luke's eyes, and he had to have spent half an hour spiking his blond hair up just enough to make it look tousled. Vince looked exactly like a jerk with money should look, and it only made him more popular.

After more than two minutes of fooling around, Vince finally started paying attention to his surroundings and saw his alpha leaning casually against the bar. His face paled and two spots of red dotted his cheeks. Luke had to hold back a smile. The kid knew that he'd fucked up if Luke was going to talk to him on the same day of the incident.

He maintained eye contact for several seconds before turning around and walking out of the bar. Vince and friends would follow him. They knew the rules.

Luke didn't wait in the parking lot. There were too many regular people in town who had no idea of the monsters that lived among them. He walked around the side of the small brick building and waited just past the tall wooden fence that separated the back of the restaurant from view of the road. In the summer they'd put out chairs and tables for vacationers to enjoy the beautiful Colorado weather. But now that fall was easing in, the tables were stacked to the side and would only be put up at special request. It made it the perfect place for meetings like this.

Vince sneaked back first, his head down and shoulders slumped. He leaned back against the fence and said nothing. Luke just waited. Nearly a minute passed before Henry and Mick joined them. All three boys waited for the alpha to speak. Luke let them stew in silence for several minutes. They were fucking up his life and he didn't care to make things easy for them.

Only after he saw a bead of sweat form on Vince's forehead did he speak. "Do you have an explanation?"

If possible, Vince's shoulders sunk even further. Any more and he'd be bent completely forward. "She wasn't using it," he mumbled.

Luke made a sweeping motion with his hand. "Do you see any snow on the ground?" He didn't raise his voice. He didn't have to.

Vince gulped and his friends winced. "No, sir."

"Did you hear sounds of distress from inside Rinna's garage? Perhaps a scared puppy?" He leaned close, just inches from the kid's face.

"No, sir."

"So would you care to explain to me why you stole a woman's snow mobile and attempted to drive it down the street, causing thousands of dollars in damage?" He ended on the slightest growl and was satisfied when Vince whimpered, the sound barely escaping the kid's throat.

Both Henry and Mick kept their heads down, refusing to make eye contact or defend their friend. Vince said nothing in his own defense.

"You all go to school and come home. If you have jobs, you do those. Each of you will owe Rinna $500 to cover the damages and you will work on her property every weekend until Christmas. If you want to do anything else, you ask me first. I catch you disobeying, and it's confinement to my place anytime you're not at work, at school, or asleep. Got it?" These three may have been nearing adulthood, but they still counted as children in the pack. They were lucky - if any one of them had been just a year older the punishment could have been much worse. And now, to drive the point home: "Do any of you know what's happening in a couple of weeks?" He let the question hang, watching the boys.

Henry finally looked up and gave a jerky nod. "The summit."

"Exactly." At least they weren't completely clueless. "First time in a century that vampires will be in this territory without a war. Don't fuck it up." Luke left them there. The kids were either going to follow his orders or not, and if they didn't, he'd deal with it. But right now he needed a drink, a woman, or a fight. He'd take any one of those, but his mind drifted back to that red head inside and he figured a drink and a woman sounded like a nice combination.

3

Sinclair already had a beer waiting for him before he sat on the bar stool. "They give you any trouble?"

Luke shook his head and swigged the beer. "The second those little shits get caught they turn into kittens. I'll be worried the day they realize that their claws can actually cut."

Sinclair smiled and moved away, wiping the other end of the bar.

Luke shot a glance back towards the table where the red head had been sitting. He'd only been outside for five minutes and hoped that she hadn't left yet. But no one was sitting there anymore. Turning back to his drink he caught a whiff of a subtle floral scent. At least, it would have been subtle if he weren't a shapeshifter.

But enhanced senses came with the game. For him it smelled like he was walking through a rose garden, but at least the scent seemed all natural. Some synthetics made him sneeze.

He looked towards the scent and smiled when he saw the red head. A part of him was disappointed that she wasn't a shapeshifter – he couldn't think of any that would wear such a strong perfume – but that didn't last long. She didn't take a seat, instead leaning against the bar and standing close. Her elbows rested on the ledge and her back arched showcasing the incredibly alluring curve of her chest.

Luke's gaze trailed down, taking in her emerald eyes and bright red lips. He expected her skin to be lighter, most red heads' were, but she wore a nice tan like she lived in the sun. A slinky dress barely covered her from shoulder to mid-thigh and he was thankful for that tight material. And he was also thankful that his jeans were hiding the effect she was starting to have on him. Damn if he wasn't half-hard just from looking at her.

She leaned closer, her shiny red lips tantalizingly near his cheek. "Buy me a drink?" She breathed into his ear.

Luke suppressed a shiver as her breath caressed his skin. Damn it had been a long time if one little human was having this effect on him. Something niggled at his senses while he stood there. Something smelled wrong, not unhealthy, not the creeping rot of a vampire or the burnt danger of a witch, just off. "What kind of drink?" He asked, still studying her. She was doing the same.

She reached around him, her breasts brushing against his chest. Luke didn't suck in a breath. He didn't tighten up. He was an alpha cat and he didn't react like a randy boy when a hot woman got close. She grabbed his beer and put the bottle to her lips, taking her time to sip it. He watched her swallow as the liquid slid down her throat. "This one." She smiled and lingered just inches in front of him.

Luke could tell she was trouble, and just the kind he wanted. He rested his hand on her hip. She smiled even further. Looking at her face he saw where the weird scent was coming from. Her hairline was wrong, it didn't line up like it should. She was wearing a wig. It seemed his red wasn't what she seemed. Disappointing, but he would live. "You've taken something of mine," he said. He grabbed for his beer but she held it out of reach, "I think that makes me entitled to something of yours."

"Does it now?" Her voice was melted chocolate, smooth, warm, everything he wanted.

He wasn't getting his beer back and he didn't care.

"It does." He put just enough command into the flirtation and saw her grin. "Tell me your name and I'll forgive you."

She swallowed the rest of his beer and leaned past him to set the empty bottle on the counter. Once again she brushed up against him. "It's Katie." That was all wrong for this woman. Katie was the name of a girl, a simple, cute girl. And just from looking he knew she was anything but simple. "Who are you?" she asked.

He leaned in closer, catching her scent, something ethereal under the flowers and synthetic hair. He wanted her naked before him, her secrets bared to his senses. "My name is Luke." He couldn't answer her entire question - any human would think his answer was crazy. But they didn't need words between them now, not when the chemistry was ramping up everything inside him. His cat was scratching inside his skin, waiting to roll around and show off for her. He pulled her close and she came with no resistance.

Just as he brushed his lips against the skin at the base of her throat he heard a voice clear behind him. Luke came back to his senses for a moment to see Sinclair standing behind the bar, twirling his rag with a smirk on his face. "What kind of store do you think I'm running here?" The gruff man asked.

While there were perks to being the alpha, he

couldn't just run roughshod over his people's territory. Luke grinned and nodded. He kept Katie close, but spoke against her ear instead of kissing her. "Want to get out of here?"

She glanced behind them, towards the opposite wall. All Luke saw were a few patrons sitting at the tables and EC's eclectic décor. A few mirrors and posters, the head of an elk, and an old clock. But when she looked back she smiled. "Now you're speakin' my language." She spoke with a bit of a drawl, her g's dropping off the ends of words. Luke couldn't wait to get her alone and hear what else she would say.

He led her out of the restaurant, one arm possessively around her waist. A few pack members eyed him, but they said nothing, their expressions carefully neutral. Luke Torres did not pick up women in local bars. Ever. But there was something about this one that he wasn't letting go.

Vince and friends were long gone and the parking lot was full of cars but no people. Katie didn't make a move to go to her own vehicle, letting him lead her to his motorcycle. If he'd known he was going to pick someone up, he would have brought a truck. But her eyes lit up when she saw the sleek black bike. Perhaps it was a good choice after all. "This is yours?" Excitement lit her words.

"For years now." He wanted to say that he'd won it in a card game or found it in an abandoned garage and restored it from a rusted heap. But the origin was far too mundane for that. He'd simply purchased it after falling in love at first sight. "Where are you—" His phone interrupted him, vibrating in his pocket. An alpha's work was never done. He gave her an apologetic glance and answered. "It's Torres." Gone was the flirtatious man he'd been with her. Now his voice was pure business.

Maya Nunez, his head of security, spoke. "We've had some anomalies tonight. I think it would be best if you come check out the security feed."

He wanted to curse. Here he had a beautiful woman who seemed to like him and his bike, and he had to go home. For a moment he considered taking her with him. But she was human, and that couldn't happen. "Got it. Prepare a report." He hung up and looked back at Katie. "How long are you in town?" She didn't live in Eagle Creek, he would have recognized her.

She shrugged, disappointment in her words, "I'll be around for a bit. Who knows?"

Oh, what the hell. He pulled her close and captured her lips with his. If this was the only time he'd ever see her, he was letting himself have that much. Her arms went around him and she opened for him, her tongue tangling with his. Damn. Luke had made a terrible mistake.

One taste of her was never going to be enough.

If he kissed her like that again Mel was in trouble. She shook her head as he drove off on a very nice looking motorcycle. There was work to be done. But her fingers drifted up to rest on the smeared lip gloss on Katie's lips. Mel wasn't the type to wear something so bright or sticky, but Katie Jenkins, one of her more fun identities, absolutely loved it. And both of them clearly had the hots for a certain dashing werecat.

But that was neither here nor there. She pulled out her phone and checked the time. Including the time it took to travel to his place, Krista and Bob should have had at least twenty minutes to get started, just like they asked. And with Luke only leaving now, there was probably a little time left.

A part of her wanted to call them and make sure that they got out safely, but that would compromise the mission and put them in even greater danger. Besides, they wouldn't appreciate the interruption. They were adults and she knew that Krista had been doing all of this at least as long as she had. Who knew how long

Bob had been in the business? No use checking in; she just needed to get back to the cabin and wait. Then they'd plan.

Mel itched to shift into her other form and cover the distance on foot. She hadn't run as a cat in weeks for one thing, and the roads out here were so bad that it would be much faster to journey through the forest. But a leopard would bring far more attention to her than the gray sedan she'd acquired for this job. At best she'd scare the shit out of someone if she was seen, at worst she'd alert the local pack. And she didn't need Luke Torres to have any idea that she was coming.

She drove out of town on the state highway keeping an eye out to make sure she wasn't being followed. Even though it wasn't that late, there were almost no other cars on the road. After a dozen miles she pulled onto a heavily forested road. The trees hung over the street, blocking out all sight of the moon and making it unnaturally dark. She could only see by the glow of her headlights. With the help of her GPS she found the second road, this one somehow even darker than the last. She saw no houses, no mailboxes, nothing to indicate that anyone lived out here.

The incline grew as she went higher up the hill. This wasn't a mountain, there weren't any so close to the city, but this foothill offered just enough wilderness for summer travelers to truly feel like they were escaping civilization. Her final road was more of a dirt path. Only one vehicle could go in a direction at a time, but since the only place on this road was their cabin, that wouldn't be an issue.

The trees gave way to open land and the bright moon illuminated the quaint wood cabin that she'd rented. Unlike the car, she'd come across the property through relatively legitimate means. There was no reason to be surprised by vacationers.

Neither Krista nor Bob were back yet, so Mel set about making dinner. She'd meant to eat something at the restaurant, but the stress of speaking with her team once more, and then the little distraction with Torres, had put a damper on that. She preheated the oven and pulled a plastic bag filled with pre-made chicken fingers out of the freezer. After a moment's thought she set out enough for the three of them. Maybe Krista and Bob wouldn't be hungry, but it seemed callous not to be prepared.

The oven had barely finished preheating when she heard the gravel crunch outside from another car coming up the road. Mel shoved the food in the oven and waited for her teammates to join her.

She heard the muffled sounds of Krista and Bob talking before they reached the door, but once they came into the cabin, they were silent other than a brief greeting. "I'm making food, if you're hungry," Mel offered.

Krista smirked, "Let me guess, chicken nuggets?" She set a large canvas bag down on the coffee table and plunked herself down on the couch. Bob joined her. Together the two of them occupied most of the couch space, leaving Mel no choice but to bring in a chair from the kitchen. Neither Krista nor Bob seemed apologetic.

"How did it go?" If her partners didn't want to make small talk, she'd be all business. Simple as that.

Krista dug around in her bag and pulled out four small red stones. She moved the bag to the floor and set the stones up as the corners of a large square on the table. With a wave of her hand and words that Mel couldn't quite understand, Krista's enchantment lit up, and light shot out of each of the stones forming a square. Slowly a picture filled in: it looked like a three dimensional blueprint with furniture layouts and shadows darting around representing people inside of the building. The enchantment was hazy, incomplete. Mel had seen Krista use this spell to create something as substantial looking as a dollhouse. What they had now was disappointing.

"It's bad." Krista said.

"Bad how?" Mel could deal with bad, hell, she loved dealing with bad.

"Very bad." Bob added.

"Their security is at least double what it should be right now. The vault is only accessible through three checkpoints where someone is sure to catch your scent, and even if we can get you in, there's no way to get you out." Krista detailed everything up to the vault, but made it clear even their magical reconnaissance couldn't get inside.

"But you can get me in?" If she could get in, she could get out. Even if she had to drill a hole through the wall to do it.

"They'll have your scent. You won't ever be able to work this area again. And that's if they don't kill you." Concern laced Krista's words. "This is bad, Mel. If we had three months and a team of seven, maybe we could pull this off. But not in two weeks, not with just us."

"If this is the only way closer to Ava, we have to take it." Mel didn't pace the room, but she tapped her fingers against the seat of the chair. Just the thought of Ava had her ready to fight.

Krista and Bob exchanged a glance. After a moment Bob excused himself. Mel heard the door close when he went outside. "Mom has done this shit to you before.

Remember the Rialto? Do you even know if the stone is scry-worthy?"

Now Mel did get up. "She wouldn't lie about that."

Krista leaned back and crossed her arms. "Have you met her? She started lying to me about when my birthday was when I was three years old. She has no concept of honesty."

"She won't lie about this because she knows that I'll never work for her again if she does. This is too important." The map on the table blinked and a new display showed up. "What's this?"

Krista gave it a look. "Alpha's quarters, far as we could tell. Directly above the vault, well, three stories above it, but there's nothing the rest of the pack can access."

Luke Torres in his own quarters, now there was a delicious thought. But Mel pushed it aside. "Does he have direct access to the vault?"

Krista picked up one of the red stones and the picture dissolved. She shoved her hand in her pocket and gave Mel a hard stare. "There isn't a plan that gets you out of that freaking fortress. Bob has been thinking about it all night. If he can't think it, it can't be done."

"Remember Phoenix?"

"That ended with you half on fire, me with a broken leg, and Bob nearly bleeding to death." Krista crossed her arms, "Of course I remember Phoenix. You're not thinking clearly about this."

"No!" Mel didn't mean to yell, but it ripped out of her. "Ava killed my parents, she killed everyone I loved. And she made me become this—this thing!" Mel bit off the rest of the thought. Krista didn't need Mel's shit piled on her own. "What I mean is this. I'm doing this job. I will succeed. But I need you and Bob if I'm going to get out of this thing. For real. So, please, help me."

Krista reached out with one hand but pulled it back before it was even fully extended, curling her fingers into a fist. "It takes two weeks to make a transportation charm that probably won't kill you. A month to make one that definitely won't, and three to make one that will ensure all of your parts end up in the right place after you use it. Without that charm, we can't get you out, they'll have your scent and running will be useless."

The problem started turning over in Mel's head. "We have to think of something. I'm doing this job, and I'm not going to kill myself getting it done."

Krista rested her head on her hand and let out a sigh. "Then let's talk to Bob. But I'm telling you, we're screwed."

4

Luke sat at his desk in the War Room while Maya explained the breach. Originally the room was just supposed to be an office, but after a few pitched battles and the necessary planning meetings that came up from running a successful pack, someone started calling it the War Room. Much to Luke's consternation, it stuck.

"Best as we can tell, it was a flock of bats." Maya said, her bright red hair was pulled back tightly into a bun, though she also had on a small elastic headband to keep some of the frizzy bits under control. The hair was obviously colored, he knew she was naturally a brunette, but he also knew why she did it. With the large scar on her cheek and the honey colored eyes of a lioness, Maya screamed predator. And she would rather have people see the hair and the stylish clothes and discount her as a threat until she was slitting their throats. Luke appreciated that about her.

"So it was the vampires?" It was half statement, half question. Vampires couldn't turn into bats - at least they never admitted it if they could. But rumor had it that they could use them as spies.

"Seems like." She spread a map out on his desk and pointed to an area about five miles from the house. "They stayed just outside the interior perimeter. Looks like a scouting party. Technically this doesn't break any agreements we have standing with them, and since we can't even prove it was them, there's no point in bringing it up."

Luke studied the map. "What tipped you off?" There were enough caves in the area to make bats common, even a colony of that size taking to wing shouldn't have brought him running back to the heart of his territory.

"Genie said they smelled dead." Maya wore a wry smile. Genie had never said something so tame in the half a decade that she'd been working for Luke.

"What did she really say?"

Maya took a moment to consider, smiling all the while. "Something like they smell like flying rats covered in shit left out to rot for three days? I don't have her way with words."

"No one does." Luke studied the map. "Double the after dark patrols. But if the vamps do show up, no violence unless they offer it first. We want to contain them, not kill."

"Already done. I'll relay your orders regarding prisoners." She rolled up the map and left without another word.

Luke followed her after a minute. Yes, the office was his, but work as the alpha rarely required long stints behind the desk. And, truth be told, he'd give up the job in a heartbeat if he was going to just be filing paperwork all day. But Maya's words put him in mind of the upcoming summit, and he made his way through the house, down two flights of stairs, and through a heavy metal door to the vault.

The vault predated the house by some time. As a matter of fact, it predated most of the buildings within Eagle Creek. But the town wasn't even a hundred years old, so that might have been bragging over nothing. He hadn't wanted to build his fortress so far out, but the former alpha kept all his goodies here, and while the man could barely keep himself standing in a fight, his home security was pretty decent. But that didn't mean that Luke hadn't made his own improvements.

After entering his security code on the keypad and stepping through the door, the lights came on automatically. It all looked a bit like a bank vault with individual lockboxes secured on the wall. At one point he'd considered moving to a digital system, but the cost didn't make sense compared to the reward. Besides, there was only one thing in the entire vault worth spending millions to protect.

The Scarlet Emerald.

He kept it in a glass case in the center of the room. All of the security in the vault was dedicated to protecting that one ugly-ass stone.

He'd first heard of the stone when he was a kid back in college. How Jaime Pascal had used it to ward off wolves and protect his clan for fifty years. It had always belonged to the alpha of these cats. And when Luke fought for his place twelve years ago, the stone became his. Whether it offered real protection or not was anyone's guess. There were stories, rumors, tall tales, but nothing definitive. And he'd never needed it or even tried to use it. If the stone was magic, there would be a price. There always was.

But in two weeks he'd finally take it out of the case and put that chunky gold chain around his neck. Vampires appreciated ostentation. Wearing a huge, cloudy, red stone the size of a baby's fist would catch their attention. He only wished he could go out and bury the stone back in the mountains and be done with it. His pack didn't need mystical protection, not when they had sharp teeth and pointy claws.

He abandoned the vault. There was nothing there but the weight of responsibility. He made his way up the inner, twisting staircase to his quarters where he planned to take a nice hot bath and think of that sexy redhead. Even now his cock stirred at the memory. He wondered what her real hair color was, how it would feel in his hands, how it would look spread out on his bed.

Oh, now there was a thought.

He was so wrapped up thinking about it he didn't notice the intruder in his room until he'd already taken off his shirt.

"Ew, gross!" Said the eighteen year old girl sitting on his couch, reading a magazine. Well, she was reading a magazine until she threw it at him and used one of the pillows to cover her face. "I'm going to have to cut my eyes out!"

Cassie was the dramatic one. His little sister was visiting while on autumn break from school. Between beautiful strangers and security risks he'd forgotten all about her. "It's a torso, I'm sure you've seen one before," but he pulled his shirt over his head anyway.

No need to court the wrath of a teenaged girl. "And what are you doing in here, brat? I thought you were given quarters down the hall."

She stood up and collected her magazine from the floor. Looking at the two of them, no one would realize they were siblings. Cassie looked far too much like her father, Luke's step-father, Scott, and not enough like their mom. His sister was as tall as him, with blonde hair halfway down her back that she usually gathered into a ponytail or bun whenever it annoyed her. She did have their mother's brown eyes, but her skin was almost pale, with little hint of their Mexican origins.

"We were supposed to grab a bite after you did your thing in town?" she suggested.

A glance at the clock on the wall showed that it was inching towards nine o'clock. She must have been waiting for hours. "Damn it, I'm sorry. I got caught up with some stuff." He didn't want to put it off any longer. "Let's go raid the kitchen."

They foraged some leftover pizza and soda which Luke insisted that they take to the balcony outside his room. It was late enough in the year that even with the lights on they weren't bothered by insects. Cassie nibbled at her slice without quite looking at him. It took Luke several minutes to realize that she was trying to work her way up to something.

"So when am I driving you to the airport?" Denver was two hours away, but that didn't mean he'd delegate that task. Cassie was his sister after all.

She took another bite, bigger than the last. She made an exaggerated motion of chewing, delaying him further. But Luke had learned how to deal with the silent treatment. He returned her silence, keeping his expression pleasant. After she swallowed, his sister pondered the crust a moment before setting it down. "I was thinking that maybe I could extend my trip a bit? We haven't really gotten to hang out." She sounded just as innocent as she had when she had sprayed bright pink paint over the walls of his room.

Luke knew she was hiding something, even if she was right about hanging out. "What about class?"

She rolled her eyes, "It's not like I have to worry about perfect attendance."

Luke took a sip of his drink before answering. "With the vampires coming I can't risk it. Not with–"

"It's because I can't shift?" Pain laced her words. "I asked you to turn me, why won't you?"

Shapeshifters weren't born with the ability to change into animals. If their parents had the ability, usually sometime in their late teens a shifter would learn. But in some cases, especially when only one parent was a shifter, it didn't happen. And Cassie was getting close to nineteen. "Because it's dangerous and we don't know that it won't happen naturally."

She held up a fist and extended her fingers as she spoke, "Alana did when she was 15, Joey at 16, Leah last year. Of all my friends, it's just me who hasn't. Why won't you, or Mom, or Dad just accept that I'm broken and fix me?" Her voice cracked, and Luke saw a tear in her eye. But Cassie tilted her head back and turned aside, discreetly wiping it away.

Scott hadn't been turned until after their mom was pregnant with Cassie. And Luke knew that Cassie didn't want her friends to know she was technically only half shapeshifter. "You're not broken." Luke leaned over and put an arm around her shoulders, hugging her close. "But it's so dangerous, and way more painful than the other way. Just wait until you're twenty, okay? If Mom or Scott won't do it then, I will." He'd made that promise to her before, but he hoped it stuck this time.

And he hoped that she changed before then. He couldn't imagine mauling his sister.

They finished up their dinner and Cassie didn't repeat her plan to stay longer. Luke forgot about it.

<h1 style="text-align:center">5</h1>

"Before we start, I just want to submit that this is fucking crazy, and one of us is probably going to end up dead. You, most likely." Krista was standing next to Mel, speaking in a low tone. They stood just on the edge of the forest that abutted Torres' property.

It had taken a week to get everything together and ready for the heist. Once a few of the details were ironed out, it seemed incredibly simple. Ballsy, but simple. As long as Mel could pull off her bit, they'd have the stone in plenty of time for Tina's deadline.

"No one's dying on this one." Mel stretched out her neck and arms, swinging her limbs in circles.

"We can get the scry stone from Mom some other

way." Krista reached into her bag, digging for charms, as she spoke.

"Tina won't give it to me another way. We both know that." Mel stopped stretching and looked at the other woman. "We're good, right?"

Krista's hand paused in the bag and she wouldn't look at Mel. "I'll do the job."

That was good enough. Mel checked her watch as the seconds ticked down. Bob should be in place at any moment. She tried to clear her head of the clutter floating around, the tension between her and her team, the stray thoughts of Luke's lips that wouldn't leave her alone. She needed everything gone but the job.

An owl hooted in the distance. Four seconds later a crow cawed. And then the owl once more. She nodded goodbye to Krista and took off through the forest at a run. She had a lot of distance to cover and not enough time to do it in. But they'd added more guards at the perimeter of the property, so Mel had to time her entrance just right. There was a thirty second window where she could cross into the territory without anyone catching the scent of an unfamiliar shapeshifter.

And then there was getting into the house itself. She activated the cloaking spell and approached slowly. Fast movements were more likely to break the illusion, but it was a risky spell to use around shapeshifters since it masked sight, not scent. But if Bob had done his job, she'd have enough time to get in and get the stone before they smelled her.

She climbed up the stone wall, her fingers finding handholds that shouldn't have been possible. Her destination was a small balcony with a simple French door. Normally it would be guarded by an alarm, but she was able to disarm that and let herself in without an issue. That was the easy part.

They could take care of the people outside the house, but they had no way of knowing who was inside. Krista couldn't leave activated charms in the house for more than a few hours, so their intel was half data, half hope. Mel didn't slink through the house. The charm kept her invisible, and even if someone caught her scent it might take them a little while to realize that it shouldn't be there. No house was without its visitors.

No one saw her, no one stopped her. She made it all the way to the vault without anyone the wiser. The lock would have been tricky, but she'd encountered it before. In her experience, most shapeshifters of note went to the same two or three consultants for home security. Consolidation like that made her job easier. She took a breath before opening the door; this was the biggest mystery. They hadn't gotten eyes in the vault yet.

But once she was through the door she let out a small sigh of relief. She'd been having nightmares about encountering some unknown enchantment, something that would kill her if she didn't have permission to go near it. Never mind that almost no shapeshifter would willingly let a witch near his belongings. The smart ones always invested in enough magic to keep their stuff safe.

It looked like Mr. Torres wasn't that smart.

She disabled the sensor on the expensive glass case and exposed the Scarlet Emerald to the air. The case looked intimidating, but it was only on par with what she would find in a museum.

She stuffed the gem into a small canvas bag tucked against her side and turned around to face the vault door. Either there was a mass of shapeshifters waiting for her on the other side or there wasn't. She only had one way to find out. Mel checked her watch. Krista and Bob were due to be in place for the grand finale.

No one was in the hall outside the vault. Good. Maybe, just maybe, Plan B would work and they'd all walk out of this scot-free. With practiced patience, she made her way through the inner staircase and up to the alpha's room. It was madness to use this as an escape point, but it was also the fastest way out of the house.

She was through the door and into his room in

seconds. Mel froze by the window when the door opened. Her enchantment should still be working, but the sudden movement of jumping through the window would break it.

A blonde head popped through the door. "Luke?" A girl asked. "Are you in there?" She stepped in and closed the door behind her.

Mel bit back a curse. She couldn't speak without revealing her position. On the other hand, either the open window or her scent would give her away before long. But Mel held still. She watched the girl look around, thankful that she didn't switch on the light.

The girl seemed to give up, muttering something and walking back through the door. Mel let out a breath. She examined the screen in the window and found one sensor. An alarm would sound if she removed it from the frame. A glance at the door to the balcony told her the same thing would happen there. But there was a simple way around the frame.

She heard accelerated steps in the hallway outside the door.

Mel pulled a small retractable knife from her pocket and sliced the screen in an X. The fall was going to hurt like hell, but it wouldn't kill her. She backed up a few steps and took the window at a run, diving through the hole she made. Just as she went through, she heard the door open behind her once more.

Showtime.

She was in the middle of the shapeshifters territory, running, and carrying their most prized possession. This shit was going to be tricky. She had to make it into the forest bordering the property and a mile away before they caught her.

Mel dropped all pretense and sprinted, covering the grass of the yard and diving into the woods. She trusted her body to find the right path, avoiding fallen branches and vines. Of course this would have all gone a lot faster if she could have covered the distance in her other form, but then she would have no way to carry the gem. She'd briefly considered holding it in her mouth, but the risk of swallowing it was too great.

The forest was eerily silent around her. But then again lions were chasing her, she'd barely be able to hear them when they caught up. She didn't look behind her, instead looking up at the thick branches overhead. If she were going to catch someone, she would pounce from above. But she was a leopard. That was her style. Luke's pack was made of lions. Who knew how they would act? This wasn't the savanna.

Her heart labored in her chest, pumping so fast that she could feel the pulse in her temple. But she covered the mile and found the little charm buried under the dirt. It resonated with the magic in her concealment charm. She pulled the concealment from the bracelet she wore and grabbed the small canvas bag with the Scarlet Emerald in it and buried both of them underneath a small layer of dirt. Krista would be able to come back for it and the charm would keep the gem hidden from the werecats.

Breaking into Torres' house wasn't that hard. Stealing the stone had been even easier than she expected, but now came the part that made this job so damned difficult. Once a shapeshifter got a scent, he didn't forget it. She would be a marked woman in this territory for as long as Luke Torres ruled, maybe longer. And that was if she could get out.

Her car was hidden another two miles away, and she had no idea what connections Torres had to local law enforcement. She and her team had taken every shortcut possible to get this thing done, and now she was going to pay the price.

Mel felt rather than saw the first cat. It was a prickle at the nape of her neck. She picked up her pace, changing to an all-out sprint. She made enough noise to scare every small animal in a half-mile radius, but speed was now more important than stealth.

A roar sounded far behind her, and she wanted to

freeze in her tracks. The alpha knew and now he was after her. She should have been scared, but Mel smiled, feeling the thrill of the hunt. Even if she was the one hunted, that alpha was a worthy opponent. And no matter what happened to her, she'd already beaten him.

Mel couldn't run any faster. There was a simple limit to how fast two legs could carry any one person, and she was there. It would take too long to shift and gain speed. That lion's roar told her she was in trouble, but she didn't give up. Escaping would be nearly impossible, but she'd been in impossible situations before. She always came out of them, somehow.

This time, though, it looked like she would need to find another way. A lioness landed behind her, claws digging into the dirt just feet from where she'd been a moment before. Mel skidded to a stop. She couldn't outrun a cat, not on two legs. Probably not even on four. Outrunning a shapeshifter in her own territory was a fool's errand.

Fight or surrender?

She knew what she was supposed to do, but her claws pricked at her fingertips, dying to be let out. She could take one cat. Even in human form. But the saner part of herself argued. It wouldn't just be one cat for long, and the fight would delay her.

"Damn it!" Mel turned around, her hands raised.

A golden lioness crouched before her, ready to leap up and subdue her. Mel bowed her head, keeping the animal in her sight. "I surrender myself to the Alpha's mercy." The words burned her tongue, but ritual words held power. They were important. Now this lioness couldn't kill her, not if she thought that honor was important. There was only one man who could do her harm now.

Luke Torres.

Luke had the account from Maya. They'd been able to reconstruct the exact path the thief had taken, captured her both on video and by scent. And yet no one could remember seeing her when she came in. A dozen people in the house and she had walked off with the proverbial crown jewels.

He walked down two flights of stairs, into a sub-basement that shouldn't have existed. It was a tiny room, really, with just an overhead light and no furniture. They called it the Cage, but the name didn't ring true. There were no bars here, just a steel door with a handle on the outside. The only other way in the room was through a five inch wide vent in the ceiling. No creature that Luke knew of could fit through it, at least nothing that could also look human. And this woman definitely looked human.

Though he found that he missed the red hair.

He let the steel door close behind him and studied his captive. Not many people threw themselves on the mercy of an alpha. In some territories it would be suicide. In others, it would be worse. Especially for a woman as beautiful as the one reclining against the stone wall. At the moment her beauty was mostly a remembered thing. She wore all black clothing which disguised her figure and yet gave her plenty of range of motion, and covered her face with a balaclava. In any other circumstance, his cats would have stripped her of the mask, but as it was, no one could touch her.

No one except for him.

That shouldn't have excited him. He wasn't that type of man, but Katie – or whoever she was – had been haunting his dreams. The things he could do to her now...But he wouldn't. There were lines that a man didn't cross.

He studied the thief. For all that she sat in a cell, she seemed relaxed. Though in her line of work he doubted that this was her first time in a cage. She had one leg drawn up with an arm resting on her knee. Her head was tilted back against the wall. And yet her eyes studied him with a calculated coldness. Then they darted away, taking in the rest of the room.

"How many ways out do you have?" He found himself asking.

The woman smiled and Luke felt his heart thump. She didn't try to hide behind a smile - she let the predator shine through. "There *is* only one door." Her voice was lower than it had been at the bar and he wondered if this was what she really sounded like.

"One door out of this room, yes. But I'm sure you've accounted for that." He almost took a step towards her, but he held himself back. There were only four feet between them already, no need to close the distance.

"You would think."

Luke slid down to sit against the door. It felt wrong to tower over her. "I take it your name isn't Katie." He felt ridiculous talking to a masked woman, and there was no way it could be comfortable to sit with that thing on her face. Luke leaned over and grabbed the balaclava, pulling it off of her and revealing brown hair and the rest of the face that he thought he knew so well. He remembered the green eyes, but without the red hair, they looked duller. And she'd covered the dusting of freckles on one cheek when they first met. But her face wasn't lopsided, if anything he liked it better. He felt himself smile. "Would you care to enlighten me?"

She opened her mouth but bit back whatever she planned to say. It was never a wise move to lie to the man who held ultimate power over life or death. "Mel."

It was a start. "Is there anything to go with that?" There had to be hundreds of Mels in the world, with no last name, no full name, he didn't know if his security squad could find out more about her.

But she only smiled. "I'm Mel," she said the words as if explaining to a child that the sky was blue.

"I'm Luke, but you already knew that." If they were explaining the obvious, he figured he'd play along. "Why did you ask for mercy?" He didn't have all night, though if he let himself forget he might stay talking to her for far too long. The ground was more comfortable here than he remembered.

Mel swallowed and looked away, this time Luke was sure she wasn't planning an escape. "My mom always told me never to fight lions. I don't know if she was being metaphorical." A strange expression crossed her face, fondness and regret. "I didn't even know what metaphorical mea..." She shook her head and flattened her expression. Mel took a second and then looked over, her eyes shining bright, "You have a reputation as a man of honor."

Luke's inner lion preened. But this wasn't the time to bask in compliments. "And a man of honor wouldn't execute a thief?" The words tasted like ash on his tongue. He couldn't even conjure up an image of her death, though he should have been reveling in plans of vengeance. Strange, and he had no idea why.

"Not without a trial." She curled her arm up so that her elbow was positioned on her knee and rested her head on her hand. "So are you honorable, Mr. Torres?"

"My sister might argue the point." He didn't want to talk about his sister with this woman. He had no reason to, but he couldn't stop himself. "Do you have any?"

Mel's eyebrows shot up and she almost recoiled. He only noticed it in the bunching of the muscles of her neck. She didn't answer for over a minute, he didn't think she would. But his Mel was full of surprises. "I suppose I don't," she said quietly.

Luke leaned toward her. He told himself that it was so that he could hear her clearly, but he could hear a possum dart through the forest from five hundred feet away. He didn't play foolish games, not even with himself. But he also didn't pull away. "You just suppose?" She smelled like the forest, mud mixed with sweat. He hadn't ever realized how alluring that was.

Mel angled her body towards his and looked at his lips while she spoke. Luke would have looked away from her face to keep himself under control, but something kept his gaze trained on her. "No, no sister. No family at all." Her hand reached up and brushed away some of the hair that had fallen into his eyes.

Luke hadn't realized that he was within touching distance. He grabbed her hand and pulled it down in front of him. The hands of a thief shouldn't have been so delicate. He traced the thin line up the center of her palm and felt her hand contract at the contact. But he only pulled her closer. Her hand was only inches from his lips when she jerked it back.

Then Luke did back up. He stood, forcing himself backwards across the room and putting as much space in between them as possible. What the hell was he thinking?

"Where is the stone?" He demanded, his voice unforgiving.

"I don't have it." She spoke so quickly that he knew she'd been anticipating the question.

He knew that Maya had caught her before she could make it anywhere and there had been no other scents to report. No one else was on his property with her. She had to be lying. "Stand up," he commanded.

Mel stood up with a bright smile. She moved languidly, stretching as she straightened to her full height. That night at the bar he thought she was much shorter than him, but now the height difference didn't seem as great. She could look right into his eyes while barely tilting her head. "Are you going to pat me down?"

That had been the plan, but looking at her, Luke reconsidered. Because he really, *really*, wanted to get his hands on her. He kept his distance. "Am I going to find anything if I do?"

She grinned, he could see the girl she must have been at some point. Bright, happy, and full of mischief. "What kind of thief would I be then?" She let her response sink in and changed the subject. "Was it the girl that tipped you off?"

Luke's brow furrowed. "Excuse me?"

Her eyes narrowed and she leaned in a little. "By my count I should have had at least thirty more seconds. A blonde girl saw me, did she tell you? Or was my estimate just off by that much?"

There were plenty of blondes in the pack, but only one who was in the house at the time. Luke advanced on Mel, slamming her against the wall and pinning her hands with his own. "You go near her, and I will kill you, do you understand?" He growled it, inside he roared.

Mel didn't look scared, she smiled, but he could feel the terrified beat of her heart with each pulse of blood through her veins. "She seemed a bit young for you. But I've got no beef with your girlfriend."

"She's not my girlfriend." Luke didn't mean to say it. He wasn't going to tell Mel anything she didn't need to know. Especially when it came to Cassie, but he didn't want her thinking there was an entanglement that didn't exist. He let go and stepped back. "Cooperate with my people. Someone will come talk to you later."

He knocked once on the door and was let out by the guards.

6

The alpha left Mel to stew in the cell for two full days. A guard came once in the morning and once at night to lead her down a pitch black hall to a bathroom with no windows. They offered her no avenue of escape. That was fine, really. She didn't need one. Mel didn't need to be given anything; she took what she wanted, and damn everything else.

The bathroom had a faucet so she tried to take in at least a few swallows of water before being lead back to her cell each time. It wasn't enough. She didn't know if they were planning to deprive her until she talked or what, but she knew that if they kept up like this another day she would be in serious trouble. She still had at least three days before any help came for her and she couldn't afford to be weak before then.

If Krista came through.

No. Mel rejected the doubt. It was only the hunger and dehydration talking. This was the job, and no matter the personal shit, Krista would get it done.

Mel's head jerked up when the door opened. She wasn't certain of the hour, but it couldn't be time for her guard to take her on her bathroom trip. And if it was, she was super screwed, that meant she'd lost all sense of time. Or they were staggering the rotations to encourage it.

But it wasn't one of the two guards she'd seen before. A short Latina woman stood in the doorway, her colorful red hair held back in a braid and her outfit nearly bright enough to blind Mel who'd grown accustomed to the dullness of her cage. "The alpha has had a meal prepared for you," the woman said. She spoke with the slightest southern drawl. "He has asked me to tell you that you are to attempt no escape and harm no one, unprovoked. Of course, if you are challenged, you are welcome to defend yourself."

Standard stuff. As the alpha's ward, Luke was responsible for her protection. And until he decided what to do with her, she was honor-bound to obey his commands. Lucky for Mel, she'd always been a bit short on honor.

It took her a moment to stand, and when she did the room wobbled for a few seconds. Mel clenched her teeth but concentrated on keeping everything else loose. These people didn't get to know that what they'd put her through had any effect on her. She would not appear weak. Once the room righted itself, Mel smiled at the woman. "That sounds wonderful." Her voice was hoarse. Nothing a little water wouldn't fix.

Her guide didn't speak anymore. She led Mel through the lower level and up one flight of stairs making no attempt at hiding their path, leading Mel directly to another small room set up with a cot and a table. They were still underground and there were no windows. But this room had a light switch inside the door and Mel could see a small bathroom.

What on Earth were they playing at?

"Were they fresh out of bars when you were building this place?" she asked.

The woman gestured for Mel to take a seat at the small table. There were two chairs, one facing the door, one facing the wall. The woman stood next to the one facing the wall. Wonderful. Mel's back prickled as she left herself exposed. But she sat up straight. Especially if she was getting fed.

Mel smelled her visitor a second before her captor looked up. Heat coiled through her, making her pulse jump. This attraction to the alpha was beyond inconvenient. And frustrating as hell. If this had been any other time she could have indulged him in a bit of play and been done with it. As it was, she was completely under his power and almost wished he would take advantage of that fact.

She'd hate him forever, but damn if it wouldn't be fun.

"Thanks, Maya." He took the other seat after Maya closed the door behind them.

Mel meant to study the room, but her entire focus was absorbed by the alpha. After more than two days he looked worse for wear. Though at least he'd eaten something. Speaking of food, she could smell something warm and delicious. Her eyes followed that scent all the way to one of his hands. He set a small plastic container down and popped the lid off. It was just some rice and chicken, but Mel had to keep herself from snatching it away. He placed a bottle of water next to the food.

He sat the container down between them and waited for her to look at him. After she did, he spoke. "You've hidden the Emerald well. I hope you're happy."

It wasn't hidden, but Mel didn't say that. She was

trying to keep her eyes off the food. If she didn't look at it, maybe her stomach wouldn't hurt as much.

"All I want is a direction." He pushed the food and water across the table and Mel's hands jerked up to keep everything from falling.

"What?"

"A direction," Luke repeated. "I'm not going to play some fruitless game with you. I know you won't tell me exactly where it is. But I hope you'll indulge me in this." He pulled a spoon out of his pocket and set it next to her food. "The food is yours either way."

After giving it a cautious sniff, Mel dug in. She wasn't waiting for him to change his mind. In two minutes she'd eaten half of what she'd been given and looked up to see Luke watching her. She didn't slow.

"You've gone hungry before." It wasn't a question.

Mel swallowed and wiped the back of her hand against her mouth, clearing away a grain of rice. "I suppose everyone does one time or another."

Luke sat on the bed, giving her the entire table to herself. "I wouldn't have withheld food if I knew. I'm sorry."

A hint of anger bubbled, "I don't need your pity." She grabbed the last bit of rice and swallowed it down.

"It's not pity," he leaned back, his entire body lying

across the small cot to rest his shoulders against the wall. "But I don't hold to torture. Not for punishment."

"That was punishment?" She couldn't stop the abrasive laugh. "Never been to the Forests of Fire, I take it?"

The alpha sat right back up, his eyes narrowing. "You're too young to make it out of there alive. No one with less than a century could do it."

Mel grabbed the plastic container and spun it around idly. "People always try to tell me what I can't do. It never works out for them." She studied Torres. He didn't pretend to be casual, didn't pretend disinterest. She slid the container back and forth and his eyes followed her fingers. There was something deliciously wicked about holding that man's attention. "So you've done your research now?" she asked. "You had no idea who I was two days ago."

He stood and crossed the room. He leaned across the table, planting his hands beside her own. "Two days ago you didn't matter."

That stung, even if it shouldn't have. "I've always mattered."

Luke got three inches from her face and did the strangest thing. He smiled. "I didn't know that before two days ago."

She caught a whiff of his scent. The room had

started to smell of him from the moment that he walked in, but now it hit her all at once. Pine, with some citrus undertone. His eyes dilated and she licked her lips. His gaze dropped and she did it once more. His mouth hung open the tiniest bit.

Oh she was in trouble. Even more than she knew.

Without thinking, she covered his hand with her own. He didn't move away, didn't try to grab her. Luke stayed rooted in place and Mel wanted to lean forward and steal those precious inches between them. They could be hers and then she would know if he still tasted as good has he smelled, as good as he looked.

His other hand covered hers.

What the hell.

She leaned forward and swiped her lips against his, only for a second, before leaning back into her chair. Mel was satisfied when the alpha leaned forward and tried to follow her. She licked her lips but kept the space between them. "I always thought an alpha would taste bitter."

He froze, an expression between horror and laughter on his face. "What?" Speaking broke the spell and he took the chair opposite her, resting his elbows on the table. It took her a moment to realize that their hands were still touching.

She didn't pull back. "I've never kissed an alpha

before you. And that makes it twice now. You're messing with my expectations."

"I've never kissed a cat burglar. I suppose that makes us even." He pulled his hands away.

Mel had no idea what she was doing. She was in no position to be kissing anyone, let alone her captor, but all she wanted to do was to smile and keep flirting. "I suppose it was better than a vampire, though." What was she even saying?

Luke seemed just as confused. But his hand crept forward. She let her fingers crawl across the table to brush against his nails. He was so close that not touching him felt wrong somehow. "You kissed a vampire?" She didn't know if his disgust was the thought of the vampire or the thought of her kissing someone else. She didn't know what she wanted it to be.

"I was sixteen and curious." She couldn't help but smile. Even being held prisoner in his castle, talking to him, teasing him, was fun.

But Luke paled. "Please tell me he wasn't... that is... how old was *he*?"

Mel took hold of one of his hands and traced a small scar that crossed between his thumb and forefinger. Her smile faded while remembering the vampire. "That doesn't matter." She didn't expect his skin to be soft.

And when she ran her fingers over his palm it wasn't, but the top of his hand was smooth except for a little hair and that one scar. "Did you ever?"

He understood the question. "Next week will be the first time I'm around vampires for more than thirty seconds without punching anyone. I hope."

Of course, the reason the job had to be done so quickly, so sloppily. "I suppose I've thrown a wrench in your plans then." She didn't want to upset him, but speaking whatever came to mind with this man felt natural. She liked it.

And Luke wasn't upset. He looked up from their joined hands and she saw a small smile playing across his lips. "Yes, you have." But in saying the words he interrupted whatever strange magic that was developing between them. The smile slid from his lips, leaving in its place a melancholy frown. "Who hired you?

Mel pulled all the way back, breaking the contact between them. "Thief/client privilege, I'm sorry."

Luke grabbed the plastic food container and stood. "When you're ready to talk, we'll talk." He left without a backward glance.

Mel felt adrift. She'd been held captive before, sometimes on purpose, sometimes not. And no matter what happened, she always had a plan, had some control of the situation. But this was something new. She wanted to talk to Luke, to tell him what was going on. She definitely wanted to kiss him all night and through the morning.

And that wasn't normal. An idea, barely more than an intrusive thought tried to suggest what was going on, but Mel pushed it away. She didn't have time for whatever it was.

To distract herself, she studied her new cage. In the short time that he'd been in the room with her, Luke's scent had begun to permeate the place, blending with hers and leaving an aroma that should not have been nearly as appealing. Then again, she'd not bathed in three days and anyone's scent might have been preferable to hers alone.

There wasn't much to the place other than the cot, the table, and the small bathroom. The most dangerous item in the bathroom was a small bottle of shampoo. While she could squirt it in one of the guard's eyes, the seconds it bought her wouldn't be enough to be useful. There were towels, which was nice, but no shower rod or curtain. She wondered if it was intelligence on Luke's part or something learned from experience that took away the easiest items to make improvised weapons. Most shapeshifters didn't worry about it. Either he was smarter than the average alpha, or he had the experience to deal with unconventional threats.

Mel's hand landed on the silver chain around her neck. The alloy combined with her relatively high silver tolerance meant that the necklace didn't bother her. She twirled the chain, tracing back and forth to the pendant hanging on it. If she had to choose between Luke having experience or wisdom, she'd hope for wisdom. Because even the smartest shapeshifter wouldn't see what she had coming.

7

aya was waiting for Luke in his office. She leaned back against his desk with her arms crossed and raised an eyebrow when he shut the door with too much force. "So the plan changed?" she asked. If she was speaking to anyone else he would say that she was mocking. "Since when do..." It was only after she began talking that she remembered that she was speaking to her alpha. "It is not customary for you to interrogate prisoners."

Luke sank into his chair and leaned back, drumming his fingers on the table. "It isn't customary for your team to let women steal from my vault." He didn't need to put venom into the remark for Maya to flinch. "Any news on the gem?"

Maya straightened, "No." If frustration could make

electricity, that one word would have powered the house for a month. "And no sign of her partners either. No scent, nothing obvious in town. Nothing at all." Maya gave up on standing and sank into the chair across from him. She hooked her ankle under her knee and leaned back.

Luke tried to remember anything from that first night they met, but he couldn't beyond red hair and soft lips. Maybe that was the point of the wig. He'd meant to ask her about it, but at some point had become distracted. How soon was too soon to go back down there?

Maya's hand waved in front of his face. Luke jerked up and swatted her away. "What?"

She quirked an eyebrow. "Do you want me to say what I'm thinking?"

"No." His head of security had at least a century on him, though she had never stated her actual age. And she seemed to think that all of that life experience gave her leave to give Luke advice when it was neither needed nor wanted. "So you know there are partners?"

Maya nodded, but didn't say more. In fact, it almost looked like the blood had drained from her face.

"What is it you don't want to tell me?"

She took a deep breath. "Not yet. It's just a stupid

hunch. And it's so far outside the realm of possibility that I don't want to get you freaked."

Right. Luke crossed his arms. "Are you suggesting that she's empowered the trees to hide my emerald? Perhaps convinced a nice bird to fly it away?"

Maya rolled her eyes. "Nothing that ridiculous."

The door opened and a familiar blonde head popped in. Luke had to keep his hand down to prevent himself from massaging a headache forming in his temple. He addressed Maya without acknowledging the new visitor. "When you've got something, let me know. I'll ask Mel some more in the meantime."

Maya looked ready to warn him off the burglar, but she thought better and left without another word to him.

Cassie took her spot. They didn't speak until Maya closed the door.

"I'm sorry about ditching my flight," she said. She didn't meet his eyes. Her fingers nervously picked at the armrest. "But I've made the decision not to go back to school."

Luke took a deep breath before speaking, and then another. He wasn't her father, just her big brother. So why on Earth was he the one stuck handling this shit? "Have you talked to Mom or Scott about that?"

She shook her head.

"Cassie..." He had no idea what to say. Her name just whooshed out of him in a helpless sigh. "I get it, I really do, but—"

"No!" She stood, stepping behind the chair and grasping the back. At least she was looking at him now. "You changed when you were sixteen! You did all this practically ten minutes after college. They still talk about what you did at that frat your sophomore year back home. And then everyone looks at me, and they just—ugh! I can see how disappointed the entire pack is. And if I could shift, at least then I could go home, you know? It would be real. I wouldn't be a failure."

"You're not a failure." He didn't yell, but only just. "Come here." He opened his arms.

"You'll do it?" She perked up.

Luke laughed. "No, brat. I'm giving you a hug." He gestured for her to come towards him. And thankfully she came. He stood and wrapped his arms around her. "You've either got to go home or to school." She stiffened when he spoke, but he didn't let that stop him. "Shit is about to hit the fan here. I've got a prisoner and will have vampires breathing down my neck soon. It's not safe. Not for you."

She pulled back. Luke let her go. "I'm not dumb, you know. I can take care of myself." She walked out of the room without a goodbye, slamming the door to his office behind her.

Brilliant.

He made it through the rest of the day without another disaster. But after a fitful night, he was no closer to solving the issue of his thief or helping his sister. He had a million things that needed doing, and only one place he wanted to be.

Mel was laying on the bed when he arrived at her room. He wanted to believe her smile was real. She quashed it so quickly that it had to be. "Clearly I'm an executive level prisoner if the Man himself keeps interrogating me." She sat up as she spoke, scooting back so that her spine rested against the wall. She pulled her legs up and casually wrapped an arm around them. "Come on over, your majesty. There's room for two."

She'd taken a shower since he'd last seen her. Though even yesterday she'd looked good enough to eat. And heat pulsed through him as he remembered the delectable dreams that had been part of the restless night.

He crossed the room and sat too close. At first it hadn't seemed so, but as her scent enveloped him he needed to muster strict control to keep her from seeing exactly how much she affected him. It shouldn't have been so hard. In more ways than one. "There's no need for titles," he said by way of greeting.

He needed to ask her about the gem, about her partners. He had a legitimate reason to be in that room with her. But it wasn't why he came.

"When did you first shift?" he asked.

Mel's eyes widened. He studied her expression, the slight pursing of her lips that pulled into a smile, heavily tilted to one side. Her gaze seemed to drift somewhere far off for a moment before coming back to the present. "You wouldn't believe me if I told you."

It was a highly personal question. Akin to asking when someone lost her virginity. But he needed to talk this out with someone, and Mel was a captive audience. "I've heard a lot of things."

She shrugged, "I was twelve."

"That's impossible." Bile rose in Luke's throat at the thought. The first shift felt like being ripped apart and then sewn back together with barbed wire. And for weeks after it felt like sand was sunk under your skin. Nothing felt right. To go through it as an adult was bad, but he'd never heard of anyone younger than fourteen surviving a change. And no one younger than fifteen had ever been a naturally born shapeshifter. "I didn't realize you were bitten."

Mel shook her head, "Nope, 100% the real deal. My

parents were leopards, my grandparents were leopards. Before that, who knows?" She smiled but her eyes shone with the first hint of tears. She tilted her head back, probably to keep them from falling.

He hadn't seen her other form yet, but he imagined a beautiful spotted beast slinking its way through the trees of his forest. He would love to run with her.

But that was beside the point, and it was never going to happen. "How did you do it, then?"

Her expression hardened, and then she grinned. It was a punch to the gut. "I was very determined." He thought she would leave it at that. She turned to him, studying his profile. Luke had to keep utterly still to stop himself from flexing or doing something else equally embarrassing. After a moment, she continued. "They died, they were killed when I was eight."

"Your parents?"

She nodded, "My whole family, as a matter of fact. I was the only survivor." He wanted to ask her what did it. Not many monsters could take out a family of leopards. But some questions couldn't be asked. She kept speaking. "The people who raised me weren't the greatest. And there was one who was convinced that she could..." She cut herself off.

Luke waited.

"She was convinced that if I wasn't around my kind,

I wouldn't become a shapeshifter. She thought that since I couldn't shift yet, it could be stopped. And she tried her damnedest to make sure that it didn't happen." Mel looked away from him and bit her lip with a smile. "I was properly motivated to prove her wrong."

Luke blew out a frustrated breath. He grabbed her hand and squeezed it. "But it's not just motivation that lets us shift."

She laced her fingers with his but didn't look at their hands. She didn't even look at him. "Are we speaking generally or specifically?"

He had to tread carefully. And he tried to remind himself that he was being a fool. There were a dozen people he could ask advice of, and not one of them had ever broken into his house and stolen a precious item from his vault. But he wanted to know what this woman thought, how she could help. Though he hadn't completely lost his head. "There's a girl in the pack, nearly nineteen, who is desperate to shift."

He didn't have to go any further for Mel to understand. "All her friends are doing it? She feels weak?"

Luke nodded. "And I don't know what to tell her." He wanted to say more, but was afraid that he'd said too much already.

Mel let out a breath. She held completely still

while she thought. But he could feel the heat of her right next to him, coiled to strike out at any threat. Apparently she didn't think that he was one. That satisfied him on a deep level, somewhere not even his worry about everything that was going on could penetrate.

"Is she full blooded?" she asked.

"Half, through her mother. Her father was turned later." He tried to keep it clinical.

"That sucks." She turned her shoulder completely towards him, placing lips just inches from his. "And I'm sorry, but I don't know what to tell you."

The regret on her face did something to him. It unfurled some long deadened emotion in his gut. Who he was seeing now wasn't different than the playful thief who'd robbed him blind, but she was showing him this other side of herself. Someone who should have been impossible in light of her life.

And yet here she was.

"You're not the only one." He almost left right then. Whatever answers he was looking for, she didn't have. But in the few minutes he'd been sitting with her, he felt more relaxed than he had in too long. That shouldn't have happened in the presence of his prisoner. He didn't care. "How many ways have you planned to escape so far?"

Mel leaned in, her breath licking against his ear. "Are you planning to forbid me from running?"

His cock twitched. He clamped a hand on the back of her neck and pulled her face to face. Their lips brushed lightly. It wasn't a kiss, only a symptom of the closeness. With each word he spoke he got the tiniest taste of her, it only made him want more. "What would be the fun in that?"

He shouldn't kiss her. He shouldn't want to kiss her. But sitting so close that they couldn't help from brushing their lips together, it wasn't a choice. It was an imperative. While the need drove him, he forced himself to go slow. His lips pressed against hers, still for a moment, waiting for her to respond. To push him away or to let him in.

Mel didn't expect the kiss. She should have. His hand was on the back of her neck and their lips were already touching. But Luke wasn't the type to take advantage of a prisoner.

Lucky for her, he'd decided to break his own rules. And she didn't know who had the advantage anymore.

He started to pull back as she sat there, frozen. She followed him, hitching one leg over his lap and straddling him. She could feel his growing hardness between them. Exactly where she wanted him. She cradled his cheeks and stole the kiss from him, ratcheting up the intensity and taking over. She opened her mouth, tasting him, devouring him.

Luke was not a man to let himself be idly devoured. He bit down on her lower lip, firm enough to hold her in place, but not rough enough to cause any pain. His hands trailed down her back. Mel wanted to moan, but she was too preoccupied with taking her fill, enjoying the wickedly masculine taste of him.

She had no idea what had come over her, had come over them. She was his prisoner, the woman who had stolen his most priceless possession. And yet she couldn't imagine *not* kissing him. To do anything else would be foolish. It wasn't even a decision, it was instinct.

And that instinct burned her to the core. She could feel herself growing wet for him, her hips grinding against his own, feeling his erection through the soft cotton of her pants. She wanted to ride him until she came, crying out in ecstasy at the pleasure they both earned.

But kissing was just as satisfying. She gripped his hair in one tight hand, her lips trailing across his cheek and down to nip at his jaw. Her breath came in panting gasps, further evidence of her arousal. And when one of his hands dipped into the waist of her pants, she hissed out something between pain and satisfaction.

That sound gave Luke pause. He pulled back for a second, examining her expression. Mel didn't want to stop. Not until she had tasted every inch of him. Twice. And even then that sounded like only a delicious prelude to something she couldn't see ending.

And that thought shook her to her core.

This time she pulled back, gliding off of him and standing up, taking two big steps back. Whatever that was, there was no room for thoughts of something serious. A moment of lust was easy, endings were easy. She didn't know anything else.

Luke took a moment to regain his bearings. He rubbed his thumb against his lip and Mel had to clench her fist to keep from crossing the room once more and picking up where she left off. But this was a job, not a date. And that she'd forgotten that for even a second showed exactly how much trouble she could get in if she wasn't careful.

There was a dark part of her that coolly examined her would-be lover's expression, took in his arousal, and calculated exactly how she could use it. The cool silver of the necklace around her throat was a heavy reminder of the risk she would have to take to get out of here, danger that might just be fatal. Unless she used this new development to her advantage.

But Luke spoke before she could lay any ground-work. "I'm not going to apologize."

Of course not, alphas never did. "A little fun never hurt anyone." She had to keep it light. For now. Playing this too hard in any direction could screw her over later.

Luke studied her, his brown eyes narrowing for a moment before his expression hardened into stone. "I have a condition in return for my continued hospitality."

Mel kept very still, careful to not change her expression in the slightest. Was he going to require that she whore herself out to him? She didn't think he was the type. She had counted on it. Her stomach turned in distaste because she knew she would do it, and hate him all the more. "That is your right."

"When you try to escape," he held up a hand to keep her from protesting, "Or in any other case, only fight my people in self-defense. If you injure or kill anyone for any other reason, I will revoke my mercy and have you torn apart."

A death threat shouldn't have relieved her. But Mel could work with that, and her respect for the alpha grew even more. "I've hurt none of your people thus far. Why would that change?"

"There are some things that I won't risk." He left

her alone in the room to contemplate what exactly those things were.

8

The next surprise came after dinner. And while she had been alternating between planning escape routes and thinking about a distressingly sexy alpha, nothing had prepared her for the newest wrinkle.

A blonde young woman sneaked in. She would have never made it as a thief, but for a novice, her stealth was serviceable. And Mel immediately recognized her as the woman from the night of the robbery. Luke's questions about the shifter girl started to make sense. So who was she to him? Not the girlfriend, according to him. While her pale skin and blonde hair threw Mel off for a moment, she took a closer look, seeing the line of her jaw, her nose, and the shape of her eyebrows. This girl's face bore a striking, feminine resemblance to the man who had begun to haunt her dreams.

A sister?

"It's a bit late for visitors." Mel sat up from the cot and motioned for the girl to take a seat at the table.

The girl's eyes widened and she shot a glance back at the door. "You're the person Luke is being all secretive about, right?" She hissed it. She didn't take a seat.

"Your brother has a lot of secrets, I'm sure." A hit with the brother comment. The girl didn't try to deny it. "I'm Mel, by the way."

"Cassie." She still whispered.

Mel almost felt sorry for this kid. Scratch that. She flat out felt sorry for her. Any young woman who walked into a prisoner's cell in the middle of the night had to be desperate. And she had no defenses against anything Mel would do to her.

"How did you get past the guards?" If the girl was going to let her lead the interrogation, then that was what she would do. Already a plan was beginning to form. And she probably wouldn't even need to go against Luke's edict. Not that she'd actually promised him anything. But what he didn't realize could be used to her advantage later.

Cassie waved a dismissive hand, her lips curling up into something unconcerned and vaguely fond. "Mick is on shit duty, so when I offered him some cookies to pass the time, he didn't question it."

One guard? She was insulted. And glad. "You drugged my guard?"

Cassie's cheeks heated. She finally sat down. Mel took the opportunity to stand, walking to the table and leaning against the side, her hip jutted out. Cassie looked up at Mel, her eyebrows drawn down. "You're not going to tell, are you?"

Desperation made the kid seem even younger. Because Mel couldn't imagine her eighteen year old self acting this way. Showing fear. But she placed a hand on the girl's shoulder and smiled her best comforting smile. When Cassie didn't flinch she knew that she'd succeeded. "Of course, not. Why don't you tell me what you came here for?" The girl looked ready to stall, so Mel kept talking. "Whatever you gave the guards won't hold for long. So open your mouth or get out."

Cassie's shoulders straightened and she sat up tall, clenching her hands together. "I would like to propose a trade." She didn't waver.

Mel had an idea of where this was going. "Yes?"

"I'll get you out of the house, if you bite me." She couldn't meet Mel's eyes.

That didn't matter. Mel tilted the girl's chin up with her own hand and waited until Cassie would meet her eyes. It took several moments. "A bite won't do the trick. Not *just* a bite."

Cassie knocked down Mel's hand. "I was speaking figuratively. I didn't think someone like you would object."

"Who exactly do you think I am?" Mel didn't let her words hurt. The girl was so far out of her depth she was mistaking the ocean for a swimming pool. "Do you even know why I'm down here?" Exactly how much of a liability was Luke's little sister?

There was a slight shake to her head, "You'd be in the Cage if you were that bad. Or he would have killed you." If Mel hadn't known Cassie was a born shapeshifter, that would have proved it. Few spoke so easily of their brothers committing homicide. "You only have a few minutes to decide. The distraction won't last long."

"What distraction?"

Cassie crossed her arms. "They don't exactly tell me shit," she scowled. "I heard something about vampires on the eastern perimeter. That means that they're not watching for people leaving right now. They're trying to stop them from getting in."

Smart, opportunistic kid. Mel could have molded her into something if she had the time. "You have a car?"

Cassie dug in her pocket and held up a set of keys. "Tank full of gas, too."

Mel pretended to think about it. "Walk me through it. You seem prepared, but I'm a professional."

Cassie's plan was straightforward. Simple, but possible. The house was nearly abandoned with the disturbance on the perimeter and reinforcements hadn't yet taken position. Mel smiled and pulled the keys from Cassie's hand. She pushed the girl's palm down to the table, holding her in place. She maneuvered herself behind the girl and wrapped her free arm around her neck, not quite hard enough to make her pass out.

"One tip, though." Cassie's pulse pumped against Mel's arm, fright flowing through the girl's veins. "Never give away the plan to a criminal all at once. We'll always betray you." She hauled the girl up and held her against the wall with one hand on her neck. "You know not to scream, right?"

Cassie nodded, her eyes wild.

Mel concentrated, letting her free hand shift, claws forming at the edge of her now furred, spotted fingers. She ripped up the sheets of the bed, giving herself usable rope and forced the girl into the bathroom. Without a word, she tied Cassie up, securing her to a bit of pipe behind the toilet.

If Cassie had already shifted, the cotton wouldn't have held her for long. But she only had human strength. It gave Mel more than enough time to get out. But something compelled Mel to say something before she left. She knelt out of reach of Cassie's feet. "Don't be an idiot about your shift. You're still a teenager. It might happen, but you just fucked up so beyond belief that no one is going to be willing to turn you even if it doesn't."

The girl flinched and Mel could see tears forming in her eyes.

Good. She needed to hear this.

"So here's my advice. Convince yourself that it's going to happen, and try and shift every day. That's all you can do."

Mel stood and left, wedging a chair under the door's handle behind her. She took a deep breath and grasped the small red pendant on her necklace between her thumb and forefinger. It didn't take much pressure to break the charm, but Krista had made sure that only Mel would be able to do that damage. If anyone else had handled the charm, it would have seemed indestructible.

By breaking the stone, Mel triggered a secondary concealment spell which acted much like the one she'd used to break in to Luke's house in the first place. It also alerted Krista and Bob that she was coming. They had a rendezvous point set up close enough that she should be able to make it before the spell failed or she was caught. As long as she could get out of the house in the first place.

Cassie's assessment of the situation was spot on. Mel's guard was asleep on one of the staircases, drool dripping down the side of his jaw. She walked slowly through the halls, up two flights of stairs until she reached the kitchen. She stopped in the hall, before entering the brightly lit room.

How big of a threat was out there? An alpha's house, especially one housing a prisoner, was always somewhat occupied. It was the cost of doing business. And she couldn't imagine he would leave his sister unprotected. Mel stopped walking and pressed her back against the wall. She waited a moment until she could hear the faint sounds above the loud beating of her heart. Standing still under a concealment charm was as close to invisible as a person could get, but she knew they could still smell her.

She heard footsteps in the distance, they were above her, on one of the upper floors. Faint, moving away from her. Nothing to worry about at the moment. So that made three people in the house: the unconscious guard, Cassie, and whoever was upstairs. If the threat was big enough, it wasn't outside the realm of possibility to leave the house under so little protection.

Sure that the kitchen was abandoned, Mel stepped inside. But she didn't let her certainty make her lazy. A thorough glance confirmed her instinct.

The light on the security panel blinked red. The alarm was active. If she wasn't worried about being heard, she would have cursed. It was set to a defensive mode. The house's interior motion sensors weren't active, but all door sensors were. Unless she put in the right code before leaving an alarm would sound when she opened the door to the garage and the garage door would be locked, impossible to open without breaking through.

That would be sure to send the lions running.

She studied the keypad. Five buttons were more worn away than the rest, but she would eat her metaphorical hat if the code wasn't at least six digits. She had no tools to hack her way through. Her options were to either look for tools to improvise rewiring the alarm or to guess the code.

Every moment she stood there was a moment wasted. The footsteps from upstairs tapped directly overhead, but Mel kept her cool. Cassie wasn't making a peep and she couldn't hear the other guard. She decided to guess the password. It was quicker than any alternative. And she hoped that she'd learned enough of her alpha in the past few days to give it a go.

Her first guess was his birth month and full year. Six digits, one repeated. Since the zero was the most worn or them all, it should have fit. But the panel beeped. She would have between three and five tries to get it right before the alarm was tripped anyway. So if it wasn't his birthday, what could it be?

She racked her brain, trying to decide what to try next. He couldn't be the only one to know the code, so it was either written down somewhere or easy to remember. She looked at the refrigerator, but there was nothing conveniently stuck to the stainless steel surface. What other information had their research shown? What was important to a pack of shapeshifters?

Of course.

She punched in 123006 and smiled when the light turned green.

Obviously they would care about when their alpha came to power. Simple enough in the end.

She opened the garage door and looked at the cars. Luckily, there were only four spots, and only two cars there. She would assume that the others were guarding the roads away from the house. There was only the long driveway and then the lonely state highway all the way back to town. If they setup a checkpoint in either direction, she would be caught.

Simple enough to fix.

Cassie's keys unlocked a dirt stained pickup truck. Mel needed to get out of the house quickly, but she took a moment to recreate the map of the outlying area in her mind. Cassie said that the problem was east, so she would go west. She could circle back east to the rendezvous point eventually, but not until she was well out of the danger zone.

There were county roads which connected to the state highway about a mile out in either direction and no other properties between those two roads. So if she were posting guards, she would leave a bit of a buffer, at least a quarter of a mile, maybe half. The night was dark enough that they would see her headlights from a distance. Any moment that she was on the road, she would be a beacon for any shapeshifter looking her way.

Of course, without the kid in tow, she didn't need to worry about a vehicle. Mel stripped down, tossing her clothes into the large trash can. Her charm was specially fitted to withstand her shift and stay around her neck, even in leopard form. She pressed the button to open the garage and crouched to change shape. It took nearly a minute to complete the shift. She'd heard that some people could do so in seconds, but she was nowhere near that level.

She took off into the forest at a run. No one was in the house to send up the alert that she'd gone. And while she kept her ears open for anyone in pursuit, she crossed over the border of Luke's property in a few minutes. But she didn't breathe easy.

She was open to the night around her. In her cat form all of her senses were improved. She could hear small branches rustle as nocturnal animals ran through them. The scent of greenery, of life, engulfed her, singing through her nose and into her veins. If she were free to do so, she would range through this forest, mark it as her own, and dance with all of the night creatures.

But she couldn't become enchanted by this animal magic. It always tried to take over in the dizzying moments after a shift, tried to lure her away from humanity with the siren song of the wild. Mel was too enamored of the finer things in life to be seduced, but that didn't mean she didn't have to fight the temptation each time.

She headed west, quickly covering miles, only slowing when her heart threatened to burst in her chest. Even in this superior running form she felt the weight of days stuck in a cage. She heard a semi-truck rumble by and knew she was close to the road. Mel was far enough west now that she no longer risked running into Luke's guards, but a leopard running alongside the road would be a strange sight in Colorado, and so she kept to the cover of the trees to hide herself.

She crossed the road to loop north and head back east. She added an extra dozen miles onto her run just to ensure that she stayed completely out of reach of whatever problems Luke was dealing with.

The first shaft of sunlight was breaking through the horizon when she met Krista and Luke at the rendezvous point, a little park in the city. It was risky, but they had needed to setup a place close enough to ensure that Mel could actually get to them before whoever was pursuing got to her first.

She skidded into the park where Bob was laying peacefully on top of a wooden picnic table, his hands clasped lightly over his stomach and his head hanging off the edge, lolling back. Krista had been sitting in their car, but when she saw Mel she got out and threw a pair of sweatpants and a tank top on the ground. Bob wasn't looking at her and Krista averted her gaze before she shifted.

Shifting didn't hurt, but it required concentration, and it sure as hell wasn't pretty when it couldn't be done quickly. But Mel came out all right and put her clothes on. It felt like a hundred pound weight had been lifted off her chest when she saw her team and she couldn't stop from smiling.

"Thanks for showing up," she said.

Krista's gaze hardened and Mel realized she had said the exact wrong thing. "Of course, we do the damned job." The shorter woman looked over at Bob and yelled, "We're ready," then got into the driver's seat.

Bob sat up without the assistance of his hands and moved across the park in a blink of an eye. Mel wished she could ask him what the hell he was, but his grin told her he wouldn't answer. And anyone would be offended by the question. She slid in the back seat while her other partner rode shotgun.

She could sleep for a week and had to fight to keep her eyes open, but there was still work to be done. "When's the meet?"

Krista blew out a breath and didn't answer, so Bob spoke for her. "Tonight."

9

They took her back to the cabin just outside of town. Tina planned to meet them at the cabin later that night. Mel wanted a shower before she had to deal with Tina again. When she walked into her bathroom she saw that bathing might be a problem.

"Krista!" It was a familiar frustration that laced her words, one that Krista had learned to embrace over the years. Mel stared at the circle of sand and candles situated in the white porcelain tub where she'd been planning to relax. The candles were a mix of black and white, the sand shared the same colors. Inside it all Mel saw a lock of what she assumed was her hair bound with an elastic hairband.

Krista took her time in joining her, but after a moment she appeared in the doorway. "What?"

Mel's jaw nearly dropped. She jerked her hand and pointed at the spell brewing in her tub. "Why is this here?"

Krista took one look at the project and smiled. "You wanted the teleportation charm. And if you had waited another day we would have pulled you out." She gestured to the center of the circle. Mel noticed that the bundle of hair was sitting on a small pile of ash. "Once it's dissolved completely it's as safe as teleportation ever is. Even half dissolved, it'll be useable in a few hours," she paused and then continued, "If you're feeling lucky.

"But why is it in *my* bathroom?" Mel persisted.

Krista huffed, "Like I was going to waste my space while you were locked up in some lion's dungeon? Please. Anyway, I'll be happy to sleep for a week once that's ready to go. I don't know if I've ever done so much magic in my life."

She walked away, but that didn't stop Mel from calling after her. "I'm glad you were so concerned for my safety!" Krista showed her worry with one finger. Mel would have laughed if she thought it was in jest. But the time for jokes was long past.

Mel gave up hope of a shower and decided that a

quick meal before bed would be almost as good. The kitchen was stocked with plenty of frozen food, and she grabbed a box at random. Taste was not her goal at the moment. Bob walked into the kitchen while she set the timer on the microwave. He sat on one of the stools and watched her without comment. Mel didn't feel like speaking, either. She let her food cook and watched the timer count down. She could practically feel Bob's eyes on her for all ninety seconds.

Only when she had pulled the tray out of the microwave and begun to blow on the steaming contents to cool them off did he start to speak. "Did you turn suicidal all of a sudden?"

Mel let the dinner drop and looked at her old partner. His dark skin seemed to drink in all of the light in the kitchen and nearly gave off an almost ethereal glow. She could see something dark slithering deep in his eyes, something ancient that he usually kept hidden. "What makes you think that?"

"Nothing you've done in the past few weeks has suggested otherwise." He laced his fingers together and set them on the counter.

She picked up her fork and stabbed at the chicken and noodles. "I don't want to die. I'm just...determined."

"How has that worked out for you?" When he said

things like that, Mel knew that Bob had to be much older than he put on. Most everyone she met was - anyone with a lick of magic lived far beyond the eighty to one hundred years that regular humans hoped for. But most magic types didn't bother to hide their years either. If she asked Bob how old he was, she knew that he'd smile and say thirty. Just like he had when they met eight years ago.

But Bob's question stung. "Are you talking about Cincinnati? Because—"

He held up a hand before she could offer her excuse. "Krista will get over it someday. You did what you had to do."

"And what about you?"

Bob unclenched his hands and stood. "You're one of the best damn thieves out there. Working with you is an honor, and I know you'll do what you have to do to get the job done. If the payment is right, we can continue to be colleagues." She thought he was done, but he continued after a moment. "But if I can't count on my friends, then I don't know what the point is." He left without another word.

Mel ate her sad looking TV dinner alone. She didn't have time to deal with all of this bullshit between her team members. They were going to get the job done, that was it. Then they would go their separate ways.

She and Krista weren't kids anymore, they didn't need to hold each other's hands and reassure themselves that no one could hurt them. Plenty of people could hurt them. That was just how it was.

Mel threw her tray of food away and went to lay down. She had earned her nap.

Before Tina was supposed to meet them that night, Krista placed a cerulean marble into Mel's hand. "It's just like the last charm," she said. "Only you can break it. Think of a place really hard and you should end up there. It'll be fresh enough to work for a month. But it might kill you."

She walked off before Mel could thank her.

Just after sunset Krista took down the ward and Tina drove up the gravel driveway in a beige sedan that was at least twenty years old. Mel hadn't even seen the gem after she buried it, and she couldn't wait to get rid of the thing and take her payment. This job had been far too weird. The faster she could leave Eagle Creek, the better.

And she wouldn't even think about that alpha.

Tina stepped out of the car. She still looked like she was in her forties and wore dark colors. Mel thought that she must have been wearing a glamour of some sort. It was difficult to make out where the woman ended and the darkness of the night began. Clever. Mel would need to see if she could purchase a charm like that off one of her contacts.

The older witch carried a small wooden box in her hands. She smiled at Krista and nodded to Mel. She refused to acknowledge Bob. "Mellie! Kris. I knew you girls could do it." Mel could have choked on the saccharine sweetness of her tone.

"Is that my payment?" Mel asked. She wouldn't be bitter, but neither would she be nice. This was purely business.

Without warning, Tina threw the box at her. Mel caught it and flipped the small metal clasp open. Inside was a small key. "And where's the safety deposit box? And why didn't you just bring it with?" she asked.

Tina grinned and held up a note card. "Written down here, my dear. And safety first. Now may I see the item?"

Mel could hear Krista heave a sigh and she looked over just in time to catch her rolling her eyes so hard that her head had to hurt. But a truck pulled up behind Tina's car before Krista could flash the stone. And judging by the frozen set of Tina's shoulders, no one was supposed to have followed her.

"Who are your friends?" Bob asked.

Tina looked behind her and when she faced them again all color had drained from her face. "Sweetie?"

She asked her daughter, "Could you put that ward back up before we have unpleasant company?"

Mel got a good look at the truck. It was dark gray with mud splattered all around the bottom. The light was dimming, but it looked like there was some kind of cover on the bed. The truck looked familiar, but she dismissed the thought. She had seen hundreds of gray trucks in her life. Why would this one be special?

"I'm spent," said Krista. "All I can do is make it so they can't hear us."

Tina pursed her lips and steeled her shoulders, but she said nothing else.

"Who is that?" asked Mel.

"You didn't think I wanted the gem for myself, did you?" Tina replied. She held out a hand. "Let's just finish the trade and nothing bad will happen.

"What's going on, Mom?" Krista bit out the words.

Tina still didn't answer. "Just give me my gem. Please."

With a huff, Krista pulled the velvet bag out of her pocket and handed it to her mother. "Fine, here's your stupid rock. We're done now." She looked at Mel and nodded to Bob. "Right? Business concluded?"

Mel nodded. "Yeah. Thanks for your help." She barely got the last word out when men stepped out of each of the trucks. Ice shivered down Mel's spine. Even a hundred feet away she could tell that there was something wrong about them. Their skin was white, nearly glowing in the dusky moonlight. And they moved with a serpentine grace that looked wrong on the human form. Mel saw Tina glance back once. "You hired us to work for vampires?" She hissed.

Krista had been about to walk away, but she stopped. "Did you want to get us killed?"

"It will be fine," Tina told them. "I've worked with some of them before. And I'm still very much alive."

Mel wasn't so confident. But she thought quickly, trying to reason out why vampires would want Luke's special gem. "Is it magical?" She asked.

The velvet bag had already disappeared from Tina's hands. "Does it matter?" Her tone suggested that it wasn't a question.

Both vampires were too close for Mel to argue further. She nodded for Krista to drop the sound ward so that they could talk. As they approached, Mel studied them. Though vampires came in all races, these two were as white as the moon. And like with every vampire she'd ever seen, there was something off about them: their skin looked as if the blood didn't pump steadily through their veins. Instead it swirled and stalled, leaving strange patches of red almost like blush all over. And they smelled wrong. It wasn't decay.

Vampires weren't undead, but it was something sickly-sweet. Whatever magic extended their life was the dark kind that required blood sacrifice. And while witches stank of magic, the vampires smelled of death.

Tina nodded toward the brunet, "Vladimir," and then towards the blond, "Ivan." Russians, great. Whether these were the kind of vamps who lived up the Dracula lifestyle or not would determine exactly how much blood was about to be shed.

"Ms. Anders," Vladimir spoke with a flat American accent. That probably made him old. Anyone younger than a hundred didn't bother or hadn't learned to cover their speech so well. The old ones could sound like they were from anywhere. "This is your girl?"

Mel wouldn't let herself be afraid, though she felt a bit ill with his eyes crawling over her.

Tina smiled, her words bright. "Best person for the job." She held up the velvet bag. "I taught her every-thing I know."

If the situation weren't so dire, Mel would have laughed at the ridiculousness of that statement. But Tina had always been the better talker, no need to test that now.

Vladimir looked at Mel. "You gave this to her, yes?" While his accent was right, his phrasing was stilted. Maybe he wasn't quite as old as originally thought.

Mel nodded.

He held out a hand to Tina. "Then you give to me."

Mel heard a car race down the highway. It had to be speeding to be so loud. The engine rumbled, disturbing some of the birds in a nearby tree. Tina placed the bag in the vampire's hand just as headlights flashed at the end of the drive, temporarily blinding Mel.

Vladimir yanked his hand away. "What the hell is this?" Now some of the Russian crept into his speech. "You have other buyers?"

"What? No!" Tina looked at Mel, but neither Mel nor the rest of her team spoke.

Ivan touched Vladimir's arm and the two spoke quietly in Russian. Mel could barely hear them over the idling engine and wouldn't have understood them anyway. She traded looks with Tina, Krista, and Bob.

A truck door flashed open and the enraged roar of a lion pierced through the night.

10

All hell broke loose. The vampires bolted, taking the gem with them and leaving Mel, Krista, Bob, and Tina to fend for themselves. Of course, the lions were blocking their way. In the blink of an eye, someone shifted from human to cat and pounced, landing on Vladimir. He used the cat's momentum against her and flipped the huge feline, pushing her aside.

For one horrible second Mel thought about running. She could take off and be out of the state before any of Luke's people knew she was gone. But Krista and Bob would be at his mercy. As far as she was concerned, he could have Tina.

"Give me the card," she told the older witch.

Tina didn't argue, she handed the note over to Mel and turned away, her form blurring into the night.

"Really?" Scorn filled Krista's voice. "I don't even know why I'm surprised."

There was nothing important in the house, but Mel was the only one who could leave on foot and hope to get away. "Bob?" She asked, "Assessment." They only had another minute before the lions were on them. They needed a plan.

"Six lions, three in human form, two shifted, one partial. They came in two trucks, both still running. Same model and dirt splatter as the one that vampire brought. He probably stole his from them. I suppose they're after him and that little rock." Bob looked at Krista, "No juice at all?"

Krista closed her eyes and took a deep breath. Mel could feel the tiniest hint of power. This was the scary kind, deep and dark and deadly. "Not much, and once I use it I'm down for the count."

He nodded and looked at Mel. "You better full shift or partial?"

"I can give you claws," she told him. "What do you need?"

"I can get Krista and myself out, but you're going to need to make a run for it." He turned to Krista, "Can you do something to disable the cars? Blow up the engines or whatever?"

Krista smiled. "I've got something."

Bob put a hand on Mel's shoulder and squeezed it quickly. "Don't worry about us once we get to the trees." Mel looked over. It was a hundred feet at least until they reached to forest with angry werecats and vampires in between. But Bob kept talking. "We meet in Illinois. Two days."

Mel took a deep breath and grinned, adrenaline flowing through her veins. "Let's do this thing."

They didn't need any more words. Mel ran the distraction while Bob and Krista got the hell out. They'd played this game a hundred times before, and Mel was happy to be working with people who understood exactly how to get out of a bad situation.

She stuffed the wooden box in her pocket and let claws grow out of one hand. Fighting wasn't her preferred response, but she could hold her own when necessary. She only shifted one hand so that she kept the dexterity of her fingers in the other. She needed to be able to pick things up and grab. Claws could prove bothersome.

Krista's hands glowed with a blue light as she chanted. Mel's ears popped and Krista slumped over, her magic exhausted. Each of the cars in the driveway let out a loud pop and one started shooting flames from under the hood. Krista had done her job - the cars were disabled. Bob picked up Krista and took off at a slow jog for the woods. Something about his magic helped him blend in. Mel had no idea why he would be safe once they reached the woods, and she wouldn't ask. Since he wouldn't answer, it all worked out.

But they had distance to cover and she needed to make sure that they weren't intercepted.

She headed straight for the roaring lion.

Some might have called it suicidal. But instinct drove her. The only person she needed on the battlefield was the alpha. The man she had just escaped who, for all she knew, was coming back for her in a rage.

She cleared the distance between where she'd been and the battlefield in a few seconds and dived straight for Luke, swiping at him with her clawed hand. That got his attention. Wordlessly, she took off, running in the opposite direction of Krista and Bob. The lion alpha followed, she knew that he would. Something told her that he couldn't resist.

Luke wasn't completely shifted, and because of that, she thought she might survive. Like her, he only had one hand full of claws, though he also had long fangs growing out of his mouth. Mel didn't have the time or the skill to mimic his shift. But her goal wasn't to fight him, it was just to get him far enough away, to distract him.

Fallen branches and brush were no obstacle for her as she broke into the forest opposite from where Bob and Krista ran to. Even in the dim light she could see well enough and at her speed she relied more on instinct anyway.

For a moment, she remembered her childhood, running through the forest with her parents. They always stayed in human form since she was too young to shift. But every week they walked through some of the densest woods on their land. As a child it seemed to go on forever. And they always ended up at that old well that had been boarded up long before she was born and had been overgrown with moss and ivy.

Mel pushed the thought away, in the midst of a chase for her life, for her freedom, she couldn't bother to remember shit from before she was old enough to remember almost anything. She could feel Luke closing in behind her. She was fast, but his longer legs and familiarity with the terrain worked against her.

But Mel had never met a problem head on when she could approach it sideways.

She jumped up, grabbing for a branch with her

claws and swung herself up into the trees. She didn't care if Luke saw her. It wouldn't matter.

The branches were thick enough that even in her clumsy, human form she could move among them, covering less ground, but well hidden. Luke finally caught up to her, pausing only a few feet before she would have pounced on him. He crouched low, better to get her scent, but they'd left her trail behind.

Mel held completely still. She didn't even breathe until he moved once more. He circled the copse of trees slowly, trying to figure out where she went. Her heart pounded, excitement singing through her veins. This was even better than her stint in Biloxi where the owner – former owner – of one of the finest collections of antique Bavarian wealth charms caught her outside his building while her bag was full of his collection.

It seemed like Luke had that effect on her.

But even though a part of her wanted to dart from the tree, tweak his ear, and take off running again - wanted to make him chase her, and catch her, and all of the fun that could go along with that - despite all that, she still kept her sense. The roar that he'd bellowed had been far too intense for one little thief. And while she loved risk, she had no desire to end up dead.

She just had to wait for Luke to doubt himself. Right now he knew that she had to be where she was, but she knew that if she waited long enough, he would convince himself that she had gone another way, that his senses were wrong.

After an interminable length of time he walked away, his senses caught by some far off sound. Mel let out a relieved breath, but still she didn't move. She couldn't until she was sure he couldn't chase her.

A snapped branch was her only warning half a second before Luke launched himself at her, jumping from a nearby tree. They crashed through the branches and down to the ground. Everything hurt when he landed on top of her, but nothing was broken. Her only advantage was that he hadn't been able to pin her clawed hand. She had her claws dug into his thigh, blood seeping hotly around her fingers.

"Where is she?" he bellowed, teeth flashing. He didn't seem to care that she was ripping his muscles apart.

Mel struggled for a moment, failing utterly to move the enraged alpha. She couldn't fight him. He was too strong, too big. "I can't say I'm surprised we ended up like this, but I thought I'd be lying on something a lot softer when I had you on top of me," she practically purred. For a moment the image crystallized in her mind, but she shoved it away before arousal could take hold.

Luke placed a hand on her throat, letting a claw grow out of his index finger. She felt it prick at the sensitive skin of her neck. "You will know pain unlike anything you have ever experienced before if you don't tell me what you did with her. Five seconds before I rip half of your throat out."

He was utterly serious. An experienced liar could recognize the truth like that, especially when it came to threats.

Mel didn't remove her claws, but she stopped digging in. "Who are you talking about?" But as she asked the question, she had a sinking feeling that she knew who it had to be. After all, she had only met two women at Luke's compound, and Maya wouldn't need an alpha to risk his life to rescue her.

"Your scent was all over the garage, I could smell her in your room." He growled. "I know you kidnapped her, so where is she?"

"Get off of me and I'll tell you everything I know." Honor was for good people, Mel was a survivor.

He didn't get off, but he did remove his hand. An improvement. "I don't believe you. You're a liar, a thief, and you would have done anything to escape." He was beyond reason. An alpha defined himself by the people he ruled and protected. Cassie was Luke's weak point. If Mel wanted to hurt him, she knew exactly where to hit.

She removed her claws and pushed at his legs, she got her hips free. It gave her more room to maneuver even if she didn't want to fight. "I'm a thief," she bit out, "But I'm not an *idiot*." She pulled her hand up, brushing against a spectacularly smooth rock on her way to push against his chest. He didn't budge. "Think about it. What would I gain by kidnapping Cassie? I wanted out. Why would I give you another reason to chase me?"

That gave him pause. Confusion flitted over his face. But he steeled himself after a moment and pinned one of her hands to the ground above her head and the other to her side, right over that rock. "Her scent was in your cell! Don't lie to me."

It wasn't a rock. Mel ignored the man on top of her and tried to curl her fingers around the teleportation charm that Krista had given her. In the frenetic run, she'd forgotten that she had it. All she had to do was break it and she was home free. But she didn't quite have the leverage. She spoke while she tried to move, keeping him distracted. "She wanted me to take her. She knocked out your guard. All I did was tie her up. I didn't need her to escape."

But Luke was too far gone to pay attention. It didn't matter anyway. Mel had the charm in her fist. She crushed it with all her might, shattering the glass and releasing the magic and thinking of someplace safe. After a pregnant second while the magic swirled around her, she dissolved into smoke with the hope that Krista's charm wouldn't kill her.

She heard her alpha roar into the void.

11

Luke fell forward as Mel evaporated beneath him. He let out a howl, rage beating through him as his thief escaped him a second time. He raked his claws through her forgotten clothes. The woman was gone, but she had left behind her a pile of fabric covered in her scent. He sliced through it, only pausing when he nearly crushed a small wooden box.

That was strange. Why would she carry something like that into battle?

He heard a twig snap as Maya joined him. "One of the vampires confessed to stealing the truck. He said your thief didn't do it."

Luke held the box close and turned to her. Maya had specks of unnaturally dark blood across her face, evidence of a triumphant battle. But he could see a bruise already forming under her eye. "There were two vampires."

She pursed her lips. "One got away."

"Is the other one still alive?" He sunk as much menace into the words as he could. In his mood, it was enough.

She paled. "More or less."

"Good."

Maya caught sight of the pile of clothes that Luke was crouched over. "So she got away?" she asked. "Naked?"

He held up the box, flashing it at Maya before flipping it open. Inside there was a safe deposit box key and a card listing an address. Probably for the bank. "I think she'll want this." He stuffed the box into his pocket and joined Maya on the walk back to their prisoner. He had a sister to rescue, a political nightmare to handle, and a thief to catch.

Life was getting exciting.

Mel materialized screaming in downtown Trent Crossing, Utah at midnight. And she only knew that because the sign on the side of the road proudly proclaimed a population of 363. Luckily for her, the town was so small that no one was there to see her little magic trick. She panted, illuminated only by the red flashing stop light and took stock of her situation.

It took her a moment to realize that she was naked.

When she did, she fell to her knees, looking to see if the safe deposit box key had miraculously come with her. "Come on, come on," she urged. "Where the fuck are you?" In the dim light she could see clearly, and that only frustrated her more.

The key was back in Colorado. Probably right under Luke Torres.

God damn it.

Mel didn't panic. She wasn't allowed to. She remembered the box number, the bank address. A loss of a key was an inconvenience, not a tragedy. Bank robbery was easy, like taking candy from a baby. Nothing to worry about there.

Headlights flashed, haloing her naked form.

A black pickup truck pulled up beside her. An old man, human and at least in his seventies looked out at her. "Looks like you're in a bit of a pickle there, kid." He said. He reached over and tossed her a t-shirt.

Mel put it on. "Thanks," she said. "Any chance you could give me a ride to the next big town?"

The man was apprehensive. She didn't blame him. Naked women in the town square were usually up to no good. "I think I can arrange that. Climb on in." She joined him, wrapping a blanket around herself before buckling the passenger side seat belt. It was a long way back to Illinois. But she was going to get her damned payment and leave the lion alpha behind her.

ENTANGLED WITH THE THIEF

1

Crystal Lake Savings and Loan sat a little off the main road in a nice office park in Crystal Lake, Wisconsin. At noon on a Wednesday, traffic into and out of the bank was fairly constant. Workers on lunch came to cash and deposit checks, and the part-time employees switched out shifts. Mel watched it all through the rear view mirror in a car parked half a block away.

Mel straightened the collar of her shirt and checked the clock. Kathy Pierson was her target and she needed to be inside before 12:30 or everything was fucked. On the bright side, this job didn't exactly stretch her skills. This was a small town bank protecting small town goods. But it meant that no one would look for Tina's safe deposit box here. Especially since Mel suspected that it was a temporary arrangement. The scry crystal was the only item of Tina's that would be found in this bank, probably in this state. But Mel didn't need anything else from that witch, not anymore. Once she had the crystal she would be well on her way to taking on the one person who had no place living anymore.

Mel was playing the role of Helen Undine, a mediocre lawyer from Milwaukee looking for a taste of the simple life. Her hair was pulled back into a tight bun, no flyaways allowed. Her suit was two shades darker than beige and particularly unflattering, though expensive. She wore a small strand of pearls and a gaudy engagement ring. Helen was a... complicated woman. And exactly what Mel needed at the moment.

She wore flats, even though Helen would normally wear heels. But some things needed to be sacrificed for convenience, and running in a skirt suit would be difficult enough, she had no desire to trip over unnecessary inches.

The inside of the bank did not give her the best impression of its security. A salesman's desk sat unoccupied in the lobby, and whoever sat there had left the computer logged in to the bank's network. The security guard greeted her with a smile and only carried a Taser, not a gun. Three women sat at teller's stations, though only one dealt with a customer. The other two were chatting and paying no attention to the entrance.

She smiled when she saw Kathy Pierson walk across the room.

The woman did a final check on the teller's twenty minutes before the end of her shift, and had been doing so each day that Mel cased the bank. Mel stepped forward quickly, clutching the briefcase and bumped into the bank manager.

"Oh! Excuse me, I'm so sorry," said Kathy. She gave Mel a quick once over, noting the jewelry and the fine leather of her case. "I didn't see you there. Is there anything I can help you with today?"

Perfect. Mel put just enough frustration into her stance and tilted up her nose before speaking. "Yes," she pursed her lips and kept her words clipped. "I need to access my safe deposit box. Are you someone who can handle that?" Condescension dripped from the tone.

Kathy's neck tightened in frustration. Mel knew that, at this time of day, she was the only person authorized to take customers to the vault, and she was minutes away from going home. But she smiled and didn't even sound put out. "Of course. Do you have your key with you? And I'll need to log your admission."

She grabbed a clipboard from one of the tellers and

handed it to Mel. Helen Undine had a beautiful, precise signature that matched her identification.

Kathy led her to the back of the building and through a barred gate. The security guard entered the vault with them. Mel had opened the account three days before and through some quick talking had been able to get the box adjacent to the one that she needed. The guard and Mel each put their keys in the lock and turned simultaneously. The guard pulled out the box and handed it to her. Mel gave a tight smile in thanks.

She was led to a small chamber inside the vault where she would be given privacy to review the contents of the box and make any necessary deposits. Both Kathy and the guard waited behind a red curtain while she got down to business. Mel checked her watch. She'd been in the bank less than ten minutes, and it was almost time to get to work.

A scream rent the air. Right on time.

Mel jerked from her chair and looked at Kathy and the guard. "Is everything alright?" she asked.

Kathy straightened, assessing the situation. She was the only manager on duty at the moment. "I should go check. Will the two of you be alright while I'm gone?"

"By all means," said Mel. "Obviously there are more important issues."

Kathy didn't know how to take that, but she hurried off, leaving Mel and the guard alone. Mel started counting down from 120, which was when the next distraction would go off. She idly sorted through the contents of the box. There were papers and some cheap jewelry, nothing of any real value. But it looked like there was enough that it would take time to find what she needed. That was the important thing.

Right on time, a blast rocked the air, followed by the hollow pop of fire crackers. Mel jerked, knocking over a few of her papers and gasping for effect. She stormed out from behind the curtain, bumping into the guard before she could stop herself. "What was that?" She demanded, a hint of panic creeping into her voice.

The security guard's hand flew to his Taser, and he looked toward the front of the bank. "It's alright, ma'am. You'll be safe here." He took off towards the commotion without further prompting.

Great.

Mel gave it a few seconds before opening her brief-case and pulling out the lock picks. The guard had closed the inner door behind him, which gave her privacy and the freedom to work without looking over her shoulder.

She went to box 109 and placed the guard's key in one of the key slots. She'd lifted it from him when they bumped into each other after the blast. Picking the other lock was easier than it should have been, and Mel had the safe deposit box containing her payment for the Scarlet Emerald job in her hands in under a minute.

She opened the box and froze, not quite understanding what she saw. She closed the box and opened it once more, hoping that her eyes were deceiving her.

There was no payment in the box.

There was only a business card.

In crisp letters the business card said "LUCIO TORRES" and listed a phone number and an email address. No business name, no physical address. But Mel knew exactly where he lived. After all, he was the one she stole the Scarlet Emerald from.

A month earlier, a witch named Tina Anders approached Mel about boosting the gem. It was a difficult job, one that only three people, including Mel, were capable of pulling off. But Tina and Mel had a long history, and Tina offered Mel a payment she couldn't refuse to pull off the job in a nearly-impossible time frame.

And she'd done it, too, except for a small mishap that made her the uninvited guest of the werelion alpha for a few days. And that should have been it. She gave Tina her stone, Tina gave her the key to this safe deposit box, and business was concluded.

Except for the vampires.

When she explained the job, Tina said nothing about vampires. And, if she had, Mel liked to think she would have refused the work outright, no matter the payment. But the vampires showed up, shit went to hell, Luke Torres accused her of kidnapping his sister, and Mel teleported away before he could tear her throat out.

Which was good, except for the part where she ended up naked 1,000 miles away, sans safe deposit box key or address. That all ended up with Luke, in a pile of her clothes in the forest back in Colorado. Only after she met back up with Krista was she reminded that a person using a teleportation charm needed to own the things they wished to teleport. Mel's clothes had been procured through other means.

So while she did own the key and the card with the address fair and square, she didn't own the clothes that had held them. Krista and Bob had both taken off after taking their payments for their parts of the job, and she was left with nothing.

And Luke had everything. Most importantly he had her scry stone.

Mel slammed the box shut and jammed it back into the correct slot. She bit her lip to keep for cursing. A scry stone would allow her to locate the stone's focus with the help of a witch. She'd have a magical GPS to find her target at any time. And this scry stone was more valuable than anything she owned.

This scry stone was linked to a witch named Ava. It would let her track down the woman who had killed her parents.

Mel straightened and sat back at the table, waiting for Kathy or the guard to return. Already a plan was forming in her mind. It was simple enough. She was just going to have to steal from the alpha one more time.

2

The lion roared. The sound shuddered through the forest outside of Eagle Creek, Colorado where the lions of his pack prowled in search of his missing sister. Mel's timing could have been better, but she hadn't known that the night she arrived back in town would be the same night he sent out his troops to find the lost lion cub.

Her heart pounded and exhilaration flowed through her with every snap of a twig. She was just one wrong move away from being imprisoned by the alpha once more. And this time she didn't have a witch to get her out of danger.

She didn't know if they were all out to find Cassie, but she couldn't imagine any other reason for them to be out there. The lions weren't a hunting party out for blood; she could hear the murmur of their words, the surety of their steps. They were tearing the forest apart methodically, covering ever inch in search of the kidnapped teenage girl. But other than the wind and the intermittent sounds of wereanimals on the prowl, Mel heard nothing else.

The nocturnal animals that usually owned these woods had gone into hiding. Even the insects were silent.

She blew away a stray strand of hair and then tucked it behind her ear when it landed in front of her eye once more. The first time she'd come to Eagle Creek, she'd been a red head, or at least she had looked that way. The wig was part of one of her identities and offered a distraction to anyone who tried to remember what she looked like. Tonight there were no distractions. She wore tight, dark clothing that moved with her like a second skin, and she had her brown hair pulled back into a ponytail. On other jobs like this one, she might have worn a mask, but she didn't need to hide her identity from the alpha. He knew she was coming. Hell, he had invited her.

She'd headed straight for Colorado after she'd finished in Wisconsin. The only pit stop involved an overnight's stay in St. Louis to pick up some supplies from a witch that she'd worked with before. For a second she'd considered calling Krista, but she threw the thought away almost as quickly as it came. Her old partners had made it abundantly clear that they were done with her.

And Mel deserved it, she just wished that she didn't. But screwing over partners had consequences that she couldn't avoid; she just had to live through them, and hope that one day Krista would forgive her. The witch was the closest thing to family that Mel had left.

But she couldn't get caught up in that. One wrong move and it was back to the alpha's compound. And that wasn't a game she wanted to play.

The sound of a broken twig was her only warning, Mel reacted, ducking behind a huge tree and keeping absolutely still when two lions walked into the tiny clearing that she'd been moving through. She heard two people enter the clearing and they couldn't be anything other than shifters. Mel took one deep breath and let it out as slowly as possible, resorting to shallow, near silent gulps of air as they moved closer.

She heard a man say "Hold up, there's something different here," and she felt sweat bead on the back of her neck. Mel wasn't breathing deep enough to draw in their scents, and they hadn't been in the area long enough for them to permeate every breath. But she'd been there for several minutes and they weren't hampered by shallow breathing.

"What is it?" asked a woman.

"I think I caught Cassie's scent." The man had a hint of New England in his voice and Mel could almost imagine what he looked like. He'd be tall, short hair that might have been blond, and a jaw strong enough to lift concrete slabs. Or not, she couldn't risk ducking around the tree to be sure.

The woman was pure Georgia south, her words a mix of peaches and honey. "Are you sure? There is something here, but I can't tell."

"It's not one of us," the man's words were certain. She heard him stepping closer. Mel only had seconds before he stepped around and discovered her. She concentrated, feeling her hands turn into leopard's paws, her claws extending. Her only advantage would be surprise, and she would try only to incapacitate, not kill. She had no reason to make the alpha any angrier than he already was.

"Wait," said the woman. "I think I've got a trail over here." The man's footsteps paused and then headed in the opposite direction. Both lions walked away, following the trail she'd left coming into these woods. She was damn lucky, and she wasn't going to risk being caught like that again. She had to get out of these woods and back to her hotel. She could reconfigure her plans then.

Mel took to the trees to get out of the woods. Her claws helped her, allowing her to dig into the bark and hoist herself onto sturdy branches. She jumped from tree to tree, travelling slowly but leaving a much more discrete scent trail. She froze when she heard another roar, this one unlike the first. The first lion's roar had been full of rage and regret, the call of an animal determined to have his revenge. This one was joyous.

Cassie had been found.

Alive.

Mel didn't let that stop her. She made it miles and miles away to the small parking lot in the national park close to the edge of Luke's territory. She sat on a large branch and waited for a few moments to turn her paws back into human hands. It wasn't a difficult task, but it took time. And as she shifted slowly, every joint in her fingers ached in protest at the task she'd put them through, climbing through dozens of trees in a form unsuited to the task.

She was ready to jump from her tree when a young woman walked out of the woods on the scenic path of the national park. She looked younger than Mel, maybe in her early twenties, with long black hair and pale skin. She wore jeans, a silky blouse, and hiking boots.

On her wrist Mel could see the glint of silver, perhaps from a watch or bracelet.

It was strange for a woman to be alone in the woods at night. Even Mel was only there for her own nefarious purpose. She was instantly suspicious of the woman. Even more so when she pulled out a cell phone and held it to her ear. Mel had to focus to hear, but she could make out the words clearly.

"Let her know it was a success. The girl has been reunited." Mel would have frozen in place if she hadn't already been still. The woman spoke again. "I'll need to reorder supplies from a local coven. Vladimir underestimated my needs... I understand. I'll be on the lookout." She hung up without a farewell.

Mel stayed in her tree until the woman drove away in a silver sedan. From the plates, she could tell it was a rental.

It appeared that Cassie hadn't been found, she had been given back. But what use did witches have for a werelion that couldn't even shift? And why would one need additional supplies?

Mel tried not to let it bother her. She climbed down from her tree and got in the rusty old pickup truck that she'd stolen halfway between Colorado and Wisconsin. She crossed off this parking lot as a point of entry for her next heist, and planned to get a new car out in Denver where she was staying.

It was a two hour drive back to that city. Mel let the miles pass, alone on the road with her thoughts. After half an hour of struggling, she turned up the radio and sang along with a popular country song she'd heard nearly every hour as she tried to find clear stations.

The distraction didn't work. But she made it all the way to Denver without deciding to go find out what the witches wanted.

Maya had gotten the tip about Cassie an hour ago. It took Luke twenty minutes to mobilize the search party and another dozen minutes for his people to pour through the woods. He let out an enraged roar, desperate to find his sister and bring her back home. She'd already been gone for too long, but he would not lose her.

The sound ripped out of his human mouth, battering against his vocal chords and leaving pain in its wake. He didn't care. There was no pain too great, no task too big that would prevent him from finding Cassie.

He found her scent and latched on, following it

through trails that didn't exist, vaulting over downed branches and crashing through the brush. His search wasn't silent – he'd scared away the normal inhabitants of this forest by bringing all of his own predators along for the ride. They'd all split up, searching the woods in groups of twos and threes. He alone traveled with four other lions. They would not leave their leader vulnerable in what could very well be a trap.

But Maya trusted her source, and Luke trusted Maya. They were going to find Cassie. Safe and sound.

The forest terminated abruptly, opening into a wide clearing. Luke spotted Cassie, moving in the middle of a ring of mushrooms only fifty feet away. He let out another roar, this one ragged and joyful and ran across the clearing, tromping on the mushrooms and gathering his sister into his arms.

Cassie would have hugged him back, but her hands were held together with silver handcuffs and her feet were bound with rope. She dug her face into the crook of his neck and he could feel her tears against his skin. "I was so scared," she said, "Thank you." She sobbed out the words, almost out of breath from the strength of his hug.

Luke patted down her hair. It was a mass of blonde knots with a few leaves stuck in for good measure, almost like she'd been in the forest for longer than the few hours that Maya's informant had said she had been. "We've got you." He kissed her forehead and pulled back to try and remove her restraints.

He heard two more of his lions enter the clearing while he worked. He had to pull back swiftly after one touch of the cuffs. The silver content was so high that he could already feel his fingers itch in reaction. He's always had a low silver tolerance, but it usually took at least a few moments for an allergic reaction to kick in. "I need a key to these cuffs!" He demanded and moved to untie Cassie's legs. She held still, and since it was normal, if thick, rope he was able to free her in no time.

"This isn't the same, I told you," said Javier, one of the lions who'd volunteered to search on short notice. He wasn't a tracker and had never hunted down a person before. But Luke needed all hands on deck.

His partner for the night, Alisha, replied. "We probably covered someone else's ground." She left Javier and approached Luke. Alisha had only moved into his territory three months before, formerly working at the CDC in Atlanta until she received a job offer too good to pass up in Denver. She didn't live within pack territory, but that hadn't stopped her from quickly becoming an important member of the pack.

Javier, on the other hand, had been born and raised in Eagle Creek and owned a small accounting firm that handled the money of several local businesses. They were the first two to join Luke and his entourage in this clearing. The rest of the pack slowly trickled in.

Mick, a boy recently in trouble for general rowdiness and for failure in his guard duty, quickly picked the locks of Cassie's restraints. For the moment Luke was happy the boy had the skill, but he made a mental note to figure out why kids in his pack were learning how to break into things.

There had been enough thievery for one lifetime.

After ensuring that Cassie wasn't booby-trapped and that there were no other nasty surprises in the clearing, Luke helped Cassie up and they made it out to where he'd parked his car to take her back home.

He expected Cassie to sleep after taking a shower, but his younger sister called him into her room to talk while she was busy drying off her hair. Now that she was no longer covered in smudges of dirt and grass, he could see black and brown bruises covering her pale skin. Violence roared within him and he wanted to run, to hunt down whoever had done that to her. But he was thankful that her only injuries seemed to be superficial. No broken bones, nothing worse.

At least, she hadn't said anything.

"How are you doing?" he asked. He sat down in the reading chair and propped his feet on the foot of her bed. The room was large, with two chairs, a writing desk, and a reading nook built in by the window. It was the guest room Luke used for his family and it was only two doors down from his own.

Cassie sat on the bed, her back resting on the headboard. "Bumped and bruised, but I'm okay." She combed her fingers through her hair gently while she talked. "I'm so sorry, I screwed up. I shouldn't have done it, please," tears pricked her eyes. "I know I was wrong—"

Luke held up a hand. "We'll talk about all that later." And he fully intended to, he knew that anger would lick at his heels once he was certain that his sister was safe. Even now, with her back in her room, he couldn't quite believe it. But come morning he expected to be in full form. She didn't need that tonight.

But she wasn't ready to stop talking. "Did you tell Mom and Dad?" He didn't think she could sound any more apologetic.

And it was Luke's turn to hesitate. His mother and stepfather had been on vacation when Cassie disappeared, and he hadn't even thought to contact them until two days later. As alpha of his territory, looking out for his people was his job, he couldn't go crying to his parents whenever something went wrong. So he had stalled and stalled. "Not yet," he finally said. "I knew that I would find you."

Cassie narrowed her eyes, but she didn't ask for more reasons. "So maybe they don't have to know?"

"We'll talk about that later."

His sister let it drop. She changed the subject. "There were two vampires that took me, though I only saw one after the first night. After that they—" she cut off and furrowed her brow. After a moment she continued as if she didn't remember pausing, "I can't remember how I got to the clearing, but I knew you were coming for me." She smiled and leaned further back, perhaps relaxing for the first time since she'd entered his house that night. But she sat back up and stiffened.

"What's wrong?" Luke asked.

Cassie shook her head. "I don't know. My back must be bruised or something."

Luke stood. "Can I take a look?" He didn't have medical training, but he thought he could tell the difference between something minor and something severe. "Or I can have Kenny come take a look. She's a paramedic."

Cassie lay down on her stomach. "Sure, take a look." She hiked up her shirt to reveal a mass of bruises centered around her spine. The ugly purple, black, and blue covered her back, Luke had no idea how she hadn't noticed it until that moment.

He gently pressed his hand down on the bruised flesh. "Does this hurt?" He asked.

Cassie's voice was muffled by the blanket. "Like it's bruised," she answered.

"I've got some ointment that should help." He left her alone for a moment to grab to bottle from his bathroom. But he'd only stepped into the hallway when the hackles on the back of his neck rose. He turned around and stormed right back into Cassie's room.

His thief, the woman who'd stolen the Scarlet Emerald right from his vault stood over his sister, one hand hovering over Cassie's back.

"What the hell are you doing here?" he snapped.

3

It was a good question. Mel had made it to her hotel before that nagging feeling in the pit of her stomach forced her to turn around and break every speed limit to get back to Luke's house. Witches didn't play nice, they didn't let their captives free, not as easily as they let Cassie go.

And once she saw Cassie's back things started to become clearer.

She froze when the alpha entered the room. It had only been a week since they'd last seen each other, but somehow she'd forgotten exactly what it felt like to stand next to him. Luke Torres took up all the space in the room when he was mad. He wasn't as hugely muscular as some men; his build was more compact, lithe. But he was taller than Mel, and exuded the confidence of a man who ruled over people who respected him.

He had brown hair long enough that Mel had to clench her fists to stop the compulsion of running her fingers through it, and dark brown eyes that locked her in place. In the yellow light of Cassie's room, his skin looked magically dark gold, though during the day it would be a more normal light brown.

Mel didn't know why she felt so drawn to him. She'd been around plenty of powerful men and women in her life and never had she felt the urge to be near them, or to do wicked things with them.

But Luke brought out something in her, something that called her to help when she knew he was being threatened by a force he couldn't understand. But she didn't answer his question. It was his sister who needed her attention. "Do you know who did this to you, Cassie?"

The blonde girl looked over her shoulder, confused. "One of the vampires, I guess?"

Mel studied the scrolling dark lines weaving over the ridges of Cassie's spine. She traced a finger over the hex. No, this wasn't the work of a vampire.

Strong hands gripped her shoulders, shoving her away from the teenager and against the wall. Luke put his forearm over her throat to hold her in place. "What the *hell* are you doing here?" he demanded.

Speaking around the vise of his arm proved difficult, but Mel made the effort. "Can't you see that no vampire did that?" She pushed against him but he didn't budge. She didn't expect him to.

"Your concern for my sister's injury is appreciated, but you have no right to be here." He crushed his arm harder against her and spoke inches from her face.

It was Mel's turn to be confused. Even with no experience with witches, how could they be stupid enough to think vampires could hex a girl? Mel let herself go limp, waiting for Luke to lower his guard just enough. When he did, she looped her ankle around his knee, kicking at the awkward angle and causing him to buckle forward.

She jumped to the side and hopped to the other side of Cassie's bed, putting the girl between the two of them. Luke wouldn't risk hurting his sister. But Mel had to talk fast before he recovered enough to avoid the girl. "This is a hex. I saw a witch in the forest. Something is fishy about this and I came to warn you."

That gave the alpha pause. "What would a witch want with my sister?"

Cassie watched the back and forth, remaining silent.

Mel didn't know the answer. But she needed some of her own. "Why did you think that this was a bruise? It's clearly magic." She waved her hand over the girl's back without touching her.

Luke took two steps closer, but he didn't move to hurt Mel again. Progress. "I know what a fucking bruise looks like. There's nothing magic there." He jerked his head up and he met her eyes. "How do *you* know so much about magic?"

It was a valid question, and one Mel hadn't meant to answer. Shapeshifters customarily kept their distance from witches. Centuries of conflict made collaboration a difficult prospect. And Mel's situation was stickier than most. "I've worked with witches," she finally said. "It's a requirement in my line of work."

His shoulders tensed and she knew she shouldn't have mentioned theft. But all ground was shaky when it came to dealing with Luke.

"Why should I believe you?" He couldn't have sounded more doubtful if he tried. But clearly something was keeping him from springing on her and locking her back up in the cell in his basement.

"Because—" The door flew open before Mel could finish speaking, and Maya Nunez, Luke's second in command, burst in, pointing a gun at Mel's face. The woman seemed older than Luke, though Luke was only in his thirties and most of their kind were older than him. She had bright red hair that she must have dyed constantly to maintain the vivid color. That hair brought out the red undertones in her brown skin and made her seem lit with an inner fire.

The other woman didn't take a shot. Seeing that Luke stood coiled to strike but unmoving, and that Cassie lay peacefully on the bed, she lowered her gun. Mel knew not to make any sudden movements. Luke might have been the strongest person in the room, but one look in Maya's eyes and Mel knew she was the deadliest.

"Are you alright?" she asked Luke, not taking her eyes off Mel. Her voice held the faintest trace of an accent, though Mel couldn't identify it.

Luke looked at Maya and seemed to come to a decision. "Is there anything strange about Cassie's back?" he asked.

Maya didn't question the request. She approached the girl and examined her exposed back. "She's been bruised, possibly slammed against a wall, based on the pattern. I'd guess this happened at least two days ago from the coloring." Maya looked at Mel. "So why are *you* here?"

Mel had to keep from gnashing her teeth. But it made a certain kind of sense that no one but her could see the hex. The more specific magic was, the more power it had. Mel pulled her phone out of her pocket and snapped a picture of the design on Cassie's spine. She tossed the phone to Luke. "Now do you see it?" she asked. She didn't know if it would work, but if it didn't, she was out of ideas.

The color drained from Luke's face. Cassie finally sat up. She adjusted her shirt to cover herself and approached her brother. "What is it?"

Luke handed the phone to his sister and looked over at Mel. "How?"

Mel shrugged, but while speaking to Luke she saw Maya shift on her feet. She spoke slowly, swinging her head to the side to make sure the window was in view. "You've caught the attention of a coven."

Maya sprang at her, but Mel was already moving, diving out of the third story window and rolling when she hit the grass below. It hurt like hell, but she couldn't let that slow her down. She sprinted for her life, hoping that Luke called off Maya before they unleashed the proverbial hounds.

She didn't let herself believe she was safe until she was halfway to Denver once more.

Maya had her gun out before Luke even realized that Mel was out the open window. "Let her go," he told his security chief. "She'll be back, I'm sure."

Cassie studied the picture on the phone. Luke couldn't quite believe it himself. When he'd looked at Cassie's back, it was clearly covered in regular bruises. But when he looked at the picture that Mel had just taken, he saw the darkly lined scrollwork which weaved its way over every visible part of her spine.

"It doesn't hurt," said Cassie. "It looks like a tattoo, but it doesn't hurt like one."

"You have a tattoo?" It wasn't the most important thing, but a big brother liked to know about what was going on in his sister's life.

Cassie – rightfully – hit him in the shoulder and stuck out her tongue.

Maya holstered her gun and shut the window, closing the curtain as well. "Your thief is hiding more than we thought."

And wasn't that the truth. Luke knew she was coming. How could she resist when he'd put his own business card and stolen her pretty necklace right out of her safe deposit box? But seeing her in his house once more, standing right over his sister – that had been a surprise. The first time they'd met, he had been caught by the sight of her hair. Bright red, coming down in perfect waves, as eye catching as neon. Of course, that was a wig. But what was underneath was so much more interesting. Not her hair, which was naturally brown. But the woman herself. He'd become entangled with a thief.

"Are you surprised?" He asked Maya.

"If she pulls a rabbit out of her hat, I'm done." Maya threw her hands up. The warning wasn't necessary. Shapeshifters couldn't create magic, witches couldn't change shape. Some things were constants in the world and Luke didn't expect that one to change.

Luke turned to his sister, "Do you remember this happening? Who did this to you?" With proof of magical involvement in front of him he had to act. "Do you know how you got to that forest?"

"You think I'm like a Trojan horse or something?" asked Cassie. She wasn't looking at either of them. Instead, her finger traced above the pattern immortalized in Mel's phone. Her voice was hollow, "I should remember this. It had to hurt, it *does* hurt a little. But I only ever saw vampires."

Luke drew his sister in to a hug, holding her lightly against him and resting his cheek against her blonde temple. She was nearly as tall as him, but it didn't mean he couldn't comfort her. He pulled the phone from her hands and handed it over her shoulder to Maya. "See what you can grab about Mel. And see if there's anything on the hex."

Maya nodded and left the siblings alone.

Cassie sniffed and backed away, wiping at her eyes with the back of her hand. "I thought it was going to be over."

So had Luke, but some things were just too convenient to work out that way. "How did you end up in the forest? Any idea?" The tip had come quickly, Maya had been so sure and Luke hadn't questioned it. And now it seemed that he should have.

Cassie sat back down, this time in one of the chairs. She rested her elbows on her legs and her head in her hands. "There was a house. After...no." She smacked a hand down and let out an anguished breath. "Let me start from the beginning." But she wouldn't look at him when she spoke.

Luke nodded. He wouldn't let himself be angry at her. Not yet, not until she was okay.

"Okay. I was in the cell downstairs with Mel." Cassie glanced over to see if he would say anything.

And Luke didn't interrupt to ask why. He was very proud of himself for that and tried not to let it show.

"She tied me up in the bathroom, lectured me about being stupid, and took off. And then I was down there for a while. But it couldn't have been too long because

Mick would have woken up. Maybe twenty minutes?" She twisted her fingers together and remembered to breathe. "And then I heard footsteps. Fast, and not nearly as graceful as anyone in your pack. So I stayed really quiet. But they found me. Two vampires. They untied me, threw something in my face, and got me out of the house. I don't remember it very well. It was all fuzzy. Almost like I was super drun..." she cut herself off and smiled at Luke.

Luke had to laugh. "I'm completely shocked that my eighteen year old sister has consumed alcohol. Please continue."

"Anyway, I was loopy. I don't remember if Mick was still in the hallway or not, and I blacked out once we were in the car. I woke up in a small house. I could see the mountains from my window. It was on the third story so I couldn't jump out. And then..." Cassie's eyes went distant, and she slumped to the side of the chair.

Luke rushed over, heart racing. He shook her shoulders, calling her name.

"And I woke up in the forest, all tied up." She straightened in the chair and met his eyes. "When did you get over here?" She looked between the far side of the room and Luke. "You're fast, but not that fast."

Icy terror flooded Luke and he did his best to keep his expression neutral while he spoke. He didn't want

Cassie to be afraid. To be *more* afraid, anyway. "You passed out. Do you remember that?"

Cassie paled. "No. I don't know what you're talking about."

Luke grabbed her hand and gave it a quick squeeze. "It's okay. We'll get this figured out."

He knew just who to call for assistance.

4

Mel didn't know how to make her next move. She had no way to enter Luke's property without being caught, and he had no reason to put her scry stone in a vulnerable enough position for her to be able to steal it. She stayed up the entire night trying to figure out a way to get into his fortress, but there was nothing she could do alone.

Sometime just before the sun crested the horizon she fell asleep.

Sometime later, a sound in her room woke her up. Mel remained perfectly still, not even opening her eyes. Any movement would alert her intruder. She breathed deeply and relaxed. The scent that permeated the room was one of comfort, of sexiness, and of home. Just like she remembered Luke.

Her eyes snapped open and she rolled to the side before he could pin her to the bed. In a fluid motion, she went backwards over the edge and landed on her feet, spry and ready to spring into action if he wanted a fight.

The alpha smiled, white teeth shining in the dark room. "Good morning, thief."

Mel was on the balls of her feet, but she didn't run. Instinct had kept her alive in dangerous situations for more than thirty years, and she wasn't going to start ignoring it now. Even when logic told her it would be wise to run from the alpha that couldn't want anything good from her. Not after all the shit she pulled.

Logic said that.

Instinct told her to smile. "Good morning, Alpha." She didn't let the fact that he was in her room, that she was in her pajamas, or that he'd tracked her down intimidate her. She didn't have time to be intimidated. "You've come a long way for a house call."

"I have your phone, didn't have a way to call you." He was waiting for her to run, she could see it in the minute shifting of his feet, the way he kept watching for the smallest twitch in her hips to see if she would move.

Of course, that explained how he found her so quickly. Mel hadn't expected to give the phone up, and she hadn't bothered to clear the search history on the GPS program. Hell, for that rookie mistake she deserved to be caught. "So, what do you want?" Mel reached over and turned on the bedside light. The small shaft of sunshine peeking through the blackout curtains wasn't nearly enough to conduct business by.

Satisfied that she wasn't going to immediately run, Luke leaned on the door, arms crossed. Mel didn't know if he was purposefully showing off his muscular arms or not, but she appreciated the view nonetheless. With the light on, it didn't look like he had gotten any sleep. Dark circles had formed under his eyes and there was a ragged hollowness to his cheeks. But Mel wouldn't let herself feel compassion. Not now, not for him. He was surely about to screw her over.

"You knew about the hex," he said. His voice didn't betray his obvious fatigue. He must have had plenty of practice. "You knew about it within seconds of seeing it."

Mel hoped he wasn't going to be stupid enough to accuse her of practicing magic. It would be a pity to lose all respect for him so quickly. Not that she was starting to respect him or anything.

"So you must have seen something like that before," he finished. "And judging by your reaction to it, I think you know it's bad."

Smart man. Dangerous, sexy, smart man. Mel didn't want to reveal her entire sob story. Besides, he knew enough of it already. But if she wasn't careful, he would cut to the heart of the matter just from her reactions. No wonder this man was an alpha at such a young age. "How old are you?" She didn't mean to ask – the research Krista had put together gave her an idea. But still, she was curious.

And for some reason Luke obliged. "Thirty-two. You?"

"The same." There were a dozen reasons to lie, none of them good. And besides, he probably wouldn't think she was telling the truth. Plenty of people in power believed anyone younger than seventy-five was an infant. "But I'm not living on borrowed time."

Alphas didn't last long in their positions. While some could rule for centuries, the average length was closer to a decade. Maybe a little less. And those were people with much more experience than Luke. He shrugged it off. "I'm not going to be overthrown just yet." Something glinted in his hand, and suddenly Mel's scry stone was dangling from its chain. "It's a pretty bauble."

"*My* pretty bauble." She didn't try to snatch it out of his hand. He would be too fast. "I see you've come to your senses and have chosen to surrender it to me. Your cooperation is appreciated."

He threw his head back and laughed. The sound filled the room and wrapped around Mel. Her heart jumped, just a little. But she ignored it.

"I think I would like you if you didn't keep stealing from me." The exhaustion had drained from his face, and he now looked almost like the young man he must have been once upon a time. She wondered what he would look like when he was really happy, not just caught off guard.

"If you're not giving me my necklace back, then what's the deal?" He didn't need to know how important it was to her. She wasn't going to drive up the price.

He slipped the necklace back into his pocket. "Help me fix Cassie."

She'd known it would come to that. From the moment he'd entered her room there was no other outcome. And a part of her was relieved. She had no reason to help Cassie out of the goodness of her heart, or out of the terror of what a hex could do. Still, she pretended to think about it. She let herself settle into the role of a femme fatale and swayed her hips as she walked across the room, clearing the distance between them.

She got up close to Luke, laying a hand on his chest. "Your sister's life is only worth a silly necklace?" she asked.

Luke's face was inches from hers, his lips dangerously close. And he was just as focused on his goal as she was. Mel needed him distracted. So she kissed him.

It seemed like a good idea at the time.

But if her goal was distraction, she missed her target. Luke wasn't a man to just let himself be kissed. Not when she wasn't playing like she was a peppy little co-ed anymore. He took control, devouring her. He pulled her close, almost crushing her, and kissed her with the intensity of a man who hadn't had a woman in centuries.

No, he kissed her like he knew her, and like he hadn't been able to kiss *her* in centuries.

It rocked Mel to her core, and she couldn't help but respond, seduced by his passion, his desperation. She met his fervor with her own, swiping her tongue against his, feeling the heat coil through her. There was almost nothing she could think about except feeling him for just a little longer, just a little more.

And then his hand closed around her wrist, crushingly hard. He pulled back and both of them panted. "Normally, I'd be happy to let a beautiful woman put her hands in my pants, but I can't help but think you have ulterior motives."

Mel let her head fall against his chest and she smiled. "You can't fault a girl for trying."

He let go of her wrist and she stepped back. Mel expected anger, or at least exasperation. What she saw stunned her, caught her off guard. She saw hunger. But with a blink it was gone, Luke flexed his hand and grinned. "Be careful, you might become predictable."

"We wouldn't want that." For some reason she was glad he hadn't let her lift the stone. How messed up was that? But if she couldn't get her stone through conventional methods, she'd have to do something a bit unorthodox. She'd work for it. "What are your terms?"

She saw his shoulders relax. He must have been on pins and needles all night. "I need your expertise. I've got the car downstairs and we'll go back to Eagle Creek. You will be my guest, and free to go with your payment once Cassie is better."

Mel knew that he thought those terms were fair. It must have been nice to be an alpha. She held up a hand and ticked off her points. "One, I will go to Eagle Creek under my own power. Tomorrow. Two, I will bring with me a team who will also require guest status and safe passage out of town. And three..." the last point was both the most painful and most important. "...Three. I will receive my payment and not be punished or imprisoned if Cassie cannot be cured. I will be your consultant, I will try to the best of my ability to help you, but I offer no guarantee. This isn't some easy theft. Witchcraft is dangerous and tricky."

"I want you in town tonight."

Mel put her hands on her hips, "I'll be there tomorrow."

Luke pointed towards the door, gesturing towards the parking lot. "Did you think I came alone? You can come with me freely or you can come with me under duress, I don't care which way it is."

Mel had to keep an even tone. Luke wasn't thinking clearly, and with his sister on the line she couldn't expect him to. "No one will believe me if I ask them to come when I'm already at your place. They'll think it's a trap. So I'll be there tomorrow and you'll just have to trust me."

He had no reason to. Mel knew that. But she wasn't going with him, not even to save an innocent life. Luke was the type of man to take every hint of surrender and expand until he took everything. As an alpha he had to be able to do that, but Mel wasn't his subject, she wasn't anything to him. And he didn't get to walk all over her.

And to her shock, the alpha nodded his head. "But if

you're not there by noon, I'm dragging you back whether you like it or not." He grabbed the cell phone that she'd thrown at him the night before out of his pocket and tossed it to her. "Thought you might need this."

Mel wanted to toss it back to him. There was no telling what tracking software he'd put on it. But she wasn't going to give him the heads up. "Thanks. I'll see you tomorrow."

Maya was waiting for Luke when he got back. She typed furiously on a tablet and tapped her foot. Without looking at him when he entered the War Room, she said "We've got a problem."

Of course they did. If he were a superstitious man he might think he was cursed. "What is it this time? And how's Cassie?" He hadn't even had enough time to check on his sister that morning. She'd still been asleep when he and two of his enforcers headed out to Denver to track down Mel. He'd left Antonio behind to track the thief by the GPS in her phone. Though Luke doubted anything would come of it, he needed to try.

"Cassie's asleep," Maya said carefully.

It caught Luke's attention. "That's nearly sixteen

hours. Did something happen?" The other crisis could wait if Cassie needed him.

Maya held the tablet close while she spoke. "She woke briefly and had an uncharacteristic outburst. I had to call in Dr. Murphy to sedate her."

Dr. Murphy wasn't a shapeshifter, but he was the town's only physician. And the story went that ten years before Luke came to town, a slew of shifter violence had made it impossible to shield the good doctor from the fact that something unnatural was happening. He'd been brought in on the secret of the shapeshifter clan and treated them when their wounds were too serious for even accelerated healing to fix.

"When was that?" He kept his tone even. He trusted Maya – if she hadn't called him at the time she had a good reason. He didn't fear leaving her in charge, but that didn't mean he wanted her making medical decisions for his sister.

Maya could clearly sense his frustration, "About three hours ago, just after you went radio silent to deal with the thief. The doctor said Cassie will probably sleep for a few hours, so she'll be up soon."

"And the other emergency?" There was nothing he could do for Cassie while she slept that he hadn't already done.

"Peklo is getting restless."

James Peklo was the least of Luke's worries, and he would have told the man to go to hell if it wouldn't have doomed the pack to war. "Restless how?" Peklo led the legion of vampires that Luke had put off meeting when Cassie disappeared. No group liked to be ignored, though, and rumor had it that Peklo was not a patient man when forced to wait.

"Threatening to cancel the meet if he doesn't hear from you by the end of the day today." Despite the severity of the situation, Maya smiled, a wicked glint in her eye. "I don't think he liked being put off by a woman."

"Nothing would shock me about him." Luke didn't want to deal with the vampire right now, but he couldn't avoid his responsibilities. "I'll call him tonight. He'll probably be happy if I just let him vent." It occurred to him that Peklo might have had something to do with Cassie's disappearance. But if the vampiric leader was as smart as rumor suggested, he would never have been so obvious. And the guest they'd captured when Mel escaped claimed the man had nothing to do with him.

That seemed to satisfy Maya. "And how did it go with the thief?" Luke wanted to give her an award for keeping the distaste out of her words. She had been absolutely opposed to his idea. And then she'd been offended when he didn't let her convince him that he was wrong.

Luke remembered that kiss. Of all the things that happened, it should have been the least important, but it made him think of impossible things like hope, the future, something outside of the life he now lived. "She'll be trouble, but just the kind we need."

After finishing with Maya, Luke went straight to Cassie. She wasn't yet awake, so he used the time to give Peklo a call. The vampire leader didn't answer. Luke left a message and considered his duty done.

His hand was on the doorknob before he had second thoughts. Sitting next to Cassie for the rest of the day wouldn't make her any better. He tried to find anything to do, but this thoughts kept ricocheting between his sister, his thief, and the damned hope that everything would turn out alright.

An hour later he heard the screams.

He ran, knocking aside one of his pack mates and barreling through the door. Cassie lay on the bed, the sheets wrapped around her knees and ankles almost forming a knot. She let out a banshee shriek, her body arching off the bed before falling back down. She cried and cried.

Luke got close, he wasn't afraid for himself, but he didn't want to hurt her. He looked behind to see the gathered crowd in the door and hallway. He met Mick's eyes. "Get Murphy, now." The boy took off running without further prompting.

Cassie breathed in and out quickly, panting on the edge of hyperventilating. Luke smoothed back her hair. She was covered in sweat and her shirt stuck to her body. He needed to get her changed into something else – it couldn't be healthy to be stuck in damp clothes. Her eyes snapped open, and for a second they were completely black. But she blinked again and they reverted to their normal brown. Luke hoped it had been a trick of the light, her pupils expanded larger than normal.

Help was coming. Tomorrow.

Cassie sucked in a breath. "It hurts," she moaned. "Trying to keep it out."

Luke had to lean close to hear, her words slurred and quiet. "What are you trying to keep out?" he asked.

She opened her mouth, but shuddered again before she could say anything. Luke didn't try to make her talk, it would only hurt her more.

He should have forced the thief to come back with him.

5

M el knew to avoid the demon horse statue at Denver International Airport. As far as she knew, it wasn't actually a demon, and she didn't think it was cursed, but plenty of lore surrounded it and she was already in enough trouble. She met Krista in the arrivals terminal. The witch's flight from Washington D.C. had arrived and the petite woman was already waiting for Mel.

Krista was power and pain in concentrated form. She stood barely over five feet tall and her spiked hair gave her another inch. If not for the perpetually confrontational look on her face, she might have seemed sweet. And Mel knew the woman would punch her if she ever called her a pixie out loud. Krista wore skinny jeans and an oversized t-shirt. She had a backpack slung over her shoulder and could have easily been one of the college students travelling over their autumn holidays.

Not even the silver protection charm she wore on a necklace that dipped to her mid-chest suggested that she was merely an adept witch.

They took a seat on one of the benches outside baggage claim and Krista put up a sound ward. "Usually when someone asks for five minutes, they don't make you fly halfway across the country to use them."

And Mel was glad that she'd come. She knew that Krista didn't have to, that the bond between them was battered on the edge of being completely torn up. But twice now she'd come when Mel called. And that meant something. "You know as well as I do that there are ears everywhere."

"You're lucky I wasn't busy," was all she said. "Now, why aren't you tied up in some lion's basement having your entrails slowly pulled out? You're too close to his territory for them not to know you're here."

"And you still came?" Mel smiled. She couldn't help it.

"Wouldn't be my first time pulling your ass out of the fire. Now talk, your time is almost up."

Mel pulled out the printout she'd made of the picture from her phone. She'd dumped the phone in a mall outside of the city after popping out the battery and sim card. So far, the tail that Luke had put on her hadn't been able to catch up. "This is a hex, right?"

She'd spoken with certainty to the alpha, but a witch would always have more magical knowledge. Krista held the printout close to her face. The quality wasn't great, Mel had used the hotel business center, and their printer had been purchased shortly after the printing press went out of style. But it should have been good enough to give Krista an idea. After a few minutes of studying the design on Cassie's back, Krista looked up, her face pale. "This was *on* someone? That is some person's back?" She sounded horrified.

And that scared Mel. Krista didn't freak easily, and her skill with magic was some of the best for her age. "An eighteen year old girl. I've been hired to find out how it happened and fix her."

Krista raised an eyebrow, she knew all of Mel's tricks. "Hired by who?"

There was no use in hiding it. "Luke Torres. The victim is his sister Cassie, it happened sometime after she was kidnapped and before she was returned safely yesterday night." Mel watched Krista carefully while she spoke. From the slight fist she made, Mel knew that Krista would have punched her in the shoulder – hard – if it weren't for the audience. "I happened to be in the area to see the markings. Luke and another one of his pack mates thought they were just bruises. I snapped a picture and they could see the hex after that."

Krista took a deep breath and held up a hand to stop Mel from speaking further. "You went... *back*... to his property? And you want me to do a job with you when you're clearly suicidal!" She spoke the last bit in a harsh whisper.

"I went back to get my scry stone," Mel explained, "I had no way of knowing that there would be a hexed teenager on the premises."

She watched Krista in silence. The witch didn't respond, but Mel could see the entire conversation happening behind her eyes. It was one of the benefits of knowing someone for more than twenty years. "What's my guarantee that he doesn't throw me in a dungeon or whatever the second we step into his territory?"

Mel had to stop herself from smiling. Krista was in. "I've negotiated safe passage as part of the deal."

Krista stood up. "Then we're wasting daylight."

The drive to Eagle Creek passed smoothly, and quietly. Each time Mel tried to start up conversation, Krista would change the radio station or turn up the volume. Except for one request to stop to use the bathroom, Krista kept her silence.

Maya met the two women and led them inside. "Who is your friend?" she asked Mel.

"I'm a consultant. My name is Krista, you don't need to know anything else." Krista smiled sweetly, and Mel decided to say nothing.

"Actually, I need a lot more. Krista Anders, right? Witch, 31, daughter of Tina Anders, and suspected thief." Maya ticked off the facts with a sense of glee.

"If you knew, why did you ask?" Krista crossed her arms. "I'm here to do the job."

"This is my home. I don't allow strangers."

A man cleared his throat. Mel smelled Luke and had to bite her lip to keep from grinning. What a strange reaction. What *wasn't* strange was the languid desire that flowed through her. She was getting used to that. "Actually, it's my home. Let them in, Maya."

Maya took a look at her alpha and stepped aside. Luke led them up two flights of stairs and down a hallway. Mel recognized it – they were right next to his quarters. "Is Cassie alright?" she asked.

Luke stiffened. "I wish you had come yesterday."

Luke led Mel and her friend into Cassie's room. He thought the small woman was a witch. Who else would

Mel call to help with a hex? And he couldn't be certain, but it was a close enough thing. This woman had helped Mel rob him. And she had probably given his thief the teleportation charm that let Mel escape him when he chased her.

And he had let them both into his house.

If that made him foolish, so be it. He'd play the fool a hundred times to save Cassie.

Neither woman reacted when he opened the door, at least, not in the extreme. He thought he saw Mel's mouth pull tight to one corner, but he blinked and it was gone. There would be no hysterics from these two. They were consummate professionals, even if his only exposure to them involved being their victim.

That meant they were good.

"We had to cuff her early this morning." Luke hadn't asked where Maya got the fuzzy pink handcuffs. Or why she had a pair of fuzzy handcuffs modified to restrain a shapeshifter. A shapeshifter could have broken out of them with little trouble, but an eighteen year old human didn't have the strength. And with her hands wrenched above her head she didn't have the leverage either.

Sweat plastered Cassie's blonde hair to her face and her eyes seemed to burn with an almost red inner light. Though she was bound to the bed, she couldn't stop moving. Right then she was almost calm, only squirming a little and not trying to break the hold of the cuffs. Even with the padding her wrists were bruised. She babbled a little when they came in, but the words made no sense, just random Spanish and English that formed no coherent thought.

Luke looked at Mel and saw sympathy in her green eyes. That was something. "She stopped talking – well, saying anything that made sense – a few hours ago."

Krista took no time in assessing his sister. She crossed the room while Mel stood back with him. Krista looked over her shoulder, "I'll need to touch her to determine the nature of the hex."

Luke nodded.

"She may scream. This will probably hurt." She didn't wait for a second round of approval. Krista grabbed a small wooden chair and sat next to the bed. The hair on Luke's arm stood on edge as something decidedly not normal entered the room. "Cassie –" The power faded and Krista looked back at Luke once more. "I need her full name."

He was surprised she didn't know it already. "Cassandra Torres-Jameson."

Krista nodded and turned back to the bed. Power swept through the room once more. Out of the corner of his eye he saw Mel fold one arm across the front of her body and grip her elbow, balling her other hand in a fist. Luke didn't know what made him do it, but he stepped just a little closer to her and brushed the back of his hand against her fist. Her hand loosened and he almost saw some of the tension ease out of her.

"Cassandra Torres-Jameson," said Krista, her voice echoing even in the small room, "Hear me."

Luke looked down when Mel grabbed his hand. She didn't. He decided not to make a big deal about it, instead turning his attention to the witch. Krista spoke in a deep voice, but he couldn't understand what she said. At first he was convinced it was English, but after focusing for a moment it seemed to morph into Spanish, and then into something else entirely. But it was all gibberish, he couldn't tell what she was doing or saying to his sister.

"Try not to focus on the words," Mel whispered. "If you can't do magic you can't understand it."

That wasn't the answer Luke wanted, but he wasn't an expert on spell craft. "How do you know so much about magic?" He didn't have a right to ask. He didn't have any rights when it came to Mel, but it wasn't going to stop him from asking.

Mel pulled her hand from his and laced her two hands together in front of her. "Cost of doing business," she said by way of explanation.

Clearly that was a lie. But asking now would get Luke nothing, and part of him thought that when it came to this thief, he would want it all. Crazy thought, but it was there anyway.

The power drained from the room once more and Krista stood, turning away from Cassie and facing Luke and Mel. Her face bore a grim expression, her eyes tired. "I can soothe Cassie's pain," she said, "And I can counteract some of the more obvious manifestations of the hex. But I will need time to put together everything to completely rid her of it."

For once Luke let himself hope. Her words belied her expression, "So you can make her better?" he asked.

Krista hesitated and Luke gritted his teeth before she answered, "I can remove the hex. But I don't know if she'll survive. Cassie has given me her consent to try."

Luke took a step toward her, but the petite witch held her ground. "If you kill my sister, you will be a marked woman." Mel placed a hand on his arm and he whirled around to face her. "What?"

"Krista won't kill Cassie. The hex will. If anything happens to Cassie, it won't be because we didn't try. So calm the fuck down right now." She looked him in the eye while she gave the command, her green eyes lit with an inner fire.

If anyone had been in the room with them Luke

would have needed to reprimand her. No one gave the alpha an order in his own territory, especially not an outsider who'd already stolen from him. But the strangest thing happened – instead of anger, Luke smiled. It wasn't completely happy, but that was in the mish-mash of emotions whirling around his head. A part of him liked that Mel was strong enough to boss him around.

And if she and her witch saved his sister, he'd be in her debt forever.

"We'll need Marco's powder." Krista addressed this to Mel, ignoring the temperamental lion between them.

Mel shrugged with a grin. "Not too hard to steal."

That shook Luke out of whatever he was feeling, at least for the moment. "Is theft your first instinct for everything? Do you knock over a gas station when you need a gallon of milk?" It came out as a criticism, but he truly wanted to know.

The only time he'd ever stolen something was when he was nine years old and at the supermarket. His mother couldn't afford the piece of candy he wanted, so he'd taken one for himself. When she found it, she'd made him write a note of apology and told him that she'd sent it back to the store. He was grounded for three weeks and forced to do extra English lessons for a month. Casually speaking about stealing anything just sat wrong with him.

"Why would I steal milk?" asked Mel, her tone confused. "I don't steal from humans." She said, "Well, not usually."

"What's Marco's powder?" he asked. They didn't have time to examine Mel's limited morality.

Krista explained, "A witch named Marco Aguilar developed this powder which can counteract hexes about a hundred years ago. It's the only thing that works if you can't get the original witch to undo the hex. And he guards it like a fucking dragon. He'll sell it to some people, but he hates other witches. And he won't sell to strangers."

"The good thing," said Mel, "Is that it's so magically volatile that it can't be protected by any magic. Krista was on a team that stole it before."

Mel and Krista shared a look that Luke couldn't decipher. He wondered what the history was between them. He turned to Krista. "So you can take it again?"

The witch shook her head and shot a quick glance back at his sister. "I need to stay with Cassie. Mel can head it up. Who do you think we bring in?" she asked. "There are a few people we can trust. Jo hates Marco enough to do it."

They wanted to bring in more members of their

thieves guild? Into his territory? That wasn't happening. "I'll go with you."

Mel laughed. "You just balked at stealing *milk*."

Luke let steel into his voice. "She's my sister. I'll go."

Behind them Cassie screamed. Luke lunged for the bed, shoving aside Krista in his race to do so. For the first time in hours her words made sense. But it wasn't her voice that emerged from her mouth. "Meet at the clearing where you found the girl. Friday. Midnight." The voice was masculine, deep, not anything that Cassie could imitate. But she repeated the words twice before slumping down into unconsciousness.

6

Mel shouldn't have laughed at the alpha, and she knew she shouldn't have challenged him in his own home. But with Cassie's pronouncement, he seemed to forget it all. After Krista put a small sleeping spell on the girl, Mel, Krista, Luke, and Maya all met in his crowded little office to discuss the game plan.

"First you tell me what the hell *that* was in there," Luke demanded.

Mel didn't like his tone. She wasn't accustomed to working so closely with her clients. Orders were for other people. But Krista could hold her own against the alpha. "It's a bridge created by the hex. Temporary and more or less one way. We could hear him, but he couldn't hear or see us. He probably sent the message knowing that the girl would be guarded at all times and that someone would hear it."

Mel hopped in before Luke could ask more questions, "Whatever they want, they're going to offer it in exchange for fixing Cassie. And judging by the effects of the hex, they want something big. It's your choice, what we do next."

Luke didn't pause to think it through. "We're getting that damned powder, fixing my sister, and then I am going to obliterate whoever thought they were allowed to hurt her in the first place."

They spoke through the logistics, but had to break up for Mel to get the proper gear to pull off the heist. For that she needed to go back to Denver, leaving Krista alone in the lion's den. But Krista insisted that she would be alright alone. Mel was shocked when Luke let her leave without an escort, and less shocked when she made her tail after driving out of town. It was difficult to tail a car down nearly deserted roads. She lost him about an hour before she entered the city.

It took a few hours and several stacks of money to get the documentation and supplies, but she was back on the road to Eagle Creek before her tail found her again.

Luke was ready to leave the moment she got back, and supremely displeased when she insisted that they delay until the morning. "It's nearly eleven," she said. "I've been running around all day." She shoved a small manila envelope in his hands. "Our flight leaves at noon tomorrow. Direct to Mexico City. Memorize the details of your passport." She brushed past him.

He covered the ground between them in two steps and was in front of her before she reached the stairs. "I didn't give you leave to wander my house freely."

Mel disdainfully looked him up and down. "I'm going to see Krista. We have some final planning to do."

"I'll escort you," he said.

She huffed, but replied, "Fine." And let him lead the way.

"There's a room right down the hall that's set up for you and Krista. I had her move your stuff into it while you were gone," he pointed to the door as they passed.

"Thank you." She'd been planning to stay at the motel in the town, but his house would be even better. And since she didn't need to hide anything from him, she didn't see a reason to refuse the invitation. "Shouldn't this place be crawling with vampires?"

Luke looked over, his expression puzzled. "How exactly do you know what's supposed to be going on in my territory?"

Mel shrugged and said nothing.

She didn't think he would answer her initial question, but he surprised her. He'd been doing that a lot. She would have never guessed that he'd volunteer to steal with her. She was more excited at the prospect than she would ever admit. "When Cassie was kidnapped we delayed our plans. For now."

"What's the meet about anyway?" Luke's territory was remote enough that he didn't need to worry about playing games if he didn't want to. He could pretend that vampires and witches didn't exist and most of the time it would have no effect on his world.

"Business. The clan I was meeting with has a proposal for a transportation company, and they want my assurance of safe passage for their trucks down the interstate." He didn't try to make it sound intriguing.

Mel laughed. "That seems like something you could handle by email."

Luke returned her smile. "You know the old ones. If it's not inscribed in Latin by monks it's not real communication." He opened the door to Cassie's room where Krista sat holding the girl's hand. He looked at his sister and spoke to Mel. "I wish they had done this to me."

It hurt to hear him say that, but not in the way that Mel was used to. She didn't know anyone who would throw themselves in front of a hex for her. She didn't want someone to do that, but for a second the thought of that level of care appealed. She pushed it aside. "Cassie will be okay," she tried to comfort him, but his expression had closed off. "Krista is an amazing witch. She'll get it done."

He left without saying goodbye, merely nodding and closing the door behind him.

Krista looked up from her patient. "Is that going to be an issue?" she asked.

Mel raised an eyebrow and looked quickly over her shoulder at the closed door and back again. "Is what going to be an issue?"

"You're making kissy faces with the alpha. I want to know if I'm going to get screwed over when he decides he doesn't like me." Steel hardened her tone and she offered no quarter.

Mel wanted to turn back around and go to her room. She didn't have time to deal with Krista's distrust. But she hadn't earned the luxury of asking her to stuff it. She kept her voice low to avoid being overheard. "I was wrong about Chance. I let myself get manipulated by him. I'm not going to do that shit again." Even saying his name hurt. Two years ago, Chance had been a kindred soul on a heist in Cincinnati. But it turned out that Mel had been the only one to feel that way.

Krista threw her hands up. "I don't give a shit about

Chance." She fussed with Cassie's blanket while she continued, "You made a stupid mistake there, so what? But if I can't trust you to have my back when other people are involved, then I can't trust you at all."

Mel crossed the room and stopped herself a moment before she would have put a hand on Krista's shoulder. "I have your back. That was one time in twenty years, and I couldn't be sorrier than I am now. But you're my best friend, Kris. I count on you."

Krista didn't turn around, and she spoke so quietly that even with Mel's excellent hearing she almost couldn't make out what the witch said. "You're not sorry. You just want everything to go back to how it was. Newsflash, Mel, we're not friends, and I can't count on you. Once this job is done, just... just leave me alone."

An argument bubbled up in Mel's throat, a plea for absolution. But it would get them nowhere and only breed resentment. Mel left the room with no idea how to make things right.

Luke was ready at the crack of dawn with only a backpack containing two changes of clothes and a small toiletry kit. Mel instructed him to pack light.

Vince, who was still on probation for a stunt involving a snow mobile, had been assigned to take him and Mel to a private airport an hour away from his territory. He hadn't even known the airport existed, and was beginning to think that a lot more shady dealings were going on around him than he had ever been aware of.

When she came down the stairs, it was evident that Mel was not a morning person. Luke wasn't either, but he tried to hide it. Her hair was pulled back in a messy ponytail and she wore no makeup. The clothing she'd chosen looked more comfortable than fashionable, but he thought she wore the hell out of it.

Given that her job more or less required a nocturnal routine, Luke had assumed she wouldn't be awake come morning. He held up a thermos and handed it over when she reached the bottom of the stairs. "Fresh, black," he said. "I don't know how you take it, but we've got time if you need to hit up the kitchen."

Mel flipped back the lid on top and took a long drink, wincing as the liquid burned her mouth. She gave it a second and smiled at him, "Black's fine. Thank you."

Vince carried both of their bags out to the car and they followed behind. They settled into the back of a discreet black SUV and Luke pulled the passport that Mel had given him out of his pocket. He flipped through the pages of the document, it drew her eyes downward. Once he had her attention, he asked, "You know I speak Spanish, right?"

"Yeah?" The vehicle pulled out and they were off while he watched Mel try to figure out where he was going with his questions.

"And that I'm Mexican?" He smiled as he continued. Mel just nodded, clearly carefully storing up her quota of words she'd speak in the morning. "So why is my passport Canadian?" He flashed the front page at her where CANADA was written clear as day.

"It was Canada or Greece," Mel replied. "Do you speak Greek?" She leaned her head all the way back against the seat, exposing the line of her throat and yawning wide.

Luke watched her as she tried to get comfortable, squirming sideways, rearranging her legs, and finally landing half on her side, resting her head on her shoulder and looking in his direction. She looked at him for a long moment before he remembered that she'd just asked a question. "No, unless you count the alphabet." She nodded, but he wanted to keep her attention. "I thought about rushing in my freshman year, but some other stuff came up."

Mel laughed. "You don't seem like the frat boy type."

Luke angled his body closer, leaning in so that his head half covered the small seat between them. The world rolling by outside didn't exist as far as he was concerned. All he could see was his thief and her big green eyes. "You're not using your imagination," he said. A strand of her hair had fallen out of her ponytail, he reached up and tucked it behind her ear. "I was eighteen years old, a continent away from home, and ready for shenanigans."

Her eyes sparkled and she bit her bottom lip, "I didn't know alphas were allowed to engage in shenanigans."

"I wasn't an alpha then. Just a dumb kid." He didn't have any malice towards his younger self, no matter how stupid he'd been as a teenager. "And California was a bit different than Connecticut."

She laughed again, the burst of sound engulfing him and loud enough to cause Vince to spare a glance back at them. But the boy quickly averted his gaze. "First it's frat boy, then Yale. How did you end up banished to the hinterlands of Colorado?" While the mirth roiled through her, she leaned closer and her hand brushed against his arm. He thought it was unintentional, but she didn't move it back.

"I went to Stanford, thank you." And he wouldn't point out that he'd gotten into both schools. There was no need to brag, at least not about that. But answering her question was complicated. "When I was a kid we had a huge territory. Miles and miles and miles, my dad was the alpha of a small pack and my mom ruled at his side. I don't remember a lot, but I remember the forest." But he didn't want to get into all that. He liked Mel against his better judgment, but he didn't need to tell her everything. "And when we came to America we had this shoebox of an apartment. Scott is great, but he lived in the city. I guess I became a city cat, but then when we came out here..." he looked over her shoulder and smiled at the mountains in the distance. "I knew I had to make it mine."

He reached for her hand and entwined his fingers with hers. It felt so right to touch her that he couldn't resist. "What about you? Shock me with stories of the honor roll."

Mel shook her head, smiling all the while. "No, I was never in any school enough to make honor roll." She thought for a moment, her eyes rolling up before settling back to normal. "Though I think I have a trophy that one high school gave out to all the honor students."

"You stole an honor student trophy?"

"Hardly the worst thing I've taken." Pride laced her tone.

It broke the spell. Luke pulled back and sat facing forward in his own chair. The only reason Mel was with him now, the only reason he was in this mess, was because she'd broken into his house and taken something that belonged to him. His sister wouldn't be in danger if it weren't for Mel. And he was about to commit several crimes just to undo the damage.

Why the hell couldn't he remember that when he was around her?

7

Mel napped for most of the trip to Mexico City after the alpha turned cold. She should have expected his reaction, though she couldn't quite figure out why it stung so much. She'd done her job, and she didn't feel bad about that. If only Cassie hadn't been hurt. No kid deserved to be dragged into shit like this.

They landed at a small, private airstrip outside of the city. Money greased the correct palms on both sides of the border, and they were on the road within fifteen minutes of stepping out of the plane and into the hot Mexican sun. The drive wasn't far, though as they got close to the city it became beyond clogged. She pulled off the highway after an hour of driving and into a nice residential neighborhood.

"Do we have a plan?" Luke asked, breaking his hours' long silence. "Or are you going to just knock on this Marco guy's front door?"

Mel should have fought when he decided to tag along. Bob had to be available somewhere, and he could work with her much better than an angry lion who had retired from a life of theft before he hit puberty. "Yes, I have a plan. I'm not exactly new at this." She pulled into the driveway of a small, yellow cottage. It would have looked at home on a postcard with two children playing in the small front yard with a dog frolicking beside them. Instead, everything looked perfectly put together, only one step away from sterile.

"Where are we?" asked Luke.

Mel turned and smiled, "My house." She turned off the car and opened her door. "Come on, we need to get ready to go."

"You have a house in Mexico City? You have a house at all?" He seemed to be having trouble with the concept as he grabbed his bag and met her on the way to the front door. Mel unlocked it and revealed the orange painted walls and old furniture that made up the living room. Luke stepped inside and took a look around. "It doesn't exactly scream thieves den."

Mel set her bag down on the couch and flipped on the lights. "Well, I keep the Picassos in the basement.

You don't just leave those out for anyone to see." When he didn't laugh she glanced over her shoulder to see his brows drawn down as he scrutinized her words. "Really?" She asked, "You seriously think I have a stash of stolen art here? It's a safe house, you know. Meant to be safe." She gestured down the hallway off the living room. "There's a bathroom down there. I keep the utilities on all the time so it should be good. Just take a shower and we'll talk once you're clean."

Luke left without another word, walking slowly, studying every inch of her house. After a few minutes she heard the bathroom door close and the water start up. Almost immediately she realized the error of her ways. Luke was getting naked, in the shower, in her house. If she had x-ray vision she could see him right now, he was that close.

Probably a good thing she didn't. Her resolve only went so far.

She tried to focus, to set things up so that she could give Luke something to study while she cleaned herself up. But the drip of the water against the tile kept distracting her and she could almost picture the water sliding down his tight abs. She'd never seen them, but she'd felt them through his clothes. Very tight.

Her hands balled into fists.

One minute of fantasy wouldn't hurt anyone. But only one minute, then she had to work. She closed her eyes and breathed deep. His hair would be plastered to his forehead and slicked back against his scalp. And his golden brown skin would be hot under the steaming water. Mel imagined running her fingers over his muscles, tracing shapes in the water and feeling him shiver under her touch.

But her hands wouldn't be satisfied to play against his arms for long. In her mind she reached down, gliding over the sharp contours of his muscles until her hand hovered right over his naked cock. If she couldn't have him in real life, she'd settle for a feel in her daydream.

A commotion rose as Luke must have knocked over a bottle on the ledge of the shower.

Mel opened her eyes. That was not part of the fantasy. But the thought of a clumsy alpha made her smile, and then immediately frown. She'd need to think over her plan one more time to ensure he wouldn't be near anything breakable that could give their plans away.

She was able to keep her attention focused after her small fantasy. And by the time Luke came out of the bathroom, toweling off his damp hair, Mel could safely ignore him. Really, the thought of what he would look like naked wasn't even a consideration. It was a good thing that being a good liar was a necessity in her job. She could almost believe it when she tried to pull one over on herself.

No matter what she was feeling, she wouldn't show it. "Read up on Marco while I clean up. We roll out at seven."

Luke sat down on the threadbare couch and picked up a folder containing all of the pertinent details on Marco's compound and the security around the powder. He glanced through the first page and looked up. "We can seriously get in there?" He didn't flash her the picture of Marco's property. He didn't need to.

Marco lived in a fortress even more guarded than Luke's. Armed guards patrolled the perimeter and with the press of a button the entire place could go on lockdown, all windows closed by steel shutters and the doors blocked by concrete. It would be nearly impossible to break in. Luckily, Mel didn't need to. "He holds a monthly gathering to which I happen to have a standing invitation." She sat down; it was better to explain this now before Luke read through the material and got spooked. "You'll go in as my plus one. Marco will think you're either sleeping with me or that you're my muscle. Or both." Luke's nostrils flared, but Mel had to ignore it. That meant nothing.

She couldn't remember the last time she'd had such trouble focusing on a job.

That thought was a bucket of ice on her train of lust. While it was unpleasant to think about, it did bring her back in line. "Anyway," she continued when she realized she'd paused for too long. "He keeps his backup supply in his office. We'll need to switch it out with something of equal weight, but the lift itself shouldn't be too hard."

"Do you get chased by a giant stone ball if the measurement is off?" he asked.

Mel smiled. "Not quite, and I don't carry a whip with me." She shrugged, "Not usually anyway. There's a three second delay on the weight sensor. Or there was a year ago. We're going to have to hope he hasn't changed that or we're boned."

"Won't this Marco guy have his shit on lockdown if he knows he's going to have guests?" Luke tossed one paper on the table and picked up another. He didn't look at Mel while he spoke. "And if you're friendly enough to have a standing invitation to his Mexican palace, why can't you just buy this powder from him?"

Mel had to be careful with her response. Men like Luke didn't like to find out the gritty details that women like her needed to know. And she wasn't interested in a moral debate. "Stealing is easier than what he'll ask me to pay. And if I give him what he wants this time, my relationship with the man will be ruined. I'll be a client, not a colleague."

"I won't ask you to prostitute yourself for my sister." The matter of fact tone, his lack of judgment, lifted a weight from Mel's chest that she hadn't realized she'd felt. He offered no censure, and didn't call her character into question. How refreshing.

But there was more for him to read than she had time to explain, so she stood up from the sofa. "We'll go over the rest once I'm cleaned up. Your clothes are in the garment bag."

Mel took her time in the shower, and even more time afterwards preparing her hair and makeup. For a simple dinner party it would have been alright for her to let her hair hang around her shoulders, but since she knew she'd muss it up in the middle of the heist, she needed to spend more time twisting it every which way and pulling it up. The makeup was simple, a smudge of color around the eyes, a lipstick that claimed it wouldn't smudge for hours, and a little bit of blush. All part of her uniform.

She pulled on a pair of tight fitting black pants and a dark top. The second Marco saw her outfit he'd be on high alert. Luckily for her, he had no reason to think that she'd steal his powder. And with Luke with her he'd expect it even less. Two shapeshifters couldn't do magic and had no need for magic potions.

She walked out of the bathroom after nearly an hour and froze in her tracks when she saw Luke. He wore the hell out of his suit. She'd asked Maya to put Luke's nicest suit in the SUV before they left. And the quality was stunning. It had to be worth at least $3000, perfectly tailored, and fit him like a glove. Mel didn't lick her lips, but she wanted to. And if the job wasn't on the line she would have done more than ruffle his hair and wrinkle the clothes.

As it was, she could do neither.

Once her thoughts were under control, she asked, "Armani?"

Luke looked down and straightened one of his sleeves. "Gucci, actually." He offered no more explanation for why he had such an expensive suit. But Mel had already filed away several details of Luke's life. The guy came from money. Maybe he hadn't been born to it, but his stepdad wasn't suffering for cash. And by that token neither was Luke, not for at least twenty years.

She didn't hold it against him. In her line of work

she had only rarely been strapped for cash. But it was important to know a partner's background, his potential weaknesses, and his potential strengths.

"Think of this like a business dinner," she said. "Marco invites anywhere between a dozen and twenty people at least once a month. A few, like me, have standing invitations. We drop in when we're in town. The rest will be people who either want something from him or who he wants something from." Mel reached down and dug through her bag. She came out with a small black box.

Luke took it when she offered and flipped open the lid. "I have my own cufflinks," he said.

Mel smiled. "Not like these." She pulled out another box and flipped it open to reveal a matching ring. There was a diamond in the middle with a small ruby set along one edge and an emerald on the other. "They're an enchanted set," she explained. "Obviously we'll need to split up at some point. We can use these if we get in deep shit."

Luke examined his cufflinks, "Do I speak into them?" His tone bordered between sarcastic and serious.

"No," Mel slipped her ring on and flashed it to him. She twisted the stones toward the ruby.

Luke jerked, tossing the cufflinks up before catching

them again. The central diamond had turned a bright red. "It's hot, what the hell?"

Mel chuckled, "Red means 'I'm in deep shit, come get me.'" She twisted toward the green and he didn't jerk this time, but his hand did tighten around the cufflinks. "Cold, right? Green is 'I'm getting out, meet me at the rendezvous point.' You just turn the stone either way. Shift back to the center until the diamond is clear again to deactivate the charm."

He studied the gems, "Clever. Do you have a definition of 'deep shit'? Or may I trust my own judgment?"

Mel bit her tongue to stop herself from saying anything that would compromise their teamwork. "You're a big boy," she settled on, "I'm sure you'll be fine."

The drive to Marco's didn't take long, though Mel didn't go directly there. She had a few more things to set up before she was ready to put her plan in play. Luke went along, only asking questions every so often and otherwise making no conversation.

As the sun set she pulled up in front of a palatial estate. Marco's home. A gold and white gate opened to let her drive down a long driveway which led to an enormous house. There were half a dozen arches made of yellow stucco and covered by a tiled roof. The double door to the main entrance was over ten feet wide when both were open. The grounds were covered in verdant grass and trees that took far more water than was natural to maintain in such a hot climate. The house screamed money, and Mel's hands itched to see what Marco had inside.

But she had to behave; this trip had only one objective.

There were already several cars parked on the driveway. Most, like her, drove dark SUVs, though there was also a Rolls Royce and a Ferrari.

Before they got out of the car, Mel put a hand on Luke's forearm. "Remember, you're not Luke Torres in there. You don't speak Spanish, and you're trying to hide the fact that we're sleeping together."

He sputtered, "What? We're... I'm—"

"Your character," she reminded him. "You're playing a roll. And red is rescue me, green is get out. Don't be a hero." She gave his arm a squeeze. "You can do this."

They left the car and walked across the long driveway to the entrance of the house. With each step, Luke loosened up. She kept shooting glances to the side, amazed at the transformation. By the time she knocked on the door he might as well have been a different man. He stood a step too close for casual comfort and let his hand fall by his side, brushing against her thigh for just a moment too long. Mel let herself smile. They were already being watched on the security camera. He was perfect.

Marco's butler, a human man nearing sixty, opened the door. His face hid any shock at seeing Mel and he led them inside to join the fray.

8

Luke wondered if Mel feared that he would wipe his mouth with the tablecloth or ask if they had a cement pond out back. Simply because he didn't live ostentatiously at home didn't mean he had no experience in the world of the rich and gaudy.

He and Mel were the last to arrive. And judging by the reactions of everyone in the house they hadn't been expected. He mentally matched names to the fact sheets that Mel had made him study before they left. There were only three people he didn't recognize. One of whom was a man with dark hair in the far corner of the room. He was the only person not at least half-angled towards the door.

But the man – the mark – he corrected himself,

approached them. Marco Aguilar should have been taller, given the way both Mel and Krista said his name. In just a day Luke had already built him up as some kind of legend in his imagination. But the man stood a little under six feet tall, stocky, and had a wicked scar that cut through half of his left cheek. Witches weren't the most hearty when it came to immortals, but that he'd survived the wound, and not bothered to cover it up, let Luke know that the man could take a beating.

Mel offered no comment on where the scar had come from. Apparently it was not spoken of in polite company.

His skin was a dark brown, and his hair shiny and black. He wore it close to his head. Marco wore no jewelry, but his suit was of the highest quality, dark gray and nicely fitted. If the house hadn't made it obvious, the clothing did. The man bled money. And from the company gathered around the white marble room, he collected power as well.

Marco approached Mel with both arms out and a huge smile on his face. He showed no surprise at the thief's presence. But from the way two security guards moved out of the corner of Luke's eye, Luke knew that the witch had notified his staff to be on high alert. Marco kissed both of Mel's cheeks and spoke. His accent was tinged with a hint of the Mediterranean, though Luke didn't know if it was African or European.

"My dearest cat!" said Marco, "After all these years you finally show up, and on such short notice."

Mel let him keep hold of her hands while she spoke. Luke was surprised they spoke in English, though it might have been the most common language given the company. "I was in the area," Mel explained. "And my companion here has begged to see what Mexico has to offer. I could think of no one better than you to stand as an example."

While she spoke, she was Mel, but not the Mel that Luke had come to think of as the real one. There was a harshness to this version of her, like cut glass, that he hadn't seen when they were alone. Yes, she could be ruthless, but it was a ruthlessness honed by determination. Here, she showed a hint of cruelty.

Was this really her?

He hoped for his own sake, for Cassie's sake, and for the sake of his pack that the cruelty was an act. Because he was trusting her with everything.

"Who is your companion?" Marco inquired. He gave Luke a once over and dismissed him.

"A friend," was all Mel said. Her vagueness did not pique the witch's interest.

Marco took Mel's arm and led her across the room.

Luke followed a step behind, their silent shadow. He didn't try to look menacing; he'd learned long ago that it was far more effective to seem aloof rather than intentionally dangerous.

Marco displayed his power through the company gathered and the objects dotting the edge of the large room. Expensive jewelry and statues stood on marble pillars. None of it was protected by obvious security, so Luke assumed there were magical deterrents. Mel seemed to be able to sense magic. Luke didn't have that talent.

He took stock of the company. Nicola Souza, the jewel of the Mexican vampire scene for nearly a century, spoke to a man with dark skin in the corner of the room. Luke couldn't place the man, and his eyes kept slipping off of him before he could get a good look at his features.

Juan and Guadalupe Mendoza were with a group of other shapeshifters. Even before reading their file, Luke had been aware of the couple. They'd made a name for themselves by carving out a chunk of territory in central Mexico and labeling it as a safe haven. No violence, no infighting. They ruled with iron claws and remained unchallenged after fifty years. Not everyone at the party was Mexican – there were several European guests and a few from Asia and Africa as well.

And everyone was speaking English.

Everyone, except for the three men on the far side of the room. In Mexico, Spanish should not have seemed out of place, but in this room it was. Luke listened for a moment, and then the man with dark hair, who he'd noted immediately when he entered, spoke. Luke's blood turned to ice.

This was Inicio Nunca – the man who'd murdered his father.

It had been more than twenty-five years since he'd last seen him. And yet the man's face was as fresh in his mind as it had been when he was six years old. Like most adult shapeshifters, he hadn't aged a day past forty. His face only bore a few wrinkles and his hair was as black as jet. He laughed at something one of his men said, throwing his head back and letting the sound echo through the room.

He had already taken two steps toward him when he felt Mel's hand on his arm. She spoke barely above a whisper. "What's up, Torres?"

His name jolted him enough to think about where he was. He almost kept quiet, a plan to ambush the man beginning to form in the back of his mind. But they were working together, now. If he didn't tell Mel, she might abandon him here, might abandon Cassie.

"The man in the corner," he nodded in Nunca's direction. "He killed my father."

Mel didn't glance directly at them. Instead, she turned her head slowly, taking in the entire room. She didn't pause when her eyes lit on Nunca, and by the time she looked back at him Luke didn't know if she knew which man he was talking about. "Braids or scar?"

"Scar," Luke hadn't noticed the man with braided hair, his entire focus had been wrapped up in the murderous shapeshifter.

Mel closed her eyes for three seconds and took a deep breath. "Inicio Nunca controls the largest pack in Mexico. Not even the cartels fuck with him." She took another deep breath, and Luke wondered what was going through her head. "Is he going to recognize you?"

"No, he hasn't seen me since I was six." He hadn't seen the fight that took his father from him. His mother had shoved him into the arms of one of the teenagers there that night and instructed them to run and hide until she came to find them. "And he might think I'm dead anyway." Twenty-six years was a long time, and they lived in a dangerous world.

The black man that Luke had noted earlier walked up to them. He addressed Mel. "It's so unexpected to see you here. And you've brought a guest?" The man looked Luke up and down. There was something familiar about him, but Luke couldn't latch onto it. It was almost like there was a disconnect between his eyes and his brain.

"A colleague," said Mel. "Would you like an introduction?"

"You've been standing in the center of the room for more than two minutes. Marco will figure out you're up to something very soon." The man turned to Luke and nodded. "I'm Bob, by the way."

It meant nothing the Luke, but the man clearly knew Mel, and was, perhaps, her friend. With deliberate nonchalance, they made their way to the side of the room where they could speak. They hadn't escaped the prying eyes of the crowd, but they were no longer the center of attention.

Mel continued their conversation as if they hadn't just added a third member to their party. That, more than anything, let him know that Bob could be trusted. At least when it came to Mel's concerns. "Choose now. Do you want revenge or to help Cassie? We can't do both tonight."

It burned him up that Nunca was in the same room as him. Luke had not hunted the man down before, but it seemed that fate had put the two of them together. But if the choice was between revenge for an old wound or acting to save his sister, it wasn't a choice at all. "I can always find him later."

Mel stared at him for a moment, their eyes locked. She quirked up an eyebrow. "Give me your word on that."

"I've made my decision; it's not my fault if you don't trust it." The gathering moved on around them, people mingling, admiring Marco's works. "Now, are we going to get to work, or are you going to spend the rest of the night worried about my focus?"

Mel considered it a great sign of character that she didn't smack the alpha hard against the cheek. But with Bob standing right there, and the rest of the room ready to latch onto anything interesting, she kept her impulses in check. Besides, the reaction wasn't entirely his fault. Things were going belly up if she didn't fix them quickly.

What the hell was Bob doing there?

She couldn't ask him in so many words. He clearly had a reason to be there, just as she did. She only hoped they weren't after the same goal.

"I'm going to go mingle," Luke said, enacting phase

one of their plan and leaving her alone to speak with Bob.

Bob spoke before she even had a chance to turn and face him. "You're keeping interesting company. And clearly it's of your own free will."

Two could play at that game. "I thought you hated fancy parties."

Bob shrugged. "Marco's a friend." And she wasn't. He'd made that abundantly clear when they worked together to steal the Scarlet Emerald. "Are you after what I think you're after?" he asked.

"Are you going to tell Marco?" she replied. She hoped Bob still respected her enough to give her a warning, and hated herself for knowing she barely deserved one.

"He knows what you are, I'd say that's warning enough." Bob took a sip of champagne from the flute he held loosely. "I've got useful information if you tell me why you've chosen your particular partner."

He wouldn't lie. It wasn't that there was honor among thieves, but they had been partners many times before, and Bob wouldn't let idle curiosity ruin a business relationship. And she trusted his discretion. "He's got my scry stone and some witches *hurt* Cassie." She couldn't say the actual word where Marco was sure to hear it, but Bob understood.

His eyes widened slightly, but he kept his expression neutral. "So are you doing it for the payment, then?"

She didn't answer.

Bob didn't press the issue. He offered his information, fulfilling their bargain. "The weight sensor is malfunctioning. He's spreading it around that he has no product available, but it's just a cover until he can fix his security."

"I could kiss you right now." She tried to keep the excitement out of her voice and probably failed miserably.

"I think your alpha would object." He walked away before she could disagree or tell him that there wasn't anything going on between them.

Luke wasn't her alpha, just as she wasn't his thief. They were business partners. And once Cassie was better they would go their separate ways. For good.

She grabbed her own wine and spoke with several of the attendees. Sitting sullenly in the corner would serve no purpose, and Marco would know it was out of character. Luke found her after a while, a smile on his face. "I've heard of the Mendozas," he said, "But I never thought I would meet them."

"Star struck?" She grinned at him, his excitement infectious.

"You do realize that some people find me intimidating?" He asked, deceptively casual. Mel couldn't wait to be alone with him the next time he took that tone.

But not just yet. "They're all fools. You're just a giant kitten."

"Let's see if you feel that way when you see my claws, thief." Menace didn't lace his words – it was seduction.

If Mel was a different person, if they were in a different place, she'd act far differently than she needed to. But lord knew she wanted to play with the alpha. "Rundown?" She asked, all business.

Luke followed her lead, switching gears. "Rotation of three security guards, they pass by every ten minutes. I couldn't get out of the immediate vicinity without arousing suspicion."

Mel nodded, "Good. Then we're still on."

"Who's Bob?" He asked. Marco signaled them all to come to dinner and they both went, sharing whispers all the way.

"An occasional colleague and former friend. He knows who you are and why we're here. He won't sell us out," saying it out loud firmed her resolve. "He's here for his own reasons, but he would have told me if they interfered with ours."

"You trust him?"

They entered Marco's dining room, though room wasn't exactly the correct term. He'd transformed the patio into a tropical paradise. A large table stood at the center, surrounded by palm trees and tropical flowers. Torches offered meager light. Even so late in the year, the weather was pleasant, with only the slightest chill in the air.

Servers brought out the first course, a spoonful of cold soup and assorted vegetables that might have been a full appetizer in a fine restaurant.

Marco called down from the head of the table, "Mel, tell us about your friend. I've always wanted to host someone of Lucio Torres' caliber. I understand he has his own roots in this fine country. And that we even have something like a family connection."

Mel didn't look over at Luke and she hoped he didn't give himself away. At this point she had to trust him to follow her lead. "I knew you would appreciate him," she said. "Though I apologize for the subterfuge. There are always layers of red tape when he travels without his entourage."

"Once I heard about your event I couldn't resist the invitation. I hope I'm not intruding." Luke held up a glass, "To a fine host."

The rest of the guests followed suit. Lupe Mendoza

was the first to speak. "What family connection is there?" she asked.

Neither Luke nor Mel answered, so Marco took over for them. "Señor Nunca is now alpha over the land Mr. Torres' father once called his own. Why, that practically makes them brothers, I think."

For the first time, Nunca studied Luke. "Torres, you say?" He looked the other alpha up and down, taking his time. Luke didn't take his eyes off of him. "I seem to recall a different name all those years ago. And you were quite young. Rumor was that you didn't survive. I'm glad to know the rumor was false."

Mel wanted to reach over and grab Luke's hand, though she didn't know if she wanted to offer comfort or beg for restraint. But she couldn't let him look weak. Even though she had brought him here, this was his battle. And he'd promised not to take his revenge. She would trust him. It was the only thing she could do.

"I was tougher than I looked," Luke said with utter calm. "And it was years ago."

The tension didn't disperse. It couldn't. But conversation turned away from a leadership challenge that took place decades ago to certain political matters in the region. Only then did Mel slowly move her hand under the table and give Luke's thigh the tiniest squeeze. He was doing well.

And it was just about show time.

Dinner broke up and it was time to put their plan into action. Mel looked at her watch. At exactly 9:32 she would leave the room. They had six minutes, at which point she'd either have the powder or she wouldn't, and they'd have to figure out something else.

Mel waited until the appointed time and ducked out of the room, trusting that Luke would do his part. She used the information that he'd given her about the guards to extrapolate their rotation and didn't meet a single one on the way to Marco's office.

The office was closed with a simple lock. Her lock picks took care of it in an instant and she was inside. Under normal circumstances, she would have disabled the security cameras or tried to avoid them. But she hadn't had time. So she hoped she could work fast enough that she would be done by the time the guards came to stop her.

The powder was stored in a fingerprint coded safe behind Marco's desk in a locked cabinet. Mel assumed that, like most people, Marco didn't remember to wipe away his old fingerprint when he accessed the safe. She covered her finger in latex and pressed down on the finger scanner. The light turned green.

Success.

Inside the safe was a clay container with the anti-hex powder inside. Trusting Bob's assessment, Mel scooped out just a little bit of powder and put it into a plastic bag. She stuffed the bag into her bra and closed the safe and the cabinet. All in all, the theft had taken less than three minutes.

She turned the stone on her ring to green and ran out of the house, continuing to avoid the guards. She got to the car first and drove away, not waiting for Luke to get to the car. He was expecting it, they couldn't risk getting locked on the property if Marco realized that she'd robbed him.

Mel drove to the rendezvous point and waited. After fifteen minutes she had nearly given up hope. Either Luke had been captured, or he had abandoned her. Or worse. Her ring wasn't lit up, so he didn't want her help. And she had no other way of knowing if he needed it.

Another five minutes passed before the passenger side door opened and he slid in the car. The alpha panted, but he'd moved with such stealth that she hadn't heard him approach.

"Did you get it?" he asked.

Mel put the car in gear and took off. "I did. Anyone following?"

He shook his head. When he moved to put on his

seat belt he winced, sucking in a pained breath. But he fastened the belt as quickly as possible.

"Are you hurt?" It came out more harshly than Mel intended.

"I'm okay, just a bruised rib. Had a bit of an altercation back there."

Mel couldn't stop the car to see if his injuries were even worse than he said. She put her foot on the gas, accelerating so that she could speed all the way back to the safe house.

9

L uke might have underestimated the extent of the damage to his side. But Nunca's goons had fists like brick walls, and even avoiding most of the hits had left him aching. Shapeshifter healing was a boon, however, and by the time they were back to the safe house he could move without wanting to wince with every step.

Mel wasn't prepared to let him tend to his own wounds. She made him sit on one of her chairs and ordered him to remove his top if he didn't want her to cut it off. He thought she was serious and moved as quickly as he could, baring himself from the waist up.

She didn't bother with a first aid kit. Instead, after taking a minute to secure their bounty in a hidden safe, she knelt down in front of him and placed her hands on the purple bruise on his naked torso.

Luke sucked in a breath, and not because it hurt.

Well, it did hurt, but the feel of her delicate fingers on his exposed flesh was enough to turn his mind in another direction. He clenched his fists at his side and tried to think of anything else, anything appropriate that wouldn't lead him down the road to another massive mistake.

"It's bruised now," she told him. She didn't poke hard enough to make it hurt any more. "Should be completely healed by morning. We'll fly out at 10."

She didn't remove her hand from his chest. "You're sure that you got enough of the powder?" he asked.

Mel rolled her eyes up and smiled. "Not my first rodeo, Alpha." She tried to slide her hand away, but he covered her fingers with his own, clasping her to him. The smile slid off her face, replaced with something hotter.

She licked her lips.

It would be incredibly stupid to do anything with her. Whatever they'd done in the past was the past. But Luke was tired of being smart.

He slid off the chair and to his knees in front of her. Only inches separated them and their hands were still locked together against his side.

"This is probably a mistake," she tried to warn him, but her eyes were glued to his lips and lit with a desperate desire.

Luke felt the same thing within himself. Something about Mel felt so right that every moment apart from her felt like something hollow, like he was missing something integral that he hadn't known that he needed to function. Ever since the first moment he saw her it had been a constant ache inside of him.

"Some mistakes need to be made," he said. And this was a mistake he couldn't go another second without making.

He closed the distance between them as she slid both of her arms around him, planting her fingers on his back. Their lips met. Luke hadn't kissed her in more than two days, and he never wanted to go so long between tasting her lips again. In this she was his equal, neither dominating him nor letting him dominate.

Fire roared inside him, hardening him, bringing him to life. If he thought that he'd been riding adrenaline earlier, it was nothing compared to this.

They tumbled to the floor, Mel careful of his wounded ribs but otherwise giving him no quarter. She lay on top of him, hands in his hair and lips mad against his own. Luke pulled her closer, his fingers digging into her sides. He needed the contact, needed to touch her.

He found the hem of her shirt and let his fingers explore under, splaying across her naked skin. It was hot, silken. He was already hard, aching for her and only her. Since the moment he'd seen her it had just been Mel. Whatever name she used, whatever disguise, he was hers in this madness.

Her own hands quested, unbuttoning his shirt, spreading her hands across his chest and stripping him. The shirt revealed his chest, but without moving he couldn't take the whole thing off. And though he was an alpha, he liked Mel on top of him.

Mel broke the kiss and Luke tried to follow, but his ribs protested the sudden jerk. Mel wasn't stopping. She kissed her way down, starting with his neck and nipping at his jumping pulse. Luke's cock twitched. Just from a little play, and he was near the edge. His thief was going to break him. He couldn't wait.

Mel took her time exploring his chest. She took each of his nipples into her mouth, licking him until he moaned, calling out her name. She smiled up at him but kept moving down, her hands finally landing on the button of his trousers. She undid them carefully, exposing him to the warm air of the room.

Luke held himself absolutely still. He was nearly

naked below her and desperate for her touch. But he felt like speaking would ruin this moment between them, break the magic and make them return to whatever their existence was before. Separate.

Alone.

Mel could sense his desire, his need. She didn't take the length of him in her mouth or even kiss the tip. She kissed his thighs, reverently moving her hands up and around, feeling every inch of him. Every inch but the ones directly in front of her.

And then, pure bliss. Luke closed his eyes, choking on another moan as she let her lips engulf his thick length. She worked him slowly, making him her slave with every stroke of her tongue. And Luke was glad of it. He bucked against her, completely spellbound and rapt with pleasure. Nothing could ruin this moment, nor prevent their joining.

His phone rang.

Luke didn't immediately hear it, so caught up in his delicious thief. But the incessant ringing cut through and Mel pulled back. "It's yours," she said, reaching into his pants pocket and handing him his phone. If not for the heat in her eyes and his own desire, Luke wouldn't have known she'd had his cock in her mouth a second ago.

But they weren't people who could afford to

become wrapped up. Especially not hours fresh from committing a theft in a foreign country. Luke looked at the caller ID and answered. "Hello, Maya." He hoped he didn't sound as frustrated as he felt.

Mel crawled off of him and straightened her shirt. Luke wanted to pull her back down, to sit with her while he sorted whatever mess Maya had to clear up. But Mel was already walking away and he couldn't afford to neglect his duties. No matter how much he wanted to.

Mel slept through the night with a clean conscience, even if her dreams were anything but. She didn't regret what she'd done with the alpha, but it had been a mistake. Not to be repeated. She thought that she'd learned her lesson when it came to mixing work and pleasure, but where Luke Torres was concerned, all bets were off. He set off something inside her that she hadn't known existed. And it wasn't just about lust. Lust she could handle. Impulse she could handle. He made her want, made her need something that she couldn't ever remember having.

And that made him far more dangerous than any small time fling.

She wasn't going to destroy herself again. Not over a man.

On the bright side, whatever passed between them seemed to clear up the animosity he'd exuded on their flight down. They ate a pleasant breakfast of fruit and coffee and set off for the airstrip just after dawn. Luke told her that Maya had things under control. Cassie wasn't better, but she wasn't any worse either. Krista had spent most of her time closeted away with Cassie when she wasn't busy driving the second in command up the wall. In Maya's words, the witch was 'difficult.' Luke laughed when he gave Mel the report.

Mel wasn't surprised when she saw a familiar face at the airport. She stepped out of the car to see Bob standing in the bright light, a ridiculously floppy hat shielding his eyes from the bright sun. It wasn't yet hot, but the day was getting there.

Luke was out of the car in a flash, standing just a foot in front of her but only one small jump away. Mel stepped up and placed a calming hand on his arm. It shouldn't have worked. No matter what happened the night before they had no real relationship. But she could feel the muscles in the alpha's arm relax. He took half a step back, standing equal with her. That freaked her out even more. Luke was silently telling Bob that she was his equal. And that meant more than any words or actions they could exchange.

"It's a beautiful morning, isn't it?" Bob asked, calling across the short distance between them.

"I suppose," she replied. "What are you doing here?"

"Need a ride out of town. Figured you had something set up already. I'll pay my portion of the bribes." He held up a thick envelope, "Courtesy of a certain mutual friend."

He tossed the envelope to Mel. She glanced inside. At a glance there was at least five grand in there. Mel looked at Luke. "You're my client. It's your call. Bob's smart and he might have some insight into the current situation."

Luke studied the other man. He grabbed Mel's hand and gave it a quick squeeze before letting go. "If you trust him."

"There's one more thing you should know," Mel didn't know what possessed her to come clean, but even lying by omission felt wrong. "Bob was the third man. Krista, me, and him lifted the Scarlet Emerald."

She didn't know what reaction she expected. Luke looked over at Bob and studied him for another moment. "They were in EC's with you. The diner in town." If anything, humor laced his words. As good a reaction as she could hope for.

"Do you plan to tell your new mate about any other jobs I've worked?" Bob asked.

Mel felt everything still inside of her, and she could feel Luke coil up right beside her. Mate. It rang through her ears, bouncing around her head and completely taking her over. Was that what was between them? Mating was one of those funny shapeshifter quirks. Even if they shifted into animals that didn't form any lifetime bonds, shapeshifters sometimes found just the right person and stayed by them forever. Not always, it wasn't even that common. But it wasn't unheard of by a long shot. Most large packs had at least one mated pair.

Bob must have meant to be glib, to taunt her into a reaction. But if Luke was her mate, that made everything even worse. She didn't want to – couldn't – stay in one place for long. And as alpha of a pack, Luke couldn't leave. They weren't mates. They couldn't be.

She recovered before the alpha, off-kilter for only a matter of seconds. Enough for Bob to notice, but not enough for him to comment. "Shut the fuck up, dude. If you want a seat, it's yours."

She grabbed her bag and walked into the hangar.

Their plane was a small, chartered machine. It could

comfortably fit eight people in huge seats, and it included a work area with picnic seating, with two chairs on each side of a table. They all sat there, Mel next to Bob. She wanted to sit next to the alpha so much that she forced herself not to. In a short time they would part ways, probably never see each other again. She had to get used to it now.

She laid out the situation with Cassie, leaving the girl's relationship to Luke out of it. All Bob needed to know was that she was a member of Luke's pack.

"Here's the main problem. Luke has never tangled with witches before, and he doesn't know of any reason why they would target him now. So why the hex? They haven't said what they want. They haven't said who they are. Krista is probably working to trace it, but that's iffy at best." Mel set her hands on the table, her fingers twined together. "You know what I think, but it's probably not her."

Luke's gaze pierced Mel. "Who do you think is doing this? Why didn't you tell me anything?"

Mel shouldn't have said anything. And she didn't want to explain in great detail. "A witch killed my parents. She's very powerful and ambitious. But there's no reason to think she's involved in this. I'm not going to be some old Roman, ranting against Carthage when it's clearly not."

Bob grinned at talk of the classics. "Ava hasn't made

any moves in Colorado. Doesn't mean she won't. But last I heard she was in New England."

"Is there some sort of supernatural Facebook that I don't know about?" Luke asked. "I could name maybe three witches off the top of my head and half a dozen vampires. How do you know everyone?" He threw his hands up and let them land on the table.

Mel reached over and grabbed onto them with a smile. "We know who we need to know. But it's not called the underworld for nothing. I bet you know shapeshifters better than I do."

"Don't patronize me." Despite his tone, he smiled.

"Do you want my help?" Bob asked, "I may have some avenues of inquiry that Krista can't access."

"Yes," said Luke. "If Mel trusts you, I want you on the case."

10

K rista gave Bob a big hug when they arrived back at Luke's house. While they'd thrown a dozen ideas back and forth over the course of the flight, nothing had stuck. Mel was ready to tear her hair out in frustration, but every time she reached the edge, Luke was there, saying the right thing, offering a small touch, making things better.

But he wasn't her mate. She didn't have a mate, didn't need one. Especially not him.

Maya came down the stairs and took a look at Krista and Bob. "We can't waste time," she turned to Mel. "Did you get your magic powder?" Something bitter tinged her words. Other than stealing from right under her nose, Mel hadn't wronged the second in command. But in just two days her demeanor had soured towards Mel. The lion's glance shifted to where Krista let Bob go.

Perhaps it wasn't Mel then.

Interesting.

Mel tossed the powder at Krista. She caught it. "Give me an hour. Bob can try his mojo while I get this ready."

Maya led Krista to the kitchen and Mel and Luke led Bob upstairs. Cassie smiled when she saw her brother. They'd taken away her bindings and she had a book sitting on the bedside table. "Luke!" She smiled, her face glowing. "Give me a hug!" She held out her arms.

Mel could see that the girl had lost weight since the beginning of this ordeal. After only a few days her cheeks were hollow, her skin far paler than it should have been.

Luke explained who Bob was and what he would try to do. With Cassie's permission, they let the other man take the seat beside her bed and stepped back to let him try to work. Without preamble, Luke grabbed Mel's hand and held it tight. Mel didn't have the heart – or the desire – to let him go.

She was in so much trouble.

Krista came upstairs a little more than an hour

later. Bob stepped back to let the witch take his place. "I've taken a psychic imprint of Cassie," he told Luke and Mel. He didn't comment on their linked hands. "If Krista is unable to find whoever did this to her, I'll do my best."

Luke nodded. "You have my thanks." He turned to Mel. "I guess we could always go meet them like they want. That vampire hasn't given up anything."

Mel narrowed her eyes. "You never said anything about a vampire."

"Because it might have nothing to do with Cassie. And he isn't talking. It was one of the guys with you that night."

Krista looked over at them. She, Bob, and Mel all knew that Krista's mother, Tina, didn't have enough power to place a hex that powerful. But that was another connection to Ava. And to the Scarlet Emerald. All three of them kept silent. They would know soon enough.

"We didn't know they would be there until they showed up," said Mel. "I don't know who they were."

Luke accepted that. And a part of Mel felt horrible for not telling him all, but she had been who she was for much longer than she'd known him. She wasn't going to change overnight. She wasn't going to change at all.

"I'll need to be alone with Cassie," said Krista. "I'll need to ward the room and I can't have you in here distracting me. I'll set the ward so that Mel can break it if anything goes wrong."

"Wrong how?" Luke took his hand from Mel's. "You didn't say anything about things going wrong."

"Magic always has risk," Krista explained. "But with Marco's powder we should be more than adequately prepared for any funny business."

Luke nodded. Krista produced a needle and pricked Mel's finger, collecting a speck of blood on a napkin. "It will only take a few minutes. If I'm not out of here in half an hour, break the ward and check on me."

Mel nodded. She and the other two men exited the room, leaving Krista alone with the alpha's sister.

Mel set her clock to time thirty minutes. Maya joined the three of them in the hallway. She gave the alpha a hug. "It will be okay." And it only helped to solidify Mel's belief that Mel wasn't Luke's mate. She wasn't jealous when another woman touched her man. And didn't that mean he wasn't hers at all?

Even she didn't buy that lie.

Luke hugged Maya back, but he couldn't stop himself from glancing at Mel. Bob's glib accusation had been flashing through his mind for hours. Mate. Mel was his mate. Of course, it made complete sense in a strange way. From the moment he'd first seen her, she hadn't been far from his thoughts. And he couldn't keep his hands off her. She seemed likewise afflicted.

But her eyes didn't narrow when he hugged Maya; he sensed no aggression from his thief. That was good. It meant that she already knew that he was hers, sensed it in her bones. At least he hoped that's what it meant. The alternative was not something he wanted to contemplate.

He'd deal with it either way later. He had to make sure Cassie was safe first. Once the hex was lifted, he was sending her home, and telling their parents what happened. He couldn't hope to keep it from them.

Just a few more minutes and the nightmare would be over.

A scream rent the air and Luke's heart tore in his chest. He bolted for the door, stopped only by Mel and Maya holding him back. "Wait," said Mel. "It hasn't even been five minutes yet."

He didn't want to wait. The lion inside of him roared to burst through the door and save his sister. Except the ward on the other end would prevent him from even entering the room. After a second both Mel and Maya took their hands off of him.

Another scream, this one filled with pain. Luke looked at Mel. "That doesn't sound right. You know it doesn't."

A roar, a leonine scream, came through the wall. Mel had her hand on the door before he could react. She placed her hand on the thickened air, opening a gash in one palm with one of her claws. The air rippled, a shockwave knocking him back a step.

Luke pushed past Mel and took in the scene.

Krista had been knocked to the floor, all of her supplies scattered on the floorboards. The witch had an ugly, bloody gash across her collar bone. She held a hand to it and tried to crawl away from the monster on the bed. But Cassie had her claws out, digging into the witch's back as she tried to move.

His sister was in the throes of her first shift, brought on by the trauma of the hex and from trying to remove it. The shift couldn't be stopped, and if they didn't act quickly, Krista was going to die. A shapeshifter's first change was a thing of madness. The animal took over, hungry for blood, for the hunt. And once blood had been spilled, they were wild until they sated their hunger or shifted back.

And Cassie hadn't even completed her first shift.

Her hands had transformed into gigantic claws and her mouth and nose elongated to form the beginnings of a snout. But the rest of her was still human.

Maya was already moving, approaching the witch and trying to get her out of the way. Luke couldn't see Mel, but he had to trust that she was trying to help. He approached his sister and put steel in his voice. Speaking as her brother wouldn't get through to her, but being an alpha might.

He roared, letting the sound fill the room. It didn't sound right coming from his human throat, but it gave Cassie pause. She tilted her head towards him. Her eyes were turning to a yellowish brown. More and more of her was shifting. He needed her to shift all the way. He could try to control her then. Maybe talk sense into her.

"Let it happen, Cass," he said. "You need to relax into it."

But she didn't understand. Only pain and hunger lived in her eyes. She swung her claws at him, growling wildly and missing by several feet. Luke jerked back anyway. Cassie wasn't this violent thing, and he wasn't going to help her by playing nice.

Maya got Krista completely out of the way, giving him more room to maneuver. Mel was still absent.

The next time Cassie swung at him, he grabbed her arm, pulling her to the floor and straddling her legs. He had full control over her in this position, but Cassie had anger. She kept scratching, making little nicks in his flesh. They stung, but Luke could handle the pain. He just had to hold her there long enough for the shift to take over.

But Cassie didn't want to be held.

She bucked at him, the sudden motion jerking him forward. With a swiftness he didn't know she possessed, she rolled out from under him, onto her feet and ran for the door where the bleeding woman was propped against the wall of the hallway.

Luke grabbed for his sister, pulling her back down. He tried to hold her again, but he couldn't do much without hurting her. Even knowing that she couldn't feel any blows on top of the pain she was already experiencing, even knowing that he wouldn't cause any permanent damage, he couldn't hit her. She was his baby sister, and she wasn't doing this on purpose.

Cassie had no such compunctions.

She swiped at him again, this time getting in a lucky shot and opening up several inches of flesh on his arm. The only positive from that was that she was now focused solely on him, no longer diving for the wounded Krista.

Fur covered his sister's arms now, though the bones beneath hadn't completely shifted. He needed to get her farther into it. No matter how much she didn't want to cooperate.

But he hesitated and Cassie took another swipe, this time making him stumble back to stop from hitting her or slamming her to the ground.

A black mass barreled into him. Mel in her leopard form. She spared a second to bare her teeth at him, growling. And Luke understood. He couldn't stop Cassie, he wasn't willing to hurt her.

Mel could. If he trusted her.

He scooted back, letting the leopard thief take over. She wasted no time, pouncing directly on his sister and letting her claws prick at the human skin. Fur bloomed on Cassie wherever she was hurt, her body healing itself into the form it wanted to shift into.

Mel got on top of the girl and planted her teeth within her. But she was gentle, making sure that whatever injury she caused wouldn't last beyond the shift. Luke scented his mate's blood and had to hold himself back. This wasn't a fight he could win.

And nearly as soon as it began, it was done. Cassie's body gave a final ripple and a lioness stood where once there had been a girl.

"Alpha, down!" Yelled Krista.

Luke ducked, rolling out of the way without seeing the threat.

Something whizzed through the air over his head, landing in the golden fur of the lioness. Cassie took two steps on her new paws before crashing to the side, the sedative knocking her out. Luke looked over at the witch.

Maya had a rag pressed gently against her biggest wound. Krista held a huge tranquilizer gun against her shoulder. She slowly lowered it. She tried to speak, but coughed before any words came out. After a moment, she tried again. "I couldn't lift the hex. Something triggered her shift before I could do anything. And the anti-hex powder's gone."

Luke looked away. He couldn't deal with that yet. He padded over to his sister and plucked the dart out of her side. She breathed evenly, probably sleeping better than she had in weeks. He laid a hand on her head and sat next to her.

Mel snuck up beside him and lay down, still in her leopard form. She rested her head on his thigh. Luke used his other hand to pet her head. It was an intimate gesture, something he would never have felt right doing to someone he didn't know.

But Mel was different.

He closed his eyes, allowing himself three seconds to wallow in defeat. Sitting on the ground, even with his mate by his side, he didn't know how anything could ever get better. Cassie was still hexed, Mel would probably try to leave him the second she got the chance, and he had no idea what enemy he faced.

But those seconds passed and he opened his eyes. He couldn't afford more than three seconds. His enemy wanted to meet.

Bring it on.

IN THE ALPHA'S BED

1

Luke Torres should have felt comfortable in his own territory. But right now the heavy branches, bare and ready for winter's first snowfall, only made him tense. Strangers lurked in these woods. Enemies of the worst sort. The cowards hadn't tried to target him. Instead, they'd gone after his sister.

And Luke wouldn't stand for that.

Darkness had long since taken over and midnight approached. Luke could feel the claws beneath his skin ready to spring into action. Soon he would know the face of his enemy and he would tear out the spine of anyone who stood against him or tried to harm his own.

Maya Nunez and Sinclair walked beside him, with

half a dozen other lions spread out in their animal forms. Usually the forest outside of Eagle Creek, Colorado teemed with life, no matter the time of day. But now all was silent except for the sound of his packmates' breathing. Predators walked the night and all the prey was hiding.

The clearing opened before them, small, perhaps twenty feet across. Less than a week before, Luke had recovered his sister here after she'd been kidnapped by a mysterious foe. So much had changed since then. And yet they were nowhere near healing her. The witch had failed to lift the hex that was killing Cassie and they lacked the supplies to try again.

His foe hadn't told him to come alone, so he made no effort to hide his backup, at least not those who walked on two legs. While he could have brought even more lions with him, past mistakes had taught him well. He would not leave his home, his sister, undefended again. If he hadn't screwed up the first time, her life wouldn't be in danger.

All of their lives, most likely.

The air in front of Luke shivered momentarily and dissolved, revealing a tall man in a black trench coat, dark pants, and black boots. He must have meant for it to look intimidating, but as it was, it just looked silly. This witch was all skin and bones, the coat hanging off of him like it was hung on a wire hanger. But power crackled through the air and Luke knew that the danger this man presented wasn't in his meager bulk.

When no other witches showed themselves, Luke grew worried. Well, more worried. How many were hiding behind a cloak of magic? His lions hid by skill, using the lay of the land to their advantage. Using magic was cheating.

The witch took a look at Luke, Maya, and Sinclair and smirked. "Too scared to come on your own, oh great Alpha?" He spoke like he should be twirling his mustache or hiding behind a cape. If the situation weren't so dire, it would have been laughable.

Luke didn't have time for humor, but as far as enemies went, this one was almost insulting. "It seems you have the better of me. Who are you?" He had no interest in playing games, not with the stakes so high.

The man gathered himself up, standing an inch taller and speaking half an octave lower. "There are those who call me..." he bent over wheezing, the witch shot a glance to his right and winced. He gave a single nod and straightened, "Tim. I am Tim."

Maya shifted beside him and Luke trusted her to be ready to take on whoever was standing next to Tim, even if that witch was hidden. He didn't take his attention from their visible enemy. "Is the wheezing part of your name? Or was that for effect?" Clearly Tim was the front man for the real power.

Tim scowled, his teeth half bared. "You mock me when you are scared to roam your own territory alone?"

Luke wouldn't get angry, but he promised himself that he would have the pleasure of tearing this man's entrails out if he made one wrong move. "I know my own strength."

"Clearly you're weaker than you thought," Tim tilted his head slightly with a smirk. He held out a hand, unfurling his fingers slowly. Once his palm faced the sky he flicked his fingers in a strange pattern and a sputter of fire appeared. The witch tossed it from hand to hand.

"What do you want?" He didn't let himself get distracted by the fire. That had to be what Tim wanted.

"A great many things," Tim tossed the fire up and caught it, closing his fist and extinguishing the light, "Few of which you can offer me." He looked to his right once more, only for a second, before focusing on Luke.

"Then why the hell did you want me here?" Luke ground it out through clenched teeth. He'd been attacked on his own land once this month, and he never wanted that to happen again.

Tim wasn't offended by his tone, at least not outwardly. "I require information."

"You have an interesting way of going about getting it." Telling the man to fuck off would get Luke nothing; in fact, it would only make things worse. A part of him didn't care. But he tamped that part down. It was useless to him at the moment. "What information?"

"Where is the Well?"

"So you can poison my water?" What use would a witch have for a well? And couldn't they find that on their own? Neither Maya nor Sinclair seemed to know what he was talking about either, though they gave no outward indication. It was their lack of reaction that made Luke positive that they had no idea what the witch was talking about.

"Are you really so clueless?" Tim scoffed.

This was getting nowhere, and he'd already revealed his ignorance. There was no reason not to go all in. "I have no idea what you're talking about. I can't give you information that I don't have."

Tim faltered for a moment and his eyes shot to the right, he gave a slight nod and stiffened his shoulders, holding his bearing tight. "Do you want your sister to die? Give us the information and we will lift the hex. Continue this feigned ignorance and she will not live out the week."

Claws exploded out of Luke's hand, ready to rip out

the throat of this impudent whelp. "Are you admitting you're the one who hexed my sister?"

Tim shrugged. "It is your actions now that decide her fate."

Luke had to cage the violence inside of him. Killing this witch would do nothing to solve his problem. It would only make it worse. "It isn't safe for you to go there right now. The river is flooded, I will need to make arrangements." A river ran south of his territory and unseasonably heavy rains had swelled the banks. There was no well in the area, but Luke hoped the bluff would buy him time.

"You have five days." Tim snapped his fingers and disappeared, the air shimmering where he had just stood. Luke has his lions scour the area, but there was no sign of the witches. It was as if they had never been there at all.

2

Cassie wasn't seizing anymore. That was progress. Mel watched Krista work over the girl. The witch could work miracles, but against an expertly laid hex and a newly turned shapeshifter who had already severely injured her, she was having a little trouble. Two days before, Cassie had shifted into her lion form unexpectedly. Even worse, she'd been so caught up in it that she'd opened a nasty gash across Krista's chest. The wound had been tended and was starting to heal, but a witch's constitution did not handle grave injury well. For now, Krista tended to the girl when she had the energy, but she was never alone in the room.

With Luke and Maya out hunting, that left Mel the babysit.

She'd been sitting there for more than an hour of nearly comfortable silence before a commotion broke out, the sound coming from the entrance. "Sounds like the alpha's back."

"Sure does," Krista didn't look at Mel when she spoke. Mel couldn't tell if the anger was due to her injury or from the history that they weren't talking about. She didn't know which one she wanted it to be.

Maybe Bob would have been able to tell her, but he was off trying to track down whoever had hexed Cassie. He had contacts he wouldn't share with either Mel or Krista, but he would go and get the information for them. That was something.

Cassie let out a pathetic mewl and turned to her side, curling in to herself. She started shaking once more and fur sprouted out of her arm, coarse and tan. Krista moved back and let Mel take over. With a now practiced hand she grabbed the manacle that they'd mounted to the wall and chained the teenager. It was degrading, a horrible thing to do, but Cassie had agreed it was the only way to keep her and everyone around her safe.

But she was so worn down from the near constant shifting over the last two days that the shaking stopped and she slumped back, the fur on her arm receding into her skin, leaving behind the tan, human flesh. The girl's brown eyes opened and she gave Mel a sad grin. "At least I'm not missing out on going to the gym."

Mel smiled, but she didn't know how to respond. "I think I heard your brother come in," was what she finally settled on. And that seemed to perk Cassie up.

Cassie scooted back until she could sit against the wall. Her arms were still clamped over her head, but she didn't ask to be unbound. Mel didn't know if she thought she would turn again or if she had simply become so used to the manacles that she didn't notice them.

Maya walked in after a couple of minutes, but there was still no sign of Luke. Mel unlocked Cassie's restraints and left in search of him. After looking everywhere else on the residential floor, she found him in his room, sitting on his bed with his head cradled in his hands. She shut the door behind her as quietly as she could, but he heard her and looked up.

For a moment he smiled, though his eyes held the shadows that had been gathering over the last several days. The smile faded when Mel didn't move towards him. She kept herself still, forcing her feet not to march across the room so that she could gather him into her arms. They hadn't touched at all in the past two days and there was an almost physical ache at the lack of contact.

But he wasn't her mate.

It was Bob's teasing comment that had put the thought in her head back when they were in Mexico. And it was completely wrong. Thieves didn't shack up with alphas; it never worked, no matter how good it felt to kiss him, to be held by him. Because it was impossible, she wasn't going to think about it. Impossible theft was one thing – with strategic planning and a solid team, she could pull off almost anything. But romance? Never.

So Luke Torres wasn't her mate and there wasn't anything that would make her say otherwise.

"I'm guessing it didn't go well?" she asked.

Luke shook his head. He moved over to one side of the bed to give her enough room to sit, though the bed was so massive that space had not been an issue. Even though she knew she shouldn't, Mel crossed the room and sat next to him.

"About as well as could be expected," Luke replied. "Threats, insults, and demanding the impossible."

"What was the demand?" Mel relaxed her leg and let it lean against Luke. She wasn't *technically* touching him since they were both wearing clothes. But it felt so good that she didn't pull herself away.

"I'd rather just tell everyone once." He stood and broke the miniscule contact between him. Mel wasn't disappointed, not at all. He walked over to his bedside table and rummaged around in the top drawer.

"What are you doing?" Mel couldn't keep the smile from flitting at the corners of her lips.

Luke pulled a small black velvet bag out of the drawer and tossed it to her. "I think you should have this back."

Without even reaching into the bag, Mel knew what it was. But she still upended it and let the clear stone suspended on a silver chain fall into her hand. The scry stone. The damned thing that had started this mess. With it, she could track down the woman who had killed her parents. Luke had stolen it from her after she'd stolen a red beryl gem called the Scarlet Emerald from his vault.

"Why?" she asked. Cassie wasn't better, the Scarlet Emerald was long gone in the hands of an unknown buyer. Everything that she had done for or to Luke had only made things worse.

Luke closed the drawer. "We had a deal. You kept up your end of the bargain, and I'm a man of my word."

If that was the case, why did it feel like she'd just been punched in the gut? Mel had gotten what she wanted and could just walk out the door right now and never look back. But that felt so wrong. "Are you telling me to go?" If the job was finished, why would she stay?

Luke let her question hang in the air for a moment. "I don't want you here because you want a payout. I don't want that kind of obligation between us."

She couldn't react to that, she didn't know how. Instead, Mel slipped the long chain over her neck and let the stone rest under her shirt right between her breasts. "Shouldn't you be keeping my priceless gems in your vault?"

Luke grinned. "You would just steal them if I left them in such an obvious place." He walked over to the foot of the bed and placed his hands on either side of her. Mel didn't give any ground, she would never surrender her space to an alpha. They never let up. But all Luke did was quickly kiss her cheek and pull back. "Let's go talk to the others. I have news."

Mel didn't say anything to him on the walk to Cassie's room. Luke was at war internally. He didn't know whether it was right to give her back her stone, but the thought of her remaining out of obligation, or just because it was a job, didn't sit well with him. Mel was not just some business associate who would disappear into the night once this was all done. She was his mate.

At least, he thought she was.

And now that she had no reason to stay, he wanted her to stick around to see if this thing between them really would blossom into something real. Ten minutes in Mexico hardly counted, and the next time he got his hands on her, he wasn't letting go. No phone call was going to interrupt the next time they had time alone together.

But at the moment he needed his head in the game. Maybe Krista would know something about this well that Tim and the other witches wanted. The pack would be meeting soon, and he needed to gather as much information about their enemy and what he was after as he could before he spoke to his inner circle. Whatever was coming would be dangerous and he needed everyone to be as prepared as possible.

He opened the door to Cassie's room and saw Krista seated on a stool next to his sister's bed. Maya was half a step behind her and Krista held Cassie's hand, speaking softly. Despite her tone, he could hear her. "It may affect your ability to shift after this is all sorted out."

"Any idea when that's going to happen?" Cassie asked.

Luke was glad to hear his sister speaking. And if it hadn't been for the horrible pressure to find some way to fix her, to make this all go away, he would have spent every moment in this room with her.

But whatever the witch was proposing put him on edge. Especially when Krista and Cassie both stiffened when they realized that he had entered the room. Maya didn't move at all and he couldn't tell if it was because she was hiding her reaction to him or that she had none to show. "What will affect her ability to shift?" He tried to keep calm. But it had taken Cassie so long to shift, she had already lost so much because of it, that he couldn't let her sacrifice it so easily.

He heard Mel lean on the door behind him. Krista half turned on her stool so that she could take a look. She moved over a little so that Cassie could see him as well. His sister smiled at him and Luke felt a pang in his chest. Ever since she'd been hexed, she'd lost weight, her cheeks hollowed, and her skin grew sallow. Part of her was fading away and there wasn't a damn thing he could do to fix it. Except give those witches something he didn't know he had.

"Hey," said Cassie, her voice hoarse and sweet. "Give me a hug." She held out her arms. At least she wasn't handcuffed at the moment.

Krista stood up and he took her place, sitting beside his sister and pulling her close. She felt like a feather in his arms, frail enough to float away on a stiff breeze. But he could also sense a core of strength within her, resolve to make it out of this thing. He kissed her cheek and let her go to ask, "What is Krista talking about?"

He expected the witch to talk, but it was his sister who answered. "Krista thinks she can stop my shifting. Maybe let me control it." She met his eyes, her brown gaze so similar to his own. Sometimes people said that it was impossible to tell that they were half-siblings. Those people never paid attention to Cassie's eyes.

"It sounds dangerous," without more information he couldn't let his sister go through with something that might cut her off from something so vital. He looked at Krista. "What are you proposing?" It came out as a rough demand.

Maya stiffened but said nothing.

Krista glanced at Mel before speaking, the smallest smile pulling at the corner of her mouth. The expression belied her words. "Think of this hex like a computer virus," she said. Luke raised an eyebrow and she kept explaining. "If Cassie were a computer, shapeshifting would be a program running in the background. It's always there, but it's not always active."

"Yes, I know how it works," and he didn't need someone without a second skin explaining it to him.

Krista tried to cross her arms, but winced and let her injured arm hang. "The hex has targeted her shifting. I think when I tried to break it, something happened. They got tied together in a big knot. I can undo the knot, block the virus from her shifting program, so to speak, but it might prevent her from shifting at all."

Luke looked at Cassie, "No, it's too dangerous. Not after—" He stopped himself from completing the sentence.

But Cassie completed it for him. "Not after I got myself into this mess because I wanted to shift so badly? Not after I let myself get kidnapped by vampires? Not after I did this to myself? Which is it, Luke?"

"That's not what I meant," it came out harsher than he intended. Cassie had only been kidnapped after she'd tried to strike a deal with Mel weeks ago when Mel was his prisoner. Vampires had used a momentary lapse in his guard to sneak in and take her. It all felt like centuries ago now, but part of that was because he hadn't had any time to truly deal with the fallout.

Her jaw hardened. "It's not your choice to make."

"The hell it isn't." Luke wanted to stand, to pace, but he stayed seated. "You're in my territory, Cass. You think I'm going to just let some witch kill you?"

"I'm dying anyway!" It should have been a shout, but it came out a hoarse cough. "The shifts are coming faster and faster. I don't know how much longer I'll last."

The hopeless sorrow in her voice stabbed Luke to the core. He wanted something he could fight, some way to make her better. Instead he was stuck here, pinning his hopes on a witch he barely knew to help his sister and save his people.

Before he could say anything else, Mel spoke. "Did the people who did this to her show up? If they want something from you, they'll probably break the hex in exchange."

Luke wanted to tell her everything. He wanted to throw caution to the wind and ask for her advice even before taking it to his trusted pack advisors. But he couldn't. He had a responsibility to his people, and at the forefront of that he could not bring confidential information to someone who had recently been his enemy.

Or, if not his enemy, she had at least been his opponent.

So he didn't quite answer her. "Even if they did, why would I believe them?" He turned to Cassie. "Are you sure that you trust Krista to do this?"

Cassie nodded gravely. "I do."

Then he would respect his sister's decision. To a point. He looked at Krista, letting just a little bit of the inner lion bleed into his eyes. To her credit, she didn't flinch. "If she dies..." He didn't finish his threat before the witch nodded.

"Got it."

3

Mel left the room before Krista started to work on Cassie. Both Maya and Luke stayed behind, which made her feel a little guilty for abandoning her partner to the potentially unfriendly lions. But the cloying sense of magic was too much for her and she could feel a weight being lifted from her shoulders with every step. Not every shapeshifter could sense magic. As a matter of fact, most couldn't. But Mel had been around witches since she was eight years old, and while she would never be able to perform magic herself, sensing it was a learned skill.

She made it to her room and pulled the diamond out from under her shirt. The silver chain pooled in her hand, warm from her skin. She rolled the diamond between two fingers. Nothing about it felt magical, there were no special markings. But in the hands of a powerful enough witch, this stone could be used to track down Ava. It would home in on her until Mel could track her down and defeat her once and for all.

And it was the only reason that she'd been sticking around Luke's compound since they got back from Mexico.

Wasn't it?

She grabbed her bag and stuffed the necklace in a hidden compartment. As far as security went, it lacked anything she would accept under normal circumstances. But she had nowhere else to hide it outside of wearing it all the time, and if Krista saw it she would wonder why Mel hadn't just packed up and left the place the moment Luke dangled the diamond in front of her.

Mel shoved her bag under the bed and hopped onto the mattress just in time to see Krista limp in. The witch was covered in a fine sheen of sweat, her normally light brown skin almost pale. She looked like she hadn't slept in three weeks.

"Did it work?" asked Mel. She hadn't heard any screams, which seemed like an improvement, but there was no telling.

Krista leaned back against the door and let herself

sink to the floor slowly. She landed with a thunk and pulled her legs in close, resting her head against her knee. "I think it did. The kid made it through. Maya's going to have one of the senior pack members come in to monitor her. I think if she doesn't change in the next twelve hours she should have enough control to survive until..." Krista didn't finish the thought. She didn't need to.

"Good, I'm glad she'll be okay." Mel wouldn't concern herself with what could happen after. They'd stopped the immediate threat, which was all they could do at the moment. "Were you able to figure out who laid the hex?" Mel was used to not knowing who she worked for, but she couldn't stand not knowing her enemies.

Krista's voice was muffled against her leg and Mel could barely see her shake her head, "Nope, I had to stop looking after Cassie started to shift."

"Do you have any idea at all?" Hexes were strange things. Almost any witch could lay one, but to do so without leaving a clear connection between the hexer and the hexed suggested someone of immense power and skill. Few witches chose to use them. They created a bond that could be manipulated and turned back on the witch responsible. Most saw it as too big of a risk to take.

"One name comes to mind." Krista rose slowly and made her way over to her own cot. The room hadn't originally been meant for two people and Mel had claimed the twin bed the second she entered. That left Krista with a makeshift cot which she claimed was actually very comfortable. Mel had tried to offer the bed after Krista's injury, but the witch would hear nothing of it. "But if it's her," Krista continued, "It would be too much of a coincidence."

"Ava." The name filled Mel with rage and a sense of purpose. If she had set the hex on Cassie, then Mel would have no reason for the stone on the chain she'd been wearing around her neck. There would be an entire pack of lions hunting the witch down, and it was only so long until they found her. But this wasn't just about Cassie. Ava had killed Mel's family, her entire pack, when she was only a child. Mel had made it her life's goal to get her revenge on the witch. And she had never been closer.

"Or someone she trained. I can't imagine any of the other major covens doing it." It all came down to politics. Ava officially controlled no territory, but she was unaffiliated with any coven. Anything she claimed was relinquished as soon as she got what she wanted. "But," Krista continued, "Even if it's her, do we really want to fight her here? Now?" She gestured to her wound, "I'm not exactly in tip top shape, and we don't know these people."

"You're seriously suggesting that we throw away potential allies? They're not exactly thick on the ground to go up against her." No one who knew Ava opposed her for long. The best course of action for fighting her was to avoid her.

"These people were our enemies two weeks ago. You don't think they're going to turn on us the second they get a chance?" Unexpected vehemence laced Krista's words. "There's nothing for us here, Mel. We should probably think about packing up before their territory burns."

Mel didn't respond. She couldn't argue with Krista, especially since Krista was probably right. Instead, she left the witch to her own devices and headed out, determined to run off some of the energy burning up inside of her.

On her way out, she saw Maya walking down the stairs carrying a tray full of steaming soup. The werelioness said nothing and Mel returned the favor. Maya didn't look to be in a great mood and Mel had no desire to cross her. Not yet.

But Krista's words haunted her. She had never been so quick to trust, so quick to give her loyalty. And yet, when it came to Luke Torres, Mel was afraid to find out what exactly she would do. Betrayal was out of the question. The thought made her ill and she could not imagine him turning on her. She simply didn't know if she could stay and hope for the best. He was an alpha, she was a thief with no pack. Their worlds did not mix.

Ever.

Mel found herself outside in Luke's backyard. A short patch of manicured lawn ended abruptly at the dense Colorado forest. She walked out into the trees, and once in their cover stripped her clothes and bent over to shift forms. It took her some time. Her full shifts were nothing special, no longer painful after years of practice, but it did take more than a minute to go from human woman to leopard.

Once complete, she stretched, letting her long claws dig into the soft earth. The tiny destruction, the reordering, felt good. She could feel every sinew of her feline body, the strength coiled into lithe, lethal lines. There was nothing better than this. Not even theft.

She took off at a run, letting the wind lead her through the forest, dodging and climbing trees as she went. It went on and on for so long that she lost all track of time, not that it mattered to her in this form. A leopard had no need for clocks.

An eternity or a second later she caught a delicious scent, feline like her but different, masculine and reeking of the savanna rather than the jungle. A lion. Her lion. He'd come out to play, and for now she wanted to see her mate.

4

Luke almost threw up watching Krista work on Cassie. He'd never seen the witch work, never seen any witch work. And now he would be happy if he never saw a witch cast a spell on another person again. Cassie had writhed and writhed, screaming and begging them to stop. But Krista warned them that the girl would do that, and that if they stopped it would only hurt her more in the long run.

Luke had wanted to put a stop to it, but Cassie wanted Krista to perform the spell. So no matter the pain, he didn't stop Krista and he held Maya back from doing the same.

Maybe Mel had the right idea. She'd escaped before the undefinable stench of magic suffused the room and he didn't know where she'd gone. Maybe back to her room, or maybe she was robbing him blind. Now that she had the stone that she'd come for, she could just take off, her one goal in working with him achieved. It had been stupid. He knew it had been stupid, but that didn't stop him.

Once the alpha made a decision, he followed through. Decisiveness was how he remained the alpha.

Fifteen minutes after the magic started, it cut off. Cassie's screams were silenced, and the only sound in the room was the panting of Krista's breath.

Luke studied his sister. Sweat plastered her blonde hair to her face and she sucked in deep breaths, her chest rising tensely with ever inhalation. She was alive, unconscious but alive. He turned his gaze to Krista. Her honey skin was pale, and like his sister she was covered in sweat. If it was possible, he thought she had lost five pounds in as many minutes. She looked drained, exhausted, horrible.

"It's done, Alpha," she said, her brown gaze hard as steel. "She lives."

Luke had no more energy for threats. Cassie was alive, that was all that mattered. They would solve the rest in the morning. "Thank you," he said and left the room. Krista followed him and stumbled down the hall to the quarters she shared with Mel.

Maya exited last. "I'll have Ginny come sit with

her." She watched Krista, "She risked her life to save Cassie."

There was something that Maya wasn't telling him, but he trusted her to keep her own secrets. "I thanked her. She and Mel are my guests." He made a decision right then that could be even worse than giving Mel back her stone if he was wrong. "I absolve Mel of her crimes, and those of her associates."

He left before Maya could question it. He needed to run.

Leaving his own house without interruption should not have been such a chore, but between the vampires, witches, and thieves running rampant, he and his lions were on high alert. Still, Luke timed it right and made it to his forest without incident. Was this how Mel felt, he wondered, when she stole into strangers' houses in the dead of night to take their belongings?

He hoped she felt more than annoyance at the task. Some mix of fear and exhilaration, the same that had taken a hold of him during their excursion in Mexico. If not for Inicio Nunca, his memories might be fonder. The man had killed Luke's father more than twenty years before. For the sake of completing the mission, Luke and Mel had let him live. Someday, Luke would hunt Nunca down and have his vengeance. But that day wasn't today. It wouldn't even be soon.

He stripped off his clothes and crouched to change. But before even the first ripple could course through him, he froze. He wasn't alone in these woods. His thief was watching. Waiting.

It was an intimate act, to change shape in front of another person. But knowing that Mel was watching didn't stop him. His shift was quick, as always. One moment he was a man crouched on the forest floor, and not ten seconds later in his place was a gigantic lion, meant more for the vast expanse of sub-Saharan Africa than the forests and mountains in the middle of the United States.

But there was nowhere else he would rather be at the moment. Especially not after a gorgeous black leopard slinked out of the trees and crossed his path. She brushed close, stroking her tail against his mane and taking off in a sprint before he could stop her.

Luke didn't roar. This wasn't a game for his pack, this was personal. And he wasn't willing to share his mate with anyone. Not now, not ever. The sooner she realized that, the better.

He chased her, startling a hare out of the bush. But he had no interest in it, not yet. His prey was not nearly so skittish. And after several minutes of running without seeing her, he realized that perhaps he, and not she, was the prey. If she thought he would stand for that, Mel had another thing coming.

Luke stopped, listening to the quiet forest. He had chased her before, but it felt like a lifetime ago. There was no rage in him now, not for her. A branch snapped ahead of him and he almost took off, but at the last moment stopped himself. His thief was clever. She wouldn't let herself be caught by such a simple giveaway.

He moved forward slowly, his body low to the ground. Her scent was everywhere, permeating his woods all around him. He could identify a trail, but it circled back on itself and went off in every direction. This was not Mel's first run in these woods. But he found the freshest trail and chased after it, his senses open.

Somehow, Mel had hidden herself away. He covered what seemed like miles without seeing her.

She was in the trees. He realized it a moment too late as she crashed down over him, swiping playfully at his side before taking off again. This time Luke had the advantage. He was bigger, faster, and absolutely familiar with this forest.

He covered the distance between them in huge strides, his paws eating up the ground under him like it was nothing. And then he pounced, landing on top of Mel and pinning her to the ground. She struggled for a moment and then lay still. He nipped at the pack of her neck, not to hurt her, but only to show her that she was caught.

After that, they ran together, chasing animals and racing each other. It went on for a long time and Luke felt happier than he had since before he had met her. The thoughts of his responsibilities had receded to the back of his mind and he focused solely on taking this time with Mel.

They lay down together in a grassy little nook he showed her, their bodies needing to rest. He rested a paw over her feline form and felt her breathing relax and even out. For once, everything felt exactly right, and he let himself sleep.

Mel was human when she woke up, which was a bit disconcerting with the giant lion's paw resting on her naked abdomen. She could feel the weight of Luke's enormous limb on her ribs but was wary of extricating herself. He wouldn't hurt her on purpose, but he was asleep and his instincts could kick into gear, eviscerating her before he knew what he was doing.

She moved slowly, lifting his paw by inches until

she had just enough room to roll out and away from the range of his claws. Or she would have had enough room if he hadn't shifted positions in the second before she moved, crushing her once more. Mel let out a little laugh.

On the plus side, his paw was no longer on her stomach and she could try and wake him without fear of serious injury. She nuzzled her head into his mane, the heat of his fur sinking into her. Even in the chill night she felt good; he was better than a giant blanket.

Luke shuddered around her and the fur receded, his form shrinking down to that of a normal sized man. A normal, naked man. He pulled her close to him with now human arms and Mel was in a completely different kind of trouble.

Luke trailed kisses up her neck and traced her jaw, "Hello," he said. "Did you have a nice nap?"

"Mmmm," She didn't feel like talking, not when his lips could be put to much better use. She tilted her head down, capturing his lips with her own, her tongue darting in to his mouth. Yes, that was much, much better. Why had she kept herself from touching him? This felt too right.

They lay entwined, kissing for some time before Mel let her hands explore the taut planes of Luke's chest. The man was built of hard, defined muscles that could lift a car over his head. Well, they could do that after you took into account the shapeshifter strength.

Her hands drifted lower and lower, brushing against the evidence of his arousal.

Luke rolled over, pinning her to the ground under him. At another time she might have objected, but right now it felt just right. This wasn't about dominance. This was about connection, pleasure. He broke away from her lips, smiling down at her.

"You're beautiful," he said, his eyes bright and a grin on his lips. "I've never wanted anyone more than I want you."

A part of Mel wanted to defend herself from that look. She could feel it invading her, changing something deep inside. That was crazy. This was supposed to be fun, nothing more. Two adults letting off steam. So she smiled back at him and told herself it was nothing serious. "Then show me," she said.

He loomed over her and then bent down, taking one nipple into his mouth and swirling his tongue around. He traced over it, imprinting himself onto her. Mel moaned and dug her fingers into his hair. That felt good. *Really* good. Luke sure as hell knew what to do with his tongue. She hitched a leg around his hip, leaving herself open to him.

She wanted him inside of her, deep and hard.

He didn't take the hint, instead content to play with her breasts. Not that she was complaining. She could feel herself purring in pleasure. It had been too long since she let herself have this.

If she was being honest, it had never felt like this.

But Mel was rarely honest.

Luke moved away from her breasts, kissing down her stomach and down one leg, coming around to the apex of her thighs. Mel shifted just a bit and felt the grass under her. One tiny movement and she felt something poke against her.

She bolted up, knocking Luke away as she went.

He sprawled back and watched her as she swatted at her butt, tossing a huge piece of bark into the trees. "What is it?" He asked, his face alight with concern.

Mel looked down at the specks of dirt on her fingers and back to Luke. Arousal still ran hot within her, but it was tamped down by the setting. "When we fuck," she said, "It's going to be in a bed. Or the floor, or a table, I don't really care as long as I don't have bark up my fucking ass." The outdoors held sway over some, and Mel loved to run as a leopard. But when she wore her human skin, she was a woman who preferred the finer things. Like blankets, and flooring. And no bark.

Luke looked around them and seemed to only realize their setting. He laughed, the sound booming out of his chest. "I've got a bed," he said. It sounded like a promise.

He stood and offered her a hand up. Mel took it and swiped a quick kiss across his lips. She felt no shame in her nakedness. It was a fact of life, and she liked her body. As she took off back towards where she had left her clothes with Luke following behind, she could almost feel his eyes on her swaying ass.

She was glad that he liked her body, too.

5

Luke was only mildly disappointed at the end of their interlude, and though he was frustrated, ardor still sang in his blood. Hell, he considered it progress. Mel was admitting that they were going to sleep together. Though he still had to work with her on the rest of it. She seemed to think they could have a little fun and be done with it.

But Luke wasn't going to settle for just one night. That would never be enough. Not with her.

They found their clothes after a few minutes and dressed in silence. Mel was about to head back to the house when Luke stopped her by grabbing her hand and gently pulling her towards him. "Wait," he said. "There's something I wanted to talk about."

Mel didn't resist his touch, instead leaning into him

and resting a hand on his chest. She looked up with a small smile. "I'm not doing it against a tree either."

He hadn't been thinking of that, not until she suggested it. And the image flashed in his mind, her legs hooked around his hips as he thrust into her. God, this was getting out of hand. But Luke looked around and reached a hand out to test one of the oaks near them. "I don't know, seems pretty sturdy. Maybe we can tie a sweater around your waist to protect your delicate ass."

She pushed back against him, taking a step back. But she laughed. "It's your delicate ass that will be on the line if you keep talking like that."

"There is something, though. Nothing to do with tree sex." He leaned against said tree and studied her. She looked at home in this forest, comfortable. But then, she rarely looked out of place. Probably one of her many skills.

"What is it?" She asked.

"Do you or Krista know what a well is?" He still had no clue. He'd meant to bring it back up once he returned from the meet, but it had fallen to the wayside with Krista's plan to help Cassie. By the end, the witch had looked so tired that he told her to rest before even remembering that he was supposed to ask her. "It's something one of the witches wanted." He could have kept that information to himself, but he didn't want to keep those kind of secrets from Mel.

God help him, he trusted her.

But Mel's face had paled and her hands betrayed the tiniest shake. She was shaking her head slowly from side to side and stumbled back half a step. "You have a *Well* in your territory?" She hugged herself, probably to stop the shaking. "You need to get your pack and run. Far away, otherwise say goodbye to living. It's bad news."

What could be that bad? "What is a Well?" He asked again, emphasizing the word. The way she said it made it sound like it should be capitalized. It was meant to push her, especially given her reaction, but for his pack's sake, he needed to know.

"I can't do this right now." She turned away and fled back to the house. Luke didn't follow. He needed to get his thoughts together. He thought that he'd gotten to know Mel pretty well in the past few weeks. And she didn't freak, not like that.

Back in Mexico she'd barely batted a lash when his father's killer had blithely walked into the room at Marco's estate. She had broken into his house on more than one occasion, and even as his prisoner she had been remarkably calm. But one mention of a Well and she was ready to run away? Ready to surrender? He was almost terrified to find out what it could do.

He took off back to the house a few minutes later, trying to catch up to Mel to offer her comfort.

By the time he got back, she had ensconced herself away with Krista in their room. He almost knocked, but stopped himself at the last minute. If she was freaking out, he wouldn't help. He had things he needed to be doing.

He found Maya in the kitchen, putting away dishes from the dishwasher. She stopped when she saw him. "What's up?" she asked.

"Call the inner circle together. We need to meet." He had been keeping the details scarce, determined to keep Cassie safe. They were long past safety now. "And I need to talk to Peklo."

Maya pursed her lips. "You're not about to do anything stupid, are you?"

Luke had planned to meet with James Peklo more than a week ago to discuss a business venture the vampire leader wanted to head up. Vampires and shapeshifters did not get along in general, and it had been nearly a century since a peaceful delegation had ventured into Luke's territory. Between Mel's robbery and Cassie's kidnapping and hex, he'd postponed the meet and put the man off. Angering him would not be a wise move.

"Just call the meeting."

Maya nodded and left him alone. Luke went upstairs to the War Room and closed the door behind him. It wouldn't stop anyone from hearing every word said inside, but it did indicate that he wanted privacy. His lions would respect that.

He dialed Peklo's number and waited for it to ring.

Many of the older members of the supernatural community were reluctant to do business over any technology that had been invented after 1600. The vampire was slightly more flexible, being willing to handle some business over the phone. But he refused to hash out the details and do the deals any way but in person.

The phone rang several times, but Luke didn't hang up. After the fifth ring, he was rewarded.

"You've reached the offices of Jim Peak, how may I direct your call?" the voice was cheery and feminine, the receptionist at his main company.

"It's Torres. I need to talk to Mr. Peak," Peklo had been alive for centuries, he couldn't continue to use his real name. It would arouse suspicion. The receptionist told Luke to wait and put him on hold.

After another three minutes, Peklo picked up, his

voice completely devoid of a foreign accent. He sounded like he had grown up in Colorado. Some feat for a man rumored to be more than 400 years old. "Good afternoon, Mr. Torres. I'm glad you could finally get in touch. Are you ready to reschedule our meeting?"

"That is still on hold. I called wondering if you would do me the courtesy of answering a few questions." Luke didn't believe that Peklo was connected with the vampires who had kidnapped Cassie, but he couldn't just ask him. However, if he ignored the possibility, he was being negligent.

"I have a few minutes. I do hope everything is alright." To the man's credit, he sounded concerned. Luke didn't buy it for a moment, but the acting was impressive.

"Have any of your associates attempted to encroach on your territory recently? I may have some information that would benefit you, if that is the case." Luke would have loved to talk without euphemism, but there were always ears in the wires. Perhaps the old ones *were* on to something with their archaic methods.

"If you think I'm going to reveal internal matters to someone like you, I think we can terminate our relationship right now." Peklo was too experienced to confirm Luke's suspicions with an incautious answer.

"I'd hate to think that you had authorized the violation of our boundary agreements by letting your own agents wander freely." It wasn't a threat. Luke wasn't in a position to launch an offensive campaign against the vampire.

"Slavic fellow?" Peklo asked. "I've had a few out-of-towners pass through. They're not mine."

"Then you don't care what happens to him?" Peklo was probably lying, something about his casual tone sounded off to Luke.

"In the interest of openness, you may want to watch your back," he didn't answer the question, but the shift piqued Luke's curiosity.

"Oh?"

"I got wind of a thief passing through. Came into town about a week ago by plane. I haven't bothered to tail her, and who knows what she's after. Keep an eye on your valuables." He was talking about Mel, he had to be.

Luke didn't respond, instead hanging up the phone and leaning back in his chair. Was that a taunt or an actual warning? Did Peklo know that he and Mel were... something complicated? Or was he bragging about being involved in the theft?

Maya knocked on the door and walked in before he could answer. "I've called the meeting. They'll be here in an hour."

Luke nodded. It was time to ask for help.

6

"It's Ava. It's fucking Ava and there's another fucking Well." Mel paced back and forth in their little room, her arms wrapped loosely around her midsection.

Krista just looked at her from where she sat on the bed. Her injury took a lot of energy to heal, and Mel knew Krista wasn't going to waste any on theatrics. "I can't think of anyone else who would want one. Too volatile."

"I've seen the craters," Mel snapped. A part of her felt eight years old all over again and she didn't know how to stop it. Any good feeling she'd had with Luke earlier had evaporated. In its place there was only fear. "I thought I could take her if we got our shot. But not when she's going to be so amped up."

"The Scarlet Emerald has to be a focus," said Krista.

Mel agreed, though she didn't have the magical chops to sense it herself. A focus let a magic user tap into the energy of a Well. But there was always a long list of rules that went along with magical artifacts. "I stole it, so if she has it, does she own it?" It could mean the difference between life and death for Luke's pack. Hell for the entire state of Colorado. Ava could use a focus she didn't magically "own" to drain a Well of its magic, but she would only get a tenth of the available power.

Krista shook her head. "No, it should still belong to Luke."

"Thank God for small favors." That alone made Mel's entire career of thievery worth it.

Krista ignored Mel's relief and continued speaking, "But even if that's the case, does it matter? We know exactly what she can do with a Well she doesn't own. She must want this one for a reason. They're too dangerous to use blithely."

That was the truth. Half of Siberia had once exploded when a witch tapped a Well. And in that case, she had owned the focus. As far as anyone knew, that woman hadn't done anything wrong, but the power had rejected her and exploded outward. Three covens were wiped off the planet in seconds.

Now that Mel had a few minutes to think, she knew what she had to do. "I need to tell Luke about Ava. He's going in blind and this is going to get bad. Fast." She paced the room, sticking her hands in her pockets before pulling them back out and crossing her arms in front of her. Despite the statement, she still felt out to sea, adrift.

"And what are you going to do when he decides to give Ava ownership of the stone in return for Cassie's life? Because you know she'll promise him that."

"He wouldn't do that." The denial sprang from Mel's lips before she even consciously thought about it.

"He won't save his sister?" Krista rolled her eyes.

"No, he'd do anything to save her." But Mel didn't think Krista was right about how. "But he's too smart to believe Ava, even without knowing about her. She's already hexed Cassie, and she's encroaching on his territory. He'd be a fool to take her at her word."

"He trusted you and me. And we've already done him wrong." Krista made her point, and shifted in her blankets. "I think we need to consider getting out of here before Ava finds us."

That had been Mel's first response, but now she wasn't so sure. "At the very least, we need to tell him what a Well can do."

Krista wasn't convinced. But she was prevented

from saying more from the sound of the front door slamming closed and a pathetic roar echoing from a human mouth. "What the hell is that?"

They left their quarters and discovered four lions in the foyer, embracing each other and sharing greetings. Mel recognized Sinclair, but the rest were strangers.

"The inner circle," Maya said from behind them. "Brynne," she pointed out a woman, "Jonas," this one was a tall black man, "and Killian," the last was a tall man with blond hair. Mel didn't jump, but she wasn't happy that the lioness had snuck up on her. "Luke has called them to discuss matters." She paused before reluctantly adding, "You both may join them, so long as you stay quiet."

Maya led them up to the War Room where the rest of the inner circle had congregated. Though a few shot curious glances at Mel and Krista, no one made an effort the introduce themselves. Mel found a corner and leaned against the wall, waiting for Luke to arrive.

A few minutes later he did. His face was grim but he shot her a nod and a small smile before greeting the meeting's attendants. It took several minutes before everyone settled down enough to get started.

The lions took their seats in the mishmash of chairs that had been set up, Mel and Krista were left standing behind all of them. No one questioned their presence; no one acknowledged them at all.

Luke brought everyone to attention with a loud clap of his hands. "We have a problem," he said.

No one moved, no one breathed. Mel studied the other members of the pack while Luke spoke. One tightened his lips when Luke stated that his sister had been hexed. Another blinked her eyes once, slowly, when she learned that witches were somehow involved in this whole mess.

Luke laid most of it out, leaving out Inicio Nunca and the exact nature of his relationship with Mel. He went over it all quickly. For all of the danger they were in, it should have taken more than ten minutes to explain.

Once he finished with the history, he concluded with, "You may be aware that Mel was the woman who stole the Scarlet Emerald." He nodded back at Mel, but none of the other lions turned to see her. "She has my full pardon."

The declaration wasn't a surprise, but Mel fought the urge to close her eyes and take a deep breath and relief. It would hurt her mysterious thief image.

Krista glanced between the two of them for a long moment before rolling her eyes and sighing. Strangely, she shot a glance over to Maya before slowly raising her hand and catching Luke's attention. "May I speak?" She asked.

Luke nodded.

"We think you're being targeted by a witch named Ava. The Well she's after will allow her nearly godlike power while she controls it. I don't know why she wants it, but she has killed for them before." Krista didn't include their history with Ava, nor did she explain the horrible lengths that the woman had gone to in the past, but the other lions in the room took her at her word.

"Where is her territory?" asked Sinclair. His lips were barely visible under his thick beard.

"She operates out of the East Coast," said Mel. "But she doesn't have an official territory.

"She's been around for ages, but no one knows exactly how long. Unofficially, she controls at least fourteen covens in six countries, but most of the other witches leave her alone. Those that don't, suffer dearly," Krista added.

"This is her MO. She finds someone's enemies or rivals and makes a deal. It's symbiotic. The rival softens the territory, making it easy for her to step in and get what she wants. The rival takes over after she leaves and then she has allies. Most people never realize that the slaughter was anything more than a simple territorial dispute." As Mel spoke she could almost smell the blood that had seeped into the ground that night so many years ago. She sucked in her breaths slowly and past tense lips to try and keep her cool.

Jonas rubbed a hand over the dark stubble on his chin. "If we didn't know about this Well, and how does she? Why can't she just find one that isn't in our territory?"

"Wells are incredibly rare," said Krista. Mel could hear the frustration in her voice at needing to explain something so simple. Krista wasn't used to working with shapeshifters other than Mel; everyone in her world knew everything there was to know about magic. "Only three have been discovered in the last 100 years. And as to how, she has people study lore. There are spells to discover such things. She's the foremost expert on finding them and she wouldn't risk coming into your territory unless she was damn sure that there was a Well here."

Brynne looked at each of the lions in the room. Her hair fell in dark ringlets past her shoulders, and she wore a pair of thick rimmed eyeglasses. "I'm just floating this idea, so no one take my head off." Her voice held a hint of something middle-eastern, though it was nearly impossible to discern. "What if we just give her the Well? We can just tell her that she can take the power and leave as soon as she's done. I realize that it's not an ideal solution, but it would avoid bloodshed."

Luke held up a hand and shook his head. "This is my home. Our home. I'm not letting someone steal what is ours." Mel decided that it wouldn't be prudent to mention that she had already stolen what was his.

"She wouldn't go for it even if you tried." Mel had to point it out. These lions had no idea how dangerous Ava truly was. "If she thought you would give it to her, she would've negotiated. *Actually* negotiated instead of doing what she has done. You know, kidnapping Cassie, hexing her, and threatening her life. At the very least she's teamed up with some vampires, presumably the people she plans to let take over the territory once she's through with you. She will not play fair."

Sinclair looked between Krista and Mel twice before speaking, his voice incredulous. "How do either of you know all of this? You are both, what, twenty-five?"

"I vouch for them," said Luke, his tone brooking no resistance.

His inner circle clearly did not like that explanation. They shifted in their chairs and huffed their displeasure.

"No, Luke," said Mel. "They aren't going to trust us if they don't know why we know Ava." And even though she knew it had to be done, it took Mel a moment to collect herself before offering the explanation. "Here's the Cliffs Notes version. When I was a child, Ava murdered my family because there was a Well our territory."

She had been too far away to hear the screams when it happened, her life only saved because she had been playing in the forest before dinner. "After that I was adopted into Ava's coven."

Krista squeezed Mel's forearm to offer comfort, and spoke the next bit to give her a moment to recover. "My mom got us out of the coven when we were 12. It was long enough for both of us to learn exactly the kind of woman that Ava is. And Mel and I have both vowed to take her down."

"I only took the job steal from your pack because the payout would've given us a shot at Ava." It wasn't an apology, but she didn't see a reason not to offer the explanation.

"Is there a way to save my sister without giving them what they want?" asked Luke. He clutched the back of the chair that he stood behind and Mel thought he was only doing it to keep himself from crossing the room to offer her comfort. She didn't know whether she would accept it or not. She was on the razor's edge between screaming and crying, and only the need to remain composed in front of these dangerous people was keeping her steady.

Krista let go of Mel's arm and looked at Luke. "If Cassie kills the person who set the hex, that might lift it. But she is weak right now, and we still don't know which of Ava's people placed the spell."

"No offense, alpha," said Maya, "but I don't think your sister can kill witch as powerful as Ava."

"She wouldn't have set the hex," said Krista. "Hexes are risky and they are a near constant drain on power. Anyone around her could have done it, though."

"Can you figure out who did it?" Asked Luke.

Krista nodded, "I can try."

"So what do we do about the Well?"

"You can destroy it," said Mel, "Once you find it. Krista and I have the spell do it, and she has the power."

Luke nodded. He looked at Krista. "Figure out how to save my sister," he said before turning his attention to Mel. "Let's kill this witch."

It burned within Luke that he couldn't console Mel after hearing her story. But it was neither the time nor the place for comfort, and she would have resented his offer if he had been stupid enough to make it.

"So how do we find the Well?" he asked Krista. There was a certain irony in the fact that the two women who had let the Scarlet Emerald fall into Ava's hands were also the only two who might see his pack safely through this mess.

Krista furrowed her brow, probably trying to come up with a way to explain how to find something inherently magical to a man who would never cast a spell. "The Well itself isn't physical. There are natural protections that ensure it remains invisible to the naked eye."

Of course there were. Luke couldn't stop his sigh, but he didn't interrupt the witch.

"But the Well will have had an effect on the land," she continued. "The plant life surrounding it will be larger than normal, trees with huge bases, mushrooms like something out of Alice in Wonderland, stuff like that. And there won't be any animals near it. Not even bugs. Logically, it must be deep into your territory if Ava and her people haven't found it. If it were on the edge she would have harnessed its power already and we would all be dead."

"Can't you just do a spell to find it?" asked Maya.

Krista shook her head, "No spell would lead me directly there. Ava's spells gave her an area. She can track it once she's close. There isn't one that would give me GPS coordinates, and even if there was, I'd be wary.

Ava is damn powerful and any magic I do is at risk of being detected by her, no matter the precautions I take."

"Then we'll find this thing by traditional means." He turned to Brynne, Jonas, and Killian, "I want you monitoring the pack. Put security on high alert and keep everyone close. I want daily check-ins from every-one. Now is not the time for a nice vacation. Update me on strangers in the territory and get some eyes on those witches."

"You've got it," said Brynne.

"Jonas and Sinclair, you two will take the eastern half of the territory. Mel and I will take the west." His advisors didn't like that, but this was the first step to easing them into accepting her. If she agreed to stay.

"Do I get a say in this?" asked Mel, her tone halfway between amused and frustrated.

"He's the alpha," said Killian, "And he gave an order."

The room went silent. Mel pivoted to face Killian. In two huge steps she was in front of him, her hands held tightly by her sides. "This isn't my pack."

Luke waited before speaking. He would protect Mel from Killian, from anyone who tried to harm her, but he would not undermine her, especially not in this first clash of authority.

Killian bared his teeth and the faint rumblings of a growl burbled in the back of his throat. "You will respect this pack and the alpha's authority while you remain in the territory," he demanded.

Mel leaned back, all tension seemingly gone from her. But Luke could still see her clenched fist and wanted to know what she would do next. He didn't think that she could beat Killian in a fight, but if she were to ever accept that she was his mate and fellow alpha, she would need to handle his inner circle without drawing blood.

She smirked and tilted her head to the side. "Seems to me that if the alpha had a problem with what I said, he'd tell me." She turned and gave Luke her brightest smile. It was utterly fake, and yet he was still affected. "Do you have a problem with me, your big bad alphaness?"

It wasn't respectful. It was downright insubordinate. But the tension evaporated and Luke saw Brynne and Jonas trying – and failing – to hide their grins. Maya didn't even try to quash her smile and only Sinclair was left looking pensive.

"See to the town," Luke told his people. "We search at nightfall." They left, each clasping his arm before heading out.

"I'd like to see to Cassie," said Krista.

"Of course," Luke nodded. He led her back to Cassie's room and noticed that Mel followed along with them. Maya split off, but he didn't question where she went. She had plenty of work to do without his meddling.

They were about to head upstairs when the front door opened. Luke thought it was one of his inner circle returning, but when a barely familiar scent hit his nostrils he stiffened. This was their third partner, Bob.

The tall black man entered and closed the door behind him. He smiled when he saw Krista and she rushed over to hug him. Mel stayed beside Luke and merely nodded at Bob. There was a good deal of history between the three of them and Luke didn't know most of it. He doubted he would completely understand the drama that went on in a band of thieves.

When Krista stepped out of the embrace, she was smiling with hope in her eyes. "What did you find out?"

"It's Ava." If Bob had dropped that bombshell a few minutes before, he might have earned a shocked gasp.

"We figured that part out," said Mel, completely recovered from the trauma of hearing Ava's name, or, at least able to hide her emotions now that some time had passed.

Bob nodded. "She's had her eye on the area for the

past three years. A group of vamps only just agreed to help her. She has no plans to stay."

Luke had spent the last eight years learning the ebb and flow of local supernatural politics. He had dedicated informants in every city in Colorado with a population greater than 100,000, and even more scattered throughout the rest of the region. He didn't know everything that went on in the supernatural world, but he was far from ignorant. Which begged the question: "How do you know that?" he asked. He didn't like the thought of missing out on so much.

Bob met his eyes and Luke saw a depth of knowledge far greater than a man of about forty should possess. He wondered at Bob's real age, though it would be beyond rude to ask. "It's what I do," was Bob's only explanation.

Krista was unfazed by that declaration. "And anything for Cassie?"

Bob let the question stretch out between them for an uncomfortable moment. He eventually spoke. "If it comes to it, there's a favor I can call in." After a pause, he added, "Let's hope that it doesn't come to that."

"She's just a kid." Luke said. And his sister at that. There wasn't anything he wouldn't do, any favor he wouldn't call in, if it meant saving her.

Bob laughed, the sound hollow and short. "You're all kids to me."

Luke took a step forward. He wouldn't be challenged in his own territory, not so blatantly.

Krista sensed the danger and spoke up once more. "Can you help me trace the hex?"

Bob broke eye contact with Luke to smile down at Krista. "Of course." The two of them went off without a farewell to Mel or Luke.

"I'll meet you at dusk," Mel said. She left before Luke could say anything to stop her. Not that he knew what to say to keep her from leaving. Mel was complicated, and Luke had a lot of learning to do before she would agree to stand by his side.

7

For the first time in years, Mel started to think about what she would do when Ava was gone. Her entire life had revolved around avoiding or destroying that woman. At least as much of her life as she could remember. Her memories pre-Ava were more flashes and dreams than substantial thoughts.

She supposed that theft would remain her job. She was good at it - very good - and the sense of accomplishment that she felt when she defeated someone's carefully placed safeguards and took her bounty was better than anything she'd ever experienced.

But when this was all over, she wouldn't need to keep tabs on Ava. There would be no looking over her shoulder when she visited the east coast. She would no longer be that weird feral girl who grew up among the witches.

She would be free.

If she survived.

Walking along the tree line not far from the house was different than Mel's run earlier. Now she was able to amble and gather her thoughts, though she didn't enjoy the company. It took her a few moments to realize that someone was near her, and another minute after that to determine that he was following her. And it was obvious that this kid wasn't Luke.

Neither Krista nor Bob were in a mood to chase her. She didn't blame them. She couldn't wait for this entire thing to be over either. She supposed that they would all go their separate ways when this was through. After all, they were still sore from Mel's betrayal and it wasn't like she didn't deserve it.

She would miss them.

At the moment she didn't have time to wallow. She grabbed a low hanging tree branch and hoisted herself up, effectively disappearing from the ground. The kid came running after her, an idiotic choice. She really needed to talk to Luke about how he trained the kids in his pack. If he didn't start knocking some sense into them, they were going to run him into the ground.

When the blond boy was right underfoot, Mel dove

for the ground, tackling him in one swift motion and gripping his throat with her hands. They both knew that she could shift at any moment and take him out for good.

Mel recognized him. He was the same boy who Cassie had knocked out on the night of Mel's escape. The night that everything had gone to hell.

Mick.

"Did Luke send you?" she asked. "I don't need a guard."

Mick sputtered, his cheeks a splotchy pink and his eyes wet with moisture he was valiantly trying to keep from turning into tears. "No!" he insisted.

"Then why were you following me?" Of all of the things that Mel hated in the world, being spied on was near the top.

"I wasn't." He tried to shake his head, but she held his neck too tightly for him to do more than weakly jerk.

Mel believed that Luke hadn't sent him. She'd known it hadn't been that simple the second she'd asked the question. But she didn't believe for a moment that this kid wasn't spying on *something*.

She crossed her arms and raised an eyebrow. Lesser men had been known to fold in under five seconds when subjected to this look. To Mick's credit, he lasted seven before he crumpled into himself, his shoulders slumping and eyes flicking down. "I saw all of the inner circle come in. I just wanted to know what they were doing."

And it wasn't Mel's place to enlighten the kid. Even if it had been, she wouldn't. They didn't need a curious teenager with a penchant for trouble messing up their plans.

Well, they didn't need *another* teenager like that.

"I'm sure Luke will talk to you if you have questions." That sounded right. Luke was incredibly reasonable, though she doubted that he would tell this kid everything that was about to go down. But given the way his face paled when she suggested it, Mel realized that there were some things about pack politics that she may never understand.

"Please don't tell him I was here!" Mick begged.

Mel had no reason to be charitable. She knew that Mick had been the one guarding her the night that she escaped. He had been the one that Cassie drugged before begging Mel to help her jump start her ability to shift. Mick must have been feeling the heat from his failure to guard Mel or protect Cassie. Maybe that was a good reason to avoid the alpha for now.

"If you don't want him to know you're here, then

don't be here." She flicked her fingers back and forth, shooing him.

Mick didn't stay for any further conversation. He ran back into the woods, disappearing from sight long before his steps disappeared from sound.

Mel leaned against a tree for a few minutes before deciding to head back to the house. The kid had spoiled her mood.

Mel found a book to distract herself once she went back to the house. Krista and Bob were still holed up with Cassie, and she had seen neither Luke nor Maya for hours. The house was strangely silent. Surely there were half a dozen people or more walking around, but in her room she was as cloistered as a monk. She got wrapped up in the story as she sat curled up on the bed.

When Luke opened the door to her room and popped his head in she nearly screamed. It was instinct to shove the book under the covers so that he could not see the title. Ava hadn't let her read at all, and Tina thought that it was more important to finish school work than to enjoy trashy novels.

"Huh," was all Luke said as she floundered. He

made no effort to take her book away from her. As he stood in the doorway, haloed by light, he could have been an angel. A dark, sexy angel. Or maybe a devil who knew his angles.

"What?" Mel asked, knowing there was no way to look cool after that. She tried to pretend that he hadn't startled her, her pose deceptively relaxed.

Luke seemed to struggle to find words. But he didn't leave her hanging for too long. "I guess I didn't picture you reading."

It was a little insulting, that statement. Mel had traveled the world, she spoke two languages, and could fake her way through another three. "Did you think that I would be picking a padlock for fun or something?" She meant it as a joke.

"Well, when you say it like that, it sounds offensive." He didn't have the grace to sound apologetic.

Mel let out a little laugh. "They're like Rubik's Cubes," she said.

"What?" Luke didn't follow.

"Simple locks," she explained. "They're like Rubik's Cubes. Once you know the trick, none of them are difficult to crack." She held up her hands in front of her and twisted them, miming solving the puzzle. "It can be comforting, but not very engaging."

But Luke was still caught on the cubes. "There's a trick to Rubik's Cubes? I spent all summer when I was fourteen trying to solve one."

She didn't ask if he had been successful; the frustration lacing his words was answer enough. "Yeah, there's a trick."

"Much as I would love for you to teach me," and this time she thought he was being sincere, "We've got to get going. It's dark out."

Mel stood up from the bed and left the book under the covers. Krista wouldn't look at it if she didn't see it. "I'm ready."

He waited for her for a moment to slip on her shoes, and then they were off. Mel thought they would go directly into the woods, but Luke lead her to the garage. He passed up all of the cars and chose a two-seater ATV. There were two separate ATVs, one sat two people side by side, the other sat them one in front of the other.

Luke chose the latter. Mel would need to hold onto him during their ride.

"Wouldn't it be faster to run?" She didn't object to the up close and personal treatment, but they had a job to do.

"If we didn't need to talk while we worked, then yes."

Mel wasn't used to surveying with a partner. The work she'd done with Krista and Bob had been compartmentalized. When Mel shifted to surveil something, she never needed to share her observations in the moment.

But she climbed onto the ATV after Luke with a smile. This was an adjustment she was more than willing to make.

"And I'm sure you took this one because it handles better?" she asked, teasing.

Luke's voice was thick with sarcasm. "Of course."

He opened the garage and they pulled out faster than Mel expected. She leaned forward, her entire front pressed tightly against his back as she gripped close and hung on.

Yes, she liked his choice very much.

She could feel every inch of him pressed against her, from her navel to her collarbone. Each bump in the road was sweet torture. Mel remembered the feel of his lips on hers, of his body pressed against hers in that erotic dance they'd dabbled in. She couldn't wait to take him.

"This isn't how I thought I'd have my thighs around you," she spoke against his ear, her lips caressing the flesh.

"Jesus," from the sound of his voice she could

imagine him gripping the handle bars tightly. "Now you decide to flirt."

Mel tightened her hold on him, feeling his abs contract under her hands. "What else are we going to do?" Her tongue darted out and licked the outer ridge of his ear.

"I'm going to crash this fucking thing if you keep that up." There was a challenge in his words, and Mel didn't think that he wanted her to stop. She was having far too much fun to be dissuaded by the thought of a fiery wreck.

Mel kept one hand anchored around Luke's chest and let the other explore, tracing the ridges of his abs through his shirt.

Luke covered that hand, holding it in place before she could distract him further. "Unless we find the Well in the next hour, what do you say to coming back to my room and forgetting our troubles for the night?"

Mel thought he would never ask. "It sure as hell beats the forest floor."

But he wasn't satisfied. "Is that a yes?"

She kissed his neck again, though only with a quick peck. "What do you think?" His proposal made her more motivated than ever to get this job done properly. They had been heading down the road to sex for too long. Maybe this would get him out of her system and clear out all of those thoughts of mates and a future and all that bullshit.

Even as she entertained the thought, she knew she was crazy. Luke wasn't the kind of man a girl got to forget. And there was no getting him out of her system. Once they were together - really, truly together - there would be nothing keeping her from falling all the way. Mate be damned.

She'd never been in love before.

Was that what this was, now? Not just lust. Lust she understood. But this desire to speak with him, to share her thoughts and learn his mind. The dull pang she felt when she was away from him. And scariest of all, the certainty she felt in her heart that with him she could defeat Ava, defeat any enemy that crossed her path.

Could love make her that strong?

She put her terror on hold once they pulled over, parking the ATV next to a particularly tall tree. Mel climbed off, taking an extra second to enjoy the feel of her hands against his chest before pulling them completely away. But once they were no longer touching, it was down to business.

She took a good look at the woods around them. Nothing seemed strange or out of place. The sounds of animals in the distance were audible, though they'd scared away most of what lived near the path with the sound of the ATV.

"It's probably best to take our section in a big circle and see if anything seems fishy." She didn't want to comb every inch of forest if they didn't need to.

"Fishy?"

Mel shrugged. "Blood raining from the sky? Weird-ass magic shit. You know." Krista had detailed it all, and she had no doubt that Luke remembered most of it.

They took off between two trees. It wasn't quite a path, but they made do, walking side by side when they could and in single file when the forest forced them. Luke held up a half-fallen log to let her pass under before he began to talk.

He kept his voice low, barely above the sound of the forest around them. "You know what I wish I could do?"

"What?" She'd understand if he wanted magic to roast Ava alive for what she was doing for Cassie. There had been plenty of times in Mel's life where she had wished for the same thing.

"I want to call my parents and ask for their advice." He spoke it as if it were a shameful secret. As if the thought of asking for help was anathema.

"Then why don't you call?" It wasn't something Mel could do. As heartless as it sounded, there were plenty of times when Mel didn't miss her parents or her family. When she was working, when she was eating a particularly good meal, when she fought or fucked. And even when she did miss them, she never thought of the things she could have relied on them for now if they were still alive.

Luke let out a hollow sound that might have been a laugh. "With Cassie hurt?" He shook his head. The forest narrowed before them and he let Mel go ahead. "I may be the alpha, but I doubt that would stop my mother from rampaging through the state and burning everything down until she rescues her precious babies."

Some righteous anger might be useful. "There are worse things she could do," Mel reasoned. "But why can't you just tell them that you've got it all under control?" Even if that wasn't exactly true. "Don't they trust you?"

This was where Mel got hung up on the parents thing. Even though Tina had rescued her, she'd never tried to be a mom. Mel couldn't imagine someone rushing in, guns blazing out of selfless protection.

But Luke didn't seem to understand her question. He sputtered a little, his sounds trying to form into a question that she couldn't decipher. Finally, he gathered his thoughts. "It's not about trust," he explained. "Cassie and I are her kids."

Mel shrugged. "Krista's mom would let us handle everything ourselves."

"Didn't she train you both to be lawless thieves?"

"Aren't all thieves lawless? Wait—" Mel stopped where she stood. She thought she spotted something under a large rock a little ways off the path. She stepped over and around several trees and knelt beside the underbrush.

"What is it?" Luke didn't follow. He trusted her to investigate.

Mel stood and shook her head. She made her way back to him. "I thought I saw something, but not so much."

"Damn."

"Yeah."

Mel didn't want to end their conversation. She felt like she was learning so much about this man. "So you've got a good relationship with your parents?"

"I guess I do. But Scott isn't an alpha, and my mom hasn't been an alpha in more than twenty years. They don't always realize the weight that I've got on my shoulders."

"That sounds—" She couldn't finish the thought.

A scream went up, ripping through the forest and sending both Luke and Mel running towards it.

Without hesitation, Luke sprinted towards the

scream, and Mel was not far behind him. He recognized the cries as one of his pack members, even if he wasn't quite sure who. The forest blurred around him as he vaulted over fallen trees and around obstructions in the path.

If he paused to think about how he was moving, he would stumble, but this wasn't Luke's first run. After a minute he made it to a small clearing, barely more than six feet across.

A vampire held Mick close, fangs buried in the teenager's throat.

Luke launched himself at the creature, letting out a roar as he went. If Mick had been human, Luke would have never tried it. It was far too dangerous of a move for someone without the hearty constitution of a shapeshifter.

They both went down under Luke's weight and the vampire let go of Mick, turning his attention to his new aggressor. Luke growled at him, showing his own fangs to the pale beast.

The vampire should have looked human. They didn't have a second form, their only supernatural trait their long fangs. But this vampire was in the midst of a hunger-crazed rage. His eyes were glassy and blood-shot, his mouth frozen in a hiss leaving his fangs on display.

Luke moved, jerking to the side and keeping the creature's eyes on him. He could tell that Mel was trying to get Mick out of the way and to safety. He didn't want to risk either one of them falling prey to this beast.

The vampire's eyes stayed glued to him, and when the vampire lunged forward, Luke dodged, pushing him to the side and watching him tumble over. The vampire rolled completely over once before springing back to his feet with a little bounce. It would have been impressive if they hadn't been locked in combat.

But the vampire was still not steady on his feet and Luke took the advantage, charging forward and pummeling him with his fists. Had he been in his other form, the vampire would have been ripped to shreds by his claws. As it was, he had no time to shift, instead using his inborn strength to inflict as much pain as he could.

Luke got in a few good hits before the vampire bucked, unbalancing Luke and knocking him to the side. At another time, the vampire might have gone in for the kill, but this one knew he was outnumbered. He turned and ran, heading deep into the forest, away from Luke's house and the way that he and Mel had come from.

If not for the injured Mick, Luke would have given

chase. But the vampire could have friends waiting and he would not run into an ambush.

Mel wiped a bit of cloth against Mick's neck. She was not particularly gentle and he winced every time she made contact with his cuts.

"Are you alright?" Luke asked.

Mick winced again and pulled away from Mel, yanking the cloth from her hands. "You're worse than that damned bloodsucker."

"What are you doing here?" she asked in a tone verging on accusatory.

While Luke wasn't happy with the boy's presence, he didn't understand the scrutiny. This was pack land and pack members were free to roam at will with very few exceptions. Mick was currently in deep shit for failing to protect Cassie, but even he was allowed periodic walks.

Mick defended himself before Luke could say anything. "I told you already that I wasn't spying!"

Even if Luke had been a dull man, that would have set off alarm bells. "I didn't realize you two had spoken." The boy's wounds were already healing and Luke's patience was running thin. While Mick was allowed to be in this part of the territory, it was strange for him to be here now.

So why hadn't Mel told him anything about Mick's espionage?

She made up for it now. "He was lurking outside the house earlier today."

"I was standing. No lurking involved." And now the indignant tones of a teenager being ignored suffused his words. He'd admit anything in a few seconds so long as they believed him.

"Why were you standing out there?" Luke asked, "And what were you doing here now?"

Mick shrugged, wincing when he jostled his still tender skin. "Just curious. Things have all gone on lockdown the past few weeks and the guys wanted to know what's up. We all want to know."

Luke didn't like it, but Mick had a point. He'd been keeping things on a need to know basis when it came to Mel and what was going on with Cassie. His inner circle knew, but the other shapeshifters that he was responsible for had no idea.

And he had to keep it that way for now.

When this was over he would tell all, but until then he needed to keep them safe. If the choice was between that and satisfying the idle curiosity of children, he'd choose safety every time.

"You're a bit deep in the woods for idle curiosity," said

Luke. "And if you or your friends wish to know what's going on, you ask. You don't spy and sneak. You're nearly an adult. Act like it if you ever want responsibility in this pack. You are still a long way from proving yourself."

Mick sputtered, but he couldn't complete a full sentence.

"Let's head back." Luke didn't have time to give the kid a full lecture, not in the middle of the woods, not when he'd just scared off a vampire.

"I can go home myself," said Mick.

Mel huffed out a laugh, "Because that vampire couldn't track your ass down and eat you alive the second we're out of view, right?"

"I can fight one stupid vampire!"

Luke shook his head. Normally, Mick was the level-headed one among his friends. He'd never had these issues with the kid before. But every teenager acted out at one time or another. "Mel's right," he said. "I don't want you getting captured or killed."

"You're trusting a goddamned thief over a member of your own pack?" Mick scowled and threw the cloth at his neck to the ground. His wound had closed, though the skin looked thin, tender, and brightly red.

Luke growled, the sound emanating from the back of his throat. "She's—"

"Right," Mel finished before Luke could say

anything damning. "And you're being dumb." She stood and had the audacity to ruffle Mick's light brown hair. "Now stand your ass up or I'll drag you back."

She turned around and headed back the way she and Luke had come, leaving the men to follow. After about three seconds and one shared, confused glance, they did.

8

Getting Mick home turned out to be a bit of a logistical problem. But Mel ended up driving the ATV with Luke running ahead, leading her into town. About a block from Mick's house, the teenager motioned for Mel to stop the vehicle. "I can make it the rest of the way myself."

She and Luke shared a look, but they let the kid go. He was more or less safe now. She shimmied back to the passenger seat so that Luke could drive them back home. He knew the way back better than she did.

But Luke wasn't ready to head back just yet. "Are you hungry?" he asked.

Now that he mentioned it, her stomach growled. "Starving."

"Let's grab a bite before we go back." He didn't wait

for her to agree. Instead, he took them down the road until they reached the main street in Eagle Creek. He pulled the ATV into the parking lot of the Eagle Creek Bar & Grille and slid off, offering her a hand.

Mel heard the laugh of a woman abruptly cut off as the door to the restaurant closed, leaving Mel and Luke alone in the parking lot. She hesitated. "It's cool if you want to just go in and pick something up." His pack mates would be in there, ones that had no idea that she existed. And they would wonder who she was and why she was with Luke. It would complicate things.

"Why?" A car door opened near them and people got out. Luke looked over and nodded, the man and woman were two other members of his pack. He looked back at her, waiting for an answer.

"Well," trying to say it out loud made it sound weird. "People will see us together."

Luke raised an eyebrow. "Yes, they will."

He didn't seem to get it. "And you'll have questions to answer. About who I am, or whatever." Did he not get it? Or did he not care?

"I'm the alpha." He said it with such authority that sent a shiver ran down her spine. "I only answer the questions that I wish to answer."

Mel persisted, "I don't want to make things difficult for you. Well, more difficult."

Luke laughed, "You've done nothing but make my life difficult." Despite the words, she knew it wasn't a criticism. "Why stop now?"

She balled up her fist and punched him lightly in the arm. "Jerk." She smiled as she spoke and gave up the argument. If he wanted her in there with him, she'd go.

The Eagle Creek Bar & Grille hadn't changed much since Mel, Krista, and Bob sat in it a few weeks before plotting how to steal the Scarlet Emerald from Luke. The only difference now was the clientele. The place was far from packed, and nearly everyone inside was a shapeshifter. Sometimes humans could pick up on the dangerous currents around them, even if they didn't know about the supernatural world. They got out of dodge before things went to hell.

Luke waved to the hostess but didn't wait to be seated. He led Mel to a booth in the back corner in a closed section of the restaurant. No one tried to stop him from sitting there. He pulled out a chair for her so that her back would be facing the wall and then he sat beside her. They would need to speak quietly to avoid being overheard. Shapeshifter hearing was far superior to a human's.

They didn't even need to order. Three minutes after they sat down a waitress put two beers on their table along with cheeseburgers with fries. "We had an order come up. Is this alright for you?"

Mel would have been pissed if she had to wait extra-long for her food just because the alpha stopped by. But no one else seemed to mind. Luke smiled and thanked her, letting her know they would wave her over if they needed anything else.

"It's good to be the king," Mel teased.

Luke took a big bite of the burger and swallowed before he answered. "I don't force any of this shit. The old alpha was a tyrant. I do my best to be fair."

"Is that why you took over?"

"If anyone asks, yes." His tone didn't invite further questioning, though Mel was now dying to know. Perhaps Luke had an impulsive streak that he had failed to suppress.

"Do you like being the alpha?" She'd never spoken to one for any length of time before she met Luke, and now that she had him to herself the questions kept coming.

"Most of the time."

But probably not when a psychopathic witch was trying to steal his land and kill his sister. Mel thought that no one would want to be an alpha under those circumstances.

"I've been wondering something." Luke eased into his question.

There were a hundred things he could ask. "Yeah?"

"Things seem tense between you and your partners."

It wasn't a question, but Mel understood just the same. "Yeah." This was a sore subject, something she hadn't fully come to terms with herself.

"Did they not want to be here?"

Of course he had no clue why things were the way they were. And as much as Mel wanted him to like her, she wasn't going to let him think that the problem was something simple. "No," she answered, "The tension is my fault."

"Oh, how—" he cut himself off, "You don't need to tell me."

"I think I want to." Only as she said it did she realize how true that statement was.

"You do?" From his skepticism, Mel doubted she came off as the type likely to share her failures easily. But today seemed the day for opening up to him.

"You probably won't like it," she warned. She didn't like it and she'd been the one to live it.

"Try me." Luke took a sip of his beer and kept his posture casual. But tension hovered in the air between them. He was just as nervous to hear her story as she was to tell it.

"I'm just giving a fair warning. I know that we've been…" How could she even phrase it? She didn't quite understand their relationship. "Flirting," she settled on. "But you might call it off once I'm done talking."

Luke lifted her hand off the table and raised it to his lips. For three seconds the restaurant went completely silent as those watching them registered what he had done. The kiss was chaste, it shouldn't have been worth noticing, but it was a public declaration or romantic intent from the alpha. "I doubt that," he said it like a promise.

Mel had to take a second to get her emotions under control. He wasn't supposed to make her feel this way, hot and cold, ready to run out the door or throw herself into his arms, the feelings changed by the second. She was scared to tell Luke; that was something that she could hold on to. It was the only familiar thing in the mishmash of her emotions.

She knew how to deal with fear. Mel embraced it, letting it sink into her and keep her sharp. She used the fear to make her strong, to allow her to tell Luke her biggest shame. "It happened in Cincinnati two years ago." She kept her voice low, aware that they were in a room full of people with extraordinary hearing. Luke was the only one who got to hear this story, not his pack. "We were on a big job, nearly a dozen people all coming together to steal a gauntlet worth a hell of a lot of money."

Luke just nodded. Unlike before when she mentioned her career, this time he didn't turn away. They were making progress. If only theft were the worst part of this story.

"I hit it off with another thief named Chance. He's human, but nearly as good as I am. He usually doesn't work supernatural jobs, though." She left out that he had been cute and funny and treated her well. The rest of the story was bad enough as it was. "Something went wrong at the end of the job. Chance and I had the gauntlet and we were in our car, we were clear. And I screwed Krista and Bob over." She still remembered the look of the bright city lights that night, how they'd glowed a sinister red in the fog.

"You don't seem like the type to betray your friends so easily." When she wouldn't look at him, Luke squeezed her hand, offering comfort.

Mel pulled her hand out of his grasp. "Don't try to find the good in me. I fucked up." And if he didn't believe it yet, he'd do so soon, "Do you remember the cuff links I gave you Mexico?" she asked.

Luke nodded.

They'd been charmed to interact with a ring she wore. If he turned the diamond to the green gem, it meant he was getting out, if he activated the red gem, it meant he needed help. "In the car, my ring started burning, the red gem glowing. Krista had activated the charm." Mel could still remember the panic she'd felt that night. She had barely been able to breathe. "I told Chance that we needed to turn around and get them. But he convinced me that we couldn't. And I let him convince me. We had the gauntlet, we were out safe. If we went back we could easily be caught or lose the take. Five minutes after she activated the charm, it went dead."

"Did you get out of range?" His posture was no longer relaxed and the inch of space between them felt like a mile.

Mel shook her head, "There isn't a range on them, they aren't like cell phones. The only reason they stop working is if they're deactivated or the wearer dies. Once I felt that, I knew it was too late. If I had signaled back, or if we had turned around, maybe I could have stopped whatever happened to them."

"But they're not dead."

"I didn't know that for six months." She skipped over what happened the rest of that night, it wasn't important, "The next morning, Chance was gone and so was the gauntlet. Everyone but me, Krista, Bob, and Chance was either captured or died on that job. I don't know if he arranged it or if he was just lucky. But he got all the money and I haven't seen him since. I think he's operating out of Miami now."

She grabbed for her beer and took a long swig. Even though it felt like she'd been telling the story for hours, the bottle was still cold. She couldn't even look at Luke. She'd never said what she'd done out loud before and now she didn't know how he'd be able to see her as anything other than a betrayer. As worthless.

"So you didn't try to see if they were alive once you were safe?" he asked. His tone was empty, she couldn't tell if he was angry or disgusted.

"I wasn't going back to Cincinnati. Going back to the scene of your crimes is how you get caught." And yet, here she was, sitting with the man she'd stolen from, in the same restaurant where she'd planned the robbery.

"You came back to help Cassie," he said quietly.

"I came back to get my scry stone." Why didn't he see how bad it was? Why was he trying to absolve her?

"But you came back and told us about the hex." Luke grabbed her hand again and waited until she looked at him, "Mel, we've all done bad things. But I don't believe for a single second that you would do that again."

This was too intimate, in this room full of people, they might as well have been the only ones there. Mel felt tears prick at her eyes, but she did her best to hold them back.

"Thanks for the vote of confidence," she clung to her sarcasm, it was the only thing preventing a very embarrassing display of emotion. "If only Krista could see it that way." Bob had forgiven her as much as he was willing to. They would never be friends again, but he would work with her.

"Did you apologize to her?"

"How does that go? I'm sorry I chose some asshole over you? I'm sorry I left you to die? It's too little too late." She wanted to warn Luke right now, to tell him that she would betray him someday, that she knew nothing else, but she couldn't make the words come out. This was his warning. If he still wanted her after this, he was crazy.

But Luke didn't move away and he didn't let go of her hand. "I trust you, Mel." He said it with the heartfelt sincerity of another confession, one she was scared to hear. "Whether we're mates or not, no matter how this all ends up, I trust you. And I know you won't betray us."

Mel didn't know if she could be trusted, but his faith made her hope that it wasn't misplaced. He deserved so much better than her, and she didn't understand why he couldn't realize it.

"Oh hell, if you keep trusting me I'll probably just rob you blind." She meant it as a warning, but she couldn't help but smile.

They both knew she was lying.

Luke put his arm around her and pulled her close, "Anything you want..." He didn't finish the offer, but she understood.

All she needed to do was reach out and he would be hers. But Mel wasn't yet sure that she could trust herself enough to take him.

They turned away from heavy topics and finished their food. Luke drove the ATV back to his house with Mel clinging behind him. But this time she kept a little distance. He could feel it in the stiffness of her embrace and from the fact that she wasn't saying anything as they rode down the bumpy path through the woods.

It had been a hell of a thing that she told him. That was enough for him to break it off between them. He knew that she wouldn't blame him for walking away.

But he was in too deep and sinking deeper. He didn't want to walk away from her.

Mel thought that her story told him that she wasn't worthy of trust, instead he only saw how much she had grown.

She wasn't walking away from his pack in their time of need, even though he'd given her what she'd come for. He couldn't claim to know her mind completely, but he understood that she had changed. She would not abandon her people a second time, and right now, she counted him among that number.

Now all he needed to do was figure out how to make her stay.

Their plan to return to his room was interrupted the moment they stepped into the garage. Luke gritted his teeth and wished that he had taken Mel somewhere else where they could be away from responsibility for one night. Hell, even for a few hours.

But Maya was waiting to talk and he couldn't ignore her.

He pulled Mel close before she could step away. "Come to me tonight," it was half command, half question. She brushed her lips quickly against his before stepping away and going into the house alone. He'd take that as a yes.

He and Maya followed Mel into the house, though

they didn't begin talking until they were in the War Room. "So is that happening?" asked Maya.

"Excuse me?" He didn't like the tone she took. He knew what he was doing and he hadn't even tried to keep his relationship with Mel a secret.

"I think I've earned the right to ask questions." They kept their voices low. The War Room couldn't be completely soundproofed, not from shapeshifter hearing.

"Not about this."

"Do you think I'm the only one who will have a problem once it gets out who she is, and what she does for a living?" Maya leaned against the wall and crossed her arms.

"So you can make eyes at the witch all day, but I can't develop feelings for someone outside the pack?" He hadn't been planning on bringing Krista into this, but this was hypocrisy of the highest order coming from Maya.

"My *feelings*," she sneered, "Have nothing to do with this. It's my actions - and your actions - that matter. There are seven billion people in this world. I'm sure most of them would be better than a woman who stole the most important pack artifact that we have and let it fall into the hands of a murderous witch." Her words were spoken with cold fury.

"Eight years, Maya. Name one time in eight years where I put myself above this pack." He would not have argued with anyone else, but Maya had earned her place as his number two and he could not so easily silence her. If he did not earn her support, he didn't know what he'd do.

"I don't doubt your commitment. But in this case, I doubt your sense."

His lion rustled beneath his skin, aching to roar. "If you wish to challenge me, you are more than welcome to."

She rolled her eyes, "I'm not going to challenge you. You couldn't pay me enough to be an alpha." Her phone beeped and she pulled it out of her back pocket. After a moment, she slid it back. "That's not actually why I wanted to talk."

"Oh?" He was primed now, ready for the argument.

"Did you find anything?" she asked.

Luke took a second and a deep breath. He could do business. "No Well. But there was a vampire, probably scouting. It attacked Mick. Mel and I got there before it could do any major damage."

A bit of color leeched from Maya's brown face, but her expression remained neutral. "What was Mick doing out there?"

A question Luke would like answered himself. "Hell if I know. Mel says he was creeping around earlier."

Maya crossed her arms. "Wonderful."

"Has anything strange been happening with him?" Luke asked. Maya monitored the pack and acted as his eyes and ears at all times. If he didn't know something, she would.

"No more than the usual teenage bullshit."

"And are the others back yet?" He didn't know what Mick was up to, but he couldn't worry about that. He'd concern himself with the kid after they defeated Ava and her murderous witch and vampire accomplices.

"Yeah. Sinclair called to say they found bupkis."

"Bupkis?"

She nodded, "Not a leaf out of place."

Luke and Mel hadn't had enough time to search their area completely, and he wouldn't be surprised to learn that it was the same for Jonas and Sinclair. "We'll search again tomorrow," he decided.

"I'll let them know."

She turned around and crossed the room, only pausing to open the door.

"What about Cassie?" asked Luke. "Have you checked on her?"

Maya looked back over her shoulder. "She was fine

last time I checked. No change for the worse." She left, closing the door behind her.

Luke followed not long after, taking a moment to duck his head into Cassie's room. Neither Krista nor Bob was with her. Instead another lion, Kyle, sat at her bedside and read a book while she slept. He started to stand when he heard Luke, but Luke raised a hand and let him know to stay put. It was late and he had no need to wake his sister now that she was resting.

He made it back to his room and the excitement of the day caught up with him. By the time he opened the door, it felt like a thousand pound weight was crushing his shoulders. It lifted slightly when he saw Mel asleep in his bed, her hair flung out across his pillow. In the darkness she was more of a shape than a person, but it felt so right that he had to force himself forward rather than stand in the doorway and just stare at her.

That would be creepy.

He crossed the room in the dark, his steps careful and nearly silent. He didn't want to wake her. Luke pulled off his shirt and his jeans, naked except for his underwear. He gently lifted the comforter and climbed in beside her.

Mel rolled toward him, curling herself up next to his warmth. Luke put an arm around her and closed his eyes. He couldn't remember ever falling asleep faster or more comfortably.

9

The arm around her was almost distressingly tight. But Luke's scent was all around her too, and as Mel woke, she remembered falling asleep in Luke's bed. No light streamed in under the curtains and the clock on his bedside table told her it was before six in the morning.

By her count, that was nearly six hours of uninterrupted sleep. No wonder she felt rested. The alpha would be worth keeping around if only to keep the nightmares at bay.

She didn't want to wake him; Luke's face had lost some of the tension that he'd been wearing for days, and he looked five years younger. It took some careful maneuvering, but Mel extracted herself from his grasp and slid out of the bed. She wore a pair of shorts and a shirt. Last night she'd been raw, not ready for physical intimacy. And she couldn't have been happier that Luke had respected that silent request.

Mel felt constrained indoors. She needed to think, to see the horizon. And, luckily for her, Luke's room came with a balcony. She let herself out silently and stood by the railing for several moments. But it still wasn't enough.

She turned around and took a look at the roof. It wasn't too tall, and the slope was climbable. Mel crouched down and sprang up, grabbing onto the gutter and swinging herself up onto the black shingles.

Mel climbed up to the ridge of the roof and straddled it, with one foot on each slope. Though the sky was dark, it was clear and she could see for miles. The streetlights in Eagle Creek were dim, but as the sun began to rise beyond them, she saw the outline of the mountains in the distance.

It was beautiful.

But that beauty did nothing to settle the tumult of her thoughts. She'd never intended to tell Luke about Chance or what happened in Cincinnati. Shame had a way of keeping her quiet. He knew she was a thief, and that didn't bother her. It was only the truth. But to let him know about her betrayal? It didn't sit well, no matter that it was the truth as well.

If she was honest, though it was something she generally avoided, Mel knew why she told Luke - why she'd had to tell Luke everything.

There was no way she could keep him if he didn't know. And she was beginning to think that keeping him was more important than anything. She was imagining her life after Ava, and in those thoughts, Luke had a place. He was beside her, living with her and loving her.

He was also inside her and behind and above and under, but their relationship was more than prurient. Though she couldn't wait for the prurient parts.

Mel heard another person on the roof and froze. She got low, rolling off the ridge and plastering herself as flat as could be. But she caught Krista's scent and relaxed. Mel climbed back up to the ridge and waited for Krista to join her.

"I felt something disturb my ward," Krista said in place of a greeting.

"I didn't feel anything." Mel's sensitivity to magic was high for a shapeshifter, and she was used to the feel of Krista's spells.

"That's the point of a defensive ward." Krista crouched on the edge of the eastern half of the roof, her hand gripping the ridge. She must have placed wards around the house to warn them of any unwelcome company.

"It's a bit early for you to be awake." Krista normally didn't rise before the sun unless her house was on fire.

"I could say the same for you."

"I wanted to think," she said, though her thoughts were still in a jumble. Even the peace of the morning was not helping.

"You didn't come back to the room last night." It wasn't an accusation, but Mel wasn't sure how to reply.

"Do you care?" It came out sharper than intended.

"Not really." But Krista didn't leave. It was as if she couldn't decide between staying and going, so she remained perched, not quite sitting on the roof.

"I was thinking about Cincinnati," Mel admitted.

Krista waved her free hand in front of her, "I don't want to hear about it."

Now that Mel had said it, she wanted it off her chest. "Just one last time, and then I'll never talk about it again." And she meant it.

Krista blew out a breath, "Whatever." But instead of leaving Mel alone on the roof, she sat on the ridge, facing east and looking towards the rapidly brightening horizon.

Mel hadn't planned to talk to Krista about this again. The last time had gone so disastrously that she had purposely not thought about it. Until she told Luke the whole story, a part of her had believed that Krista would eventually just get over it. But saying what she'd done out loud, actually remembering that night, brought it to the forefront and made her aware of just how wrong she had been.

"I'm sorry for not being there when you needed me," and once Mel began, the words just poured out. "And I'm sorry for taking off afterward. I was wrong. Completely, totally wrong, and I should have punched out Chance and come after you myself. Barring that, I should have—"

"I don't care about what you should have done." Krista cut her off. "I care about what you did."

It brought Mel up short, but she nodded. "You're right. And if we survive this shit, I hope that you can forgive me one day." She doubted that it would ever happen. She didn't know if she could forgive Krista if their situations were reversed.

"And if I can't?"

Mel shrugged. "I guess that's that, then."

Krista took a deep breath, "I'm not actually pissed about you not coming back that night."

"What?" Mel had left her to die and Krista didn't hold it against her? That made no sense.

"I deactivated the charm. Bob found us a way out and I knew you couldn't make it in time." She hadn't been looking at Mel, but now she turned to face her. "When you didn't show up at the rendezvous a week later I thought something had happened."

At the time, Mel had convinced herself that Krista and Bob were dead and she couldn't face going to the meet and having it confirmed. Instead, she'd taken a job in Poland and stayed out of the country for months.

"I thought you were dead!" Krista's eyes blazed with an inner fire. "And when I found out you weren't, I wanted to kill you."

"I'm—" Mel cut herself off before apologizing again. She knew that Krista didn't want to hear it.

"You did something that my mom would do." Krista leveled the accusation with no malice, but Mel felt the knife all the same.

"What can I say? She taught me everything I know." Everything that Ava hadn't taught her.

"If you ever pull a stunt like that again, you're dead to me."

It wasn't forgiveness, but it was a bigger step then Mel expected. She didn't answer Krista; Krista wouldn't want one. But they sat on the roof for a long time in silence, watching the sunrise. Once the light of day stretched around them, Krista crawled back down the roof. Mel followed soon after.

It was time to face the alpha.

Luke tried not to be disappointed that Mel wasn't with him when he woke up. Her scent was still wrapped around him, a warm touch that reached all the way to his heart, and the sheets were still warm. She hadn't been gone for long.

He didn't hear her in the bathroom, so he thought she must have gone downstairs to get breakfast. Or perhaps she had some sort of thief ritual that she couldn't do in front of him.

If she wasn't there to ring in the morning with him, he saw no reason to stay in bed. He threw the covers off and crossed the room to his bathroom, where he started the water for a shower. He took of his underwear and stepped under the hot stream. Luke let out a hiss as he adjusted to the change in temperature. It was almost painful for a few seconds until the water soaked into his skin and he could feel his muscles relax.

Over the sound of the water hitting the gray tile, he heard the door open and a person step in. He turned around. The shower was enclosed by a glass door, rather than a curtain, and he saw Mel step in. She gave him the once over, her eyes flicking down quickly before looking back up at his face.

Luke smiled and stepped a little out of the spray's

range so that water wasn't running into his eyes. "Good morning."

Mel smiled back. "Right back at you."

She stayed where she was and Luke started to feel a bit on display. "Keep staring and I'll need to charge admission."

"What? You don't like to let girls look at you when you're all wet and pretty like that?"

"Just you." There were no other women, he wanted no one but Mel. "Care to join me?"

She hooked her thumbs into the waistband of her shorts and pulled them down along with her underwear. Then came her shirt and she was standing naked before him, her skin golden in the bathroom light. She stalked across the bathroom, her hips swaying.

It was a show for him, and Luke was already hard.

She opened the door and stepped in carefully, wincing the slightest bit when the water hit her. "Do you normally make it hot enough to get third degree burns?" She stepped close, putting her hand on his chest.

That wasn't enough. Luke had been thinking about her, about what he would do when he had her, since the moment they met. An inch between them would be too much. He leaned down, trailing kisses down her neck and across her collarbone. "I think it feels good."

"Mmmm," she let out a little moan and her fingers curled in, "You might have a point."

The sound she made sent a spear of pleasure right to the heart of him. He laced his fingers through her hair and tilted her head up, taking her lips in a searing kiss. The water pouring down around them may as well have not existed. He was too wrapped up in her to notice or to care.

His cock was an insistent monster, jutting out in front of him and pressing against her.

Her fingers played on his chest, stroking down along his abs and tracing their outline. All Luke could do was kiss her harder, mark her as his with his tongue. He couldn't say the words to her, not yet. But he put everything he wanted into that kiss.

And Mel responded. She was just as hungry as he was, and just as desperate.

When her fingers made it even further and brushed against the head of his erection, he groaned. She took him in hand, gripping his shaft and stroking.

It was too much for Luke and he pulled back, breaking their kiss. "Keep that up and I'll give you anything you ask for," he gasped.

Mel smiled, her eyes bright stars. "I'll give you a list."

Luke's hand slid from her hair and palmed her

breast. Even under the hot stream of the water her nipples were hard. Luke's lips followed his hands, tracing a trail of kisses down her neck until he closed his lips around one of her nipples.

Her hands were at his sides now, gripping him tight.

In this moment, Luke felt closer to her than he had ever felt to another person. There was no outside world, no past, no future, it was only the two of them, trapped together in pleasure. He wanted nothing else, no one else. If he could take one moment and freeze it for all time, it would be this one, with Mel writhing in pleasure as he tasted her.

But he wasn't satisfied with just teasing her breast. His fingers dipped lower, swiping against her sex and finding her wet. For him.

"Fuck me, Luke," she begged.

Luke didn't need to be told twice. "Wrap your legs around me," he commanded. She did so, and held on tightly when he backed her up against the wall.

Luke guided himself to her entrance and slid in, watching her bite her lip as he filled her. He kept his eyes on her the entire time, watching for any hint of discomfort, any sign that she wasn't with him. But Mel's face was awash with pleasure, and Luke was in heaven.

Mel leaned forward and kissed him. This was perfect. He moved inside her, moved with her, their very breaths in sync. There wouldn't be anyone else for him. Before he met Mel, that might have scared him, but the feel of her against him was everything that he wanted.

He was her mate, her lover, and the man deliriously in love with her. He didn't mean to say it, for all the strength of his emotion, he didn't want to scare her away, but as he moved within her, the words slipped out. "I love you," he breathed against her lips.

Mel didn't pull away. Maybe she didn't hear it, or maybe she felt the same but couldn't yet say it. She gasped, quivering around him as she came.

Luke could feel the orgasm building. He thrust into her, back and forth, his heartbeat racing in his chest until at the last second he pulled out completely, spilling his seed outside of her.

Mel lay her head against his shoulder, "Let's remember a condom next time." She stood on wobbly legs, but didn't let him go.

Luke smiled, "This was a hell of a way to wake up."

"Don't get used to it," Mel warned. "I'm not a morning person."

His smile got even wider. It wasn't a declaration of

love, but it was something. "We still need to try the bed." But they had no time that morning.

They washed together in the shower, Luke helping Mel wash her hair, Mel soaping him off. And only once the water got cold did they get out. Mel was off to patrol the woods once more and Luke had to go into town to prepare for the oncoming battle.

If he had been another man, he would have gladly laid in bed all day, making love to Mel. But he was an alpha, and they both had their duties.

10

This trip into the woods was not nearly as pleasant as the last one. And Mel was including the vampire attack in her assessment. Maya's grand idea had been to hike out four miles into the woods rather than take one of the ATVs.

The stony silence was almost a blessing.

After their interlude in the shower, Mel went back to her room for a change of clothes. By the time she came down for breakfast, Maya was waiting for her, her face suffused with frustration.

Mel hadn't known that she had been waiting, but that hardly stopped Maya from holding it against her. But Mel hadn't lived to please anyone but herself for a very long time, and she wasn't going to let Maya walk over her. So she took her time eating her bagel and then insisted on changing her shoes.

It added at least ten minutes and filled Mel with childish glee.

But Maya tried to one-up Mel's pettiness by taking them through the densest brush, walking just far enough ahead to let dozens of branches swat at Mel as she made her way through the thick greenery.

After thirty minutes of nearly running through the forest, Mel had enough. "What's your problem?" She knew she sounded frustrated.

Maya stopped, her bright red hair the only way Mel could keep her in sight. "I don't know what you're talking about."

Mel pushed aside a particularly thick branch to bring herself equal to the lioness. "I thought we were supposed to be allies or whatever now." She wasn't sure what they were, or what they would be when this was all over.

"Allies don't steal from us."

Mel threw her hands up. "It wasn't anything personal."

Maya took a threatening step towards Mel. "You think that makes it alright? If it weren't for you, we wouldn't be on the brink of war." She poked a finger towards Mel's chest, but kept it a few inches from actually poking her.

"No," Mel stepped toward her until her chest bumped against Mel's hand. "If it weren't for me, you'd be dead already. I'm to only reason that you knew trouble was coming."

"So you've made yourself the hero, how wonderful." She pressed her finger firmly into Mel's chest before pulling away, but she didn't take a step back. If Maya was Luke, they would have been close enough to kiss. As it was, aggression was the only thing in the air between them.

"Is this jealousy?" Mel asked. "Did I take the place you wanted?" She didn't mean to go there, but something about Maya was rubbing her the wrong way.

But Maya surprised her by tipping her head back and laughing. "Oh, my silly, silly girl. I've never needed to fuck my way—"

Mel didn't let her finish. Her fist went flying before she even decided to fight, but it took Maya by surprise, hitting her on the side of her skull and forcing her to bend sideways and take a step back. Maya spit out a mix of blood and saliva and straightened, wiping at her mouth with her thumb. "Oh, it's on."

She rushed Mel so fast that Mel was on her ass before

she realized she was under attack. But that didn't last long. Mel wasn't normally a fighter, but she could hold her own when it was life or death. And though she and Maya were fighting for the same pack against Ava and her coven, Mel wasn't under any misconception that they would be anywhere near friends once this all was over.

This was a fight of pure instinct and pent up rage. It poured through Mel and she let it flow, pounding her fists against Maya, rolling in the dirt, and not feeling the pain of the blows that landed.

They rolled in the dirt, neither able to claim dominance over the other. When Mel landed on her back, she pulled her legs in close and kicked out, launching Maya several feet back to where she slammed into the trunk of a nearby oak.

Mel let out a scream and charged at her, but Maya was ready for it and swept Mel's legs out from under her. She landed on top, straddling Mel's waist. Maya's red hair was a tangled mess around her face, making her look more demon than human. Mel reached up and dug her hands deep, pulling as hard as she could, making Maya yelp.

They weren't using claws. As angry as both of them were, as desperate to have this out, neither was willing to escalate it to that level. Once their claws came out, only one of them would walk away.

Besides, it would take far too long to shift properly, and whoever did it first would be vulnerable to attack in the meantime.

Mel struggled out from under Maya and kicked her again. Maya must have tripped over a branch because she fell backwards and then down a ravine behind the trees.

The fight was over.

Neither of them had won.

Mel stayed where she was, waiting for Maya to climb back up. When several minutes passed, she grew concerned. She could still hear Maya moving, so she wasn't dead, but she might have been stuck. Of course, Mel knew that Maya would drop dead before asking for Mel's help. Mel wanted to let her stew a little longer, but they had work to do and every minute they wasted was another minute that Ava could bring the hurt down on them.

So she walked to the edge of the ravine and looked down. No wonder Maya hadn't come back up. She's found an expired witch's circle – a spot where a witch or group of witches had performed magic. And by the look of the burnt out plants, it had been done recently.

Mel sat on the edge of the ravine and eased herself down, half-sliding in the dirt. She walked over to Maya, beginning to feel every bruise and cut that had just been inflicted upon her.

"This is witch crap," Maya announced.

Mel nodded, "Probably looking for the Well."

"This is too close to the house. One of our patrols should have sensed them." It wasn't arrogance. Four miles from Luke's house, in the heart of the pack territory, was far too close for the witches to make it without detection.

"There are spells that mask scent," Mel said. "They don't work for long, though."

"Wonderful." Maya edged around the circle, staying out of the main ring. It was about ten feet wide and nearly bare of vegetation. It looked almost like someone had set the entire thing on fire, but it abruptly stopped with plants half-charred in a perfect circle. "So is this the Well? Did they find it?"

Mel shook her head. She crouched down and traced her fingers through the dark, dry dirt. It had rained a few days ago, but the dirt here was bone dry. Another after-effect of whatever spell they'd used.

She looked back up at Maya and her heart jumped, beating rapidly. "Maya, freeze!" A vine had snaked its way down one of the trees and ran over Maya's foot. The werelioness hadn't even noticed.

But Mel recognized the sickly yellow-green of that

vine, and she could almost taste the foul magic in the air. And luckily for both of them, Maya held still.

"Look down," Mel instructed, keeping her voice even, "But don't move an inch."

Maya looked down and then back up at Mel, "It's a vine." She didn't sound impressed, but she didn't move.

"It's magic," Mel explained. "And as soon as you try to get it off you, it's going to dig in and string you up." Mel remembered the yank of one as it had grabbed onto her when she'd been a child. She'd been left to hang for more than a day before Krista snuck out and set her free.

"It looks like a normal vine." Maya was trying to either convince Mel or herself.

"I grew up around witches, okay?" Mel didn't want to have this argument. "So please just trust me on this."

Maya nodded. "What do I do?"

Without a witch to deflect the spell, the only way to escape was to act quickly before the magic could take hold. "Do you have a knife?" Mel hadn't brought a weapon. Normally her claws were more than enough.

Maya crouched down and her left foot slipped, skidding a few inches behind her. But it was her right foot covered by the vine and she held steady. She rolled up her jean leg and pulled a knife out of the sheath. It was four inches with a black handle and small hilt.

She could have killed Mel anytime during their fight.

Mel didn't let herself dwell on it. Dwelling would only get them killed. She edged around the circle and took the knife from Maya. "I'm going to cut the vine, and I need you up and out of the ravine in three seconds." She put steel in her voice because she had no idea if this would work.

"What about you?" Maya asked.

"I'm limber, it'll be fine."

Maya raised her eyebrows, skeptical. But she didn't argue.

"It'll be a count of three. Go on three. Got it?" At Maya's nod, Mel took a deep breath. "One. Two." She swung down quickly, slicing through the thick vine where it was plastered to the tree. "Three!"

Maya ran, vaulting up the edge and rolling up back onto the path. Mel didn't watch, instead flipping backwards and taking off in the other direction.

She heard a huge blast and after a second felt a jolt force her back. She whipped around, but the circle looked just as it had.

That wasn't a magic blast.

Maya ran over to her, "Jesus! What the fuck did you do?"

But Mel was shaking her head and getting up. She

handed the knife blindly back to Maya. "That wasn't me. That was in town."

Through the dense trees, they couldn't see anything, but the smell of soot was already in the air and it was eerily quiet, the animals gone silent.

Without another word, Mel and Maya took off running towards the direction of the blast.

The blast knocked Luke back and sent loose twigs flying. One scraped across his cheek, tearing a gash that started to bleed. But he barely felt it. His ears were ringing from the power of the explosion and it had triggered a headache so bad it was difficult to see.

But he got up. He'd been walking alone at the edge of the woods and there would be other people, both pack members and the human citizens of Eagle Creek, who would need his help.

As he made his way towards the south, his mind was racing. The explosion had come from that direction, where the main bridge out of town. It was the fastest way to the interstate, crossing over a deep gorge over the river. He knew without checking that it had been the bridge that had blown.

It had to be the witches. His only other idea was

that a tanker truck had blown up, but that would be too much of a coincidence. For some reason, they were trying to trap him and his people inside the limits of Eagle Creek.

Sinclair found him a few minutes later. The two of them had gone out into the woods to scout out a minor evacuation route. Brynne and Jonas were in town preparing EC's for an emergency meeting. The townsfolk didn't know what the pack was, but they understood enough to follow its orders when danger was afoot.

The older man was filthy with dirt clinging to his beard, but he appeared unhurt. "The bridge," was the first thing he said.

Luke nodded. "Looks like the battle's about to come to us." Luke brushed some dirt off of his shirt. "I need you to go check it out," he told Sinclair. "Is the bridge passable? What caused the explosion? Are there a dozen witches chanting destruction upon Colorado? Stay out of sight."

Sinclair nodded and was off without another word. Luke headed back into town.

This couldn't be the witch's declaration of war. If they were allied with the vampires, they would wait until nightfall to attack. It would be foolish to attack when their forces were not at full capacity. Unlike the legends said, vampires could function during daylight, but the sun sapped their powers. Normally they had the speed and strength of shapeshifters along with limited psychic abilities. But in the sunlight they were no stronger than humans and their mental capabilities were dimmed to the point of non-existence.

It had been a sunny day when Luke went into the woods, but a gloom hung over the town by the time he escaped the cover of the trees. He could feel the clouds hanging heavy in the sky, ready to vomit forth a deluge of water.

This wasn't natural. And with the overcast sky, it would be dark enough for the vampires to attack with their power intact.

Luke sped up, running into town.

It was chaos. A car was on fire in the middle of the street. Half a dozen people were sprinting away from it. There were dozens of panicking humans, running towards their homes or cars, but no visible threat.

Their panic was contagious and he found himself glancing behind himself, unable to shake the feeling that he was being watched, stalked. None of his senses were picking up anything. There was no imminent threat, but sweat beaded on his brow and his heart sped up.

There was a crash behind him and Luke nearly

jumped out of his skin, but when he jerked around to see what it was, it looked like a trash can had fallen over.

What was wrong with him? Luke didn't react like this, not ever. His existence as leader of his pack depended on him being level-headed, ready to meet out violence only when necessary. A jumpy alpha did not survive for long.

It was a sobering thought, but it helped to bring him under control. Something was wrong. Something wasn't natural about what he was feeling. And now that he knew it, he could try to control it.

He made it to EC's and though his heart kept pounding and the sweat didn't stop, he was okay. Not great, still on edge, but strong enough to examine his emotions and keep them in check.

Brynne and Jonas were waiting for him along with a few other pack members.

"Are we under attack?" Luke asked. His words came out even. No one commented on his appearance. He could see that the rest of them weren't fairing much better. Jonas's claws had sprung when Luke slammed the door open and the other man had yet to retract them.

Brynne seemed the most in control, though half of her hair had fallen out of her ponytail and she was shifting from foot to foot rather than standing still. "Three vampires were spotted. No one's dead yet. I've got all of the pack adults in town rounding people up and getting them into their homes."

Luke nodded. "Sinclair's checking out the explosion. Where's Maya?" And Mel, he added silently. But he knew not to ask about her, not while they were in crisis mode.

"She went out with Mel and hasn't reported back," said Jonas. "They were due back at the house not too long ago."

But Luke didn't need to worry about that for long. About thirty seconds after Jonas spoke, the door to the restaurant slammed open once more and Mel and Maya ran in. The lions in the restaurant all tensed, but Mel paid them no mind and launched herself across the room, rocking Luke back with the force of her hug.

Luke clamped his arms around her and took a second, breathing in her scent, letting it calm him. For a moment, the panic that had been eating at his heels abated and all he cared about was Mel.

"We came as soon as we heard the explosion," she said, easing herself down.

Luke loosened his grip, but didn't let her go. He couldn't quite make himself. "Good thinking." He turned his gaze to Maya and nodded his greeting. Her lips were pursed and she wasn't pleased with Luke's possessive grip on Mel, but Luke didn't care about that. Not right now.

He noticed an ugly purple bruise blossoming on Maya's cheek and a glance at Mel's hands showed they'd been torn up. They'd clearly fought, but Luke said nothing. They'd run here together, so whatever their issue was, they'd put it aside for the moment.

"They've got us all here, so why aren't we being attacked?" asked Brynne.

Luke didn't know. "Maybe they're waiting until nightfall." The overcast sky would give them some power, but they wouldn't be at full strength until after sunset.

"Or they're just waiting for the spell they've got hanging over town to drive everyone crazy." Mel spoke like her words made sense, but everyone turned to her with a question in their eyes.

"What spell?" asked Luke. He'd had enough of this magic shit.

"You don't feel jumpy?" She raised an eyebrow. "I'm about ready to burst out of my skin. Magic is damn near coating the town."

It made more sense than a spontaneously occurring panic disorder. "We need Krista," he said. He thought that Mel's other associate, Bob, might also be of use, but that man hadn't revealed the extent of his powers or what kind of creature he was. Maybe he was a witch like Krista, but Luke doubted it.

"I'll go get her," Mel volunteered.

"No you won't," Maya insisted.

Mel stepped away from him, stepping towards Maya and invading her space. "Do you have a problem with that?"

"You can't be trusted."

Mel flashed her teeth and her hands were fists at her side. She jerked infinitesimally, looking ready to throw down all over again, and Luke jumped between them. He'd been too optimistic about their fighting.

Before he could speak, the door to the restaurant opened again and Krista stepped inside. She held up a hand, "Before you get pissed, Alpha, I didn't have a choice."

Cassie walked in behind her, and Bob walked close beside her, a hand steady on her elbow.

He should have been mad, but he was raw and the only thing he could feel about his sister was that he was glad she was safe.

"I know where they're going," said Cassie. "They found the Well."

The beast inside of Luke roared.

11

It was chaos in the restaurant. Mel had no idea how Cassie knew where the Well was. She'd been confined to her bed for days and Krista had put a magical block on her. She should have been safe from any additional magical influences from Ava's coven.

But Cassie looked about ready to collapse. Luke rushed her to a chair and sat beside her, gently swiping back a loose lock of her hair. He left Mel standing by herself, but she didn't mind. Seeing him care for his sister like this warmed something deep inside of Mel. It made her ache to be loved like that.

Cassie took a moment to speak, she needed to catch her breath. "I've been having nightmares," she confessed. "I've been seeing the witches."

Luke's head snapped toward Krista. "I thought you said that you blocked the connection between them."

Krista crossed her arms and bristled. "I thought I had."

"I didn't realize I was actually seeing them at first," Cassie continued, dragging the attention back to herself. "I thought they were memories of when they had me or something. But when I saw the blonde woman wearing this really ugly red necklace, I knew that it was stuff that's going on right now."

No one objected to calling the Scarlet Emerald ugly, and Mel had to suppress a smile. It was a fucking garish piece.

"Where are they?" Luke asked.

"I'm not sure exactly." The disappointment was palpable once Cassie spoke. "I'm having psychic visions," she snapped, "It's not freaking GPS."

"It's okay, Cassie," Maya reassured.

"They're by a burned out cabin. I think they're south of the river and in the forest. I could hear a truck drive by before I woke up, so they can't be that far from the road."

"South of the river?" asked Maya.

Cassie nodded.

"That's not in our territory," said Brynne.

Of course it wasn't. Mel wanted to bang her forehead against a wall. They'd been so focused on the incursions into Luke's territory that it hadn't occurred to anyone that the witches could be working outside of it. The evidence they'd gathered had meant to lead them to think the territory was being invaded. Ava had played them. "So who's territory is it?" asked Mel.

Luke shook his head. "No one's. Pack territory only stretches to the river. Beyond it is unclaimed, though no one will touch it with us so close."

The intricacies of territorial law were lost on Mel. She much preferred living where she liked without a thought for the politics. "Then let's roll the fuck out and put the hurt on Ava and her minions."

"We need a plan," Maya objected.

"She's right," said Krista. "Unless you want to be cursed into oblivion."

Mel had a plan. Kill as many of those fuckers as possible. How hard could it be?

"So what do you suggest?" asked Luke. "As I assume you'd be the best equipped to fight witches."

Krista took a seat at the bar. "My idea is damn near suicidal."

Mel perked up. Dangerous was good. They'd never beat Ava by playing it safe. But she glanced over at Luke and saw that his face was a mask of concern. Maybe suicidal wasn't what she wanted. Not if it meant that the morning in the shower was the last time that they would be together.

Mel stepped next to Luke and grabbed his hand. She didn't want to be alone. Luke gave her a squeeze as they listened to Krista lay it out.

"The margin for error is zero," Krista warned. "But it's our best shot to hit Ava when she tries to draw power from the Well."

"You mean let her take power from some magic freaking nuclear bomb?" Brynne scoffed. "How do we know that you're not working with her again?"

Luke held up his free hand to silence Brynne. No one dignified her accusation with an answer.

Krista continued. "There will be at least thirteen witches and they're all going to be focused on Ava. Frankly, I doubt she brought many more than that. The vampires are her firepower, her cannon fodder. They're going to keep hitting town, trying to keep us here."

"It's her MO," said Mel. "Why waste her people when there are others to spare?"

"She can't pull the full power of the Well unless Luke gives her ownership of the Scarlet Emerald. But she'll have more than enough power to destroy this county before we even realize we're dead. The ritual to pull in the power takes seven minutes from start to finish. We need to break through the circle and incapacitate or kill as many members of the coven before it's finished."

"How many?" asked Maya. "And how?" The concern in her eyes was for more than just the battle. She was looking at Krista the way Luke looked at Mel. It seemed that both she and Krista might have something more to live for after this was all over.

"It takes a minimum of seven witches to survive pulling magic from a Well," said Bob. Even Mel hadn't known that.

"Do you know when they're going to do it?" Luke asked. The tension in the room was thick. All of these lions hated being forced to react and Mel agreed. She wanted to punch someone, claw something, just fight and win. Standing around while their enemy got more powerful was the last thing she wanted.

"They'll act at dusk." Krista didn't sound sure, but she didn't try to couch her statement.

"How do you know?" Maya asked gently. She surreptitiously glanced around the room as if waiting for anyone to doubt Krista.

"It's magic 101. The four best times to do any major spell are midnight, noon, dawn, and dusk. We've passed noon and by midnight we would have had enough time to regroup." Krista glanced down at her watch. "We've got three and a half hours until full-dark. If I were Ava, I'd act as soon as possible."

"Alright," Luke sunk a world of authority into his voice. "Jonas, I want every fighter that we've got. Split them into two groups. A quarter to guard the town, three quarters into battle. Brynne, get everyone who isn't a fighter and station them in town. They're to be the second line if our fighters fail. They get the humans out if the town falls. We gather in one hour."

Brynne and Jonas jumped up, their duties assigned. The half a dozen other lions scattered about the restaurant went with them, leaving Luke, Maya, Mel, Bob, Krista, and Cassie alone.

Krista and Bob both sat down besides Cassie. Bob looked up at Mel, Luke, and Maya expectantly. The three shapeshifters sat down.

"How the hell is Cassie out of bed?" Mel asked. "And how is Krista healed?"

"Have you healed her?" Luke asked at the same time.

Cassie's gaze dropped to the table and her shoulder sunk. Both Krista and Bob shook their heads.

"We've a temporary solution at the moment," said Bob. "I've bound my life-force to Cassie."

"And that means what?" asked Maya.

"That we're desperate."

Krista nodded, "Bob's actions allowed me to dedicate some of my magic to a healing spell for myself."

"I asked them to do it," Cassie said, suddenly. "I agreed."

"Why?" Even without knowing the details, Mel could tell this was a bad idea. If it had any hope of curing her, they would have tried it days ago. This wasn't a solution, it was a Band-Aid on a broken bone.

"Because the witch who cursed her is going to be with Ava." Krista said it like it mattered.

"So I can kill him and we'll be done with it?" Luke's questions was more of a statement.

Krista and Bob shared a glance and Mel felt a cold shiver snake down her spine. She tried to ignore it, she trusted them to do right by Cassie. "Not exactly," said Bob.

Krista continued for him. "We think the Cassie can break the hex if she kills the witch who hexed her. That witch will be wearing a charm made of something of Cassie's, probably her hair. If she does as we've instructed her, commits the deed exactly right, she should be freed."

Cassie was pale, and Krista spoke with a tone of voice Mel had heard many times when they spoke to Krista's mother as children. She was hiding something big. But Mel kept her mouth shut. If they were keeping something secret they had a damn good reason.

"Absol—" Luke held up a fist, but Mel reached over and put her hand on top of it, cutting him off.

"We can't fight Ava and kill this witch." She looked over to Krista and stared her in the eye long enough to let her friend know that she suspected she was being kept in the dark. After the moment passed, Mel spoke. "Is there any other way?"

"No," said Krista. "This is it."

Luke relented. "What do you need me to do?"

"Once we find the witch, don't let anyone but Cassie near him." Said Bob. "We think it's a woman, and we doubt that she'll be one of Ava's thirteen. The charm binding Cassie to her is most likely a lock of hair braided around her wrist. If we can isolate her and let Cassie do her thing, this just might work."

Luke turned to Maya. "Help them," he said. "Anything they need is theirs." And that was it.

They sat in silence for a moment, but when Luke stood up, Mel followed, leaving the other four behind. She and Luke didn't go far, just to a small patio behind the restaurant. Luke pulled her close, letting her lay her head on his shoulder and breathe in the reassuring scent of him.

Mel wanted to stay there forever, breathing him in,

being held by him. If she ever needed to describe the feeling of home, it would be here, in his arms. She hadn't known that he was what she wanted, she hadn't known that this feeling was what she was looking for. But now that she had it, she'd fight heaven and hell to keep it close.

Was it love? She didn't know. But it was strong, and real, and the damned most important thing that she'd ever felt.

After a wordless minute they broke apart. It was time to go to war.

Despite the gravity of the situation, Luke was calm. Everything was riding on the next few hours – his sister's life, his future with Mel, and the fate of his pack – but he only felt the stilling sense of calm.

Nearly everyone who could fight was gathered in the dining room of EC's. Maya had given the non-fighters their orders. The lions who would be staying behind were already outside, patrolling the streets and picking off the few vampires that dared to attack.

It was dead silent. No one spoke, no one fidgeted in their seat. They all simply waited for Luke to say the word.

"Things have gone crazy over the past few weeks," he said. A few of his lions leaned forward, coming to attention. "And tonight is the consequence. There is a coven of witches out there who thinks that they have the right to come in and take this territory from us. Are we going to let that happen?"

As one voice, the lions replied, "No!"

"You are the warriors of this pack," Luke's voice grew louder and his heartbeat sped up, adrenaline pumping through him. "It is you who will protect our weak, our innocent. And you will protect all of those people in this town who do not know that they need protection. If any one of you has doubts in this moment, let them go. We are mighty, and we are right. We cannot lose."

The pack cheered, surging to their feet, ready for the battle ahead.

"We know where they are, and our witch says that the magic they're preforming means they cannot dedicate a lot of protective magic to defend themselves against us. Their sentries will not have wards, and we will show no mercy."

His words took a moment to sink in; these lions had never fought witches before. But he didn't see fear in the eyes of his pack members. He saw excitement.

"YOU KNOW YOUR PART!" Luke brought it home, yelling now. "SO ON TO BATTLE!"

The shapeshifters along with Krista and Bob poured out of the restaurant, splitting off in half a dozen directions. With Cassie's help, they knew where the witches were. And coming at them in every direction would be the only way to distract them.

Forty shapeshifters ran after the coven. Luke knew the name, knew the family, and knew the history of every single one of them. Whoever he lost tonight would pierce his heart.

But he could not focus on that now.

He ran with Maya, Krista, and Bob. Mel had gone off with Brynne. Those two had taken no others with them, their first goal to find Sinclair and confirm that the bridge was passable. It was the fastest way to the witches and the fastest way to the expressway. If the bridge was out, they'd still be able to face the coven, but they would need to relay the information back to town to ensure that they could get out through the back roads. Jonas and Killian would lead their own teams of lions behind Mel and Brynne.

Luke wasn't headed for the bridge. He and his contingent took to the woods, headed downhill. They moved slowly. Krista and Bob weren't shifters, they couldn't move as quickly as lions. Cassie, despite the bond with Bob, was still slow. So they moved at an even slower than human pace.

They made it to the river as the darkness started to stretch under the trees. Dusk approached.

"We need—" Maya cut herself off when Luke shot her a look. He knew they needed to move faster. But there was nothing to be done.

He looked up to the sky. It was still overcast, but not threateningly dark. Sunset made the shadows in the forest long before the sun hit the horizon. He also looked out for flares in the sky.

There were none.

Good.

It was Mel's sign that the bridge was impassable or booby trapped. She and Brynne must have reached the bridge by now. So whatever the witches had done to cause that explosion, it hadn't taken out the road.

An unfamiliar scent tickled at his nose and the air felt thick. Luke held up a hand, stopping his group. He pointed at Krista and mouthed, "Witch?"

She closed her eyes and loosened her shoulders. The air swirled around her, rustling her shirt. After a moment, she opened her eyes back up, they glowed golden for a moment before settling back to their normal color. She nodded.

They'd discussed this in their plan. The path they

took was bound to be well guarded. It was the only forest trail that led directly to the burned out cabin that Cassie had seen in her dream. Luke and Maya were to subdue the witches they encountered while Krista and Bob would check to see if anyone of their enemies had hexed Cassie.

All of the witches would die tonight.

Luke let his claws grow long as he padded out in front of the group. Maya had stepped behind a tree to disrobe and shift. She'd walk as a lion until this was finished.

The witch wasn't far away, and Luke recognized him immediately. Tim, the man that had demanded the ownership of the Scarlet Emerald. Instead of coming at him from the ground, Luke bent low and sprung up, grasping a tree branch and wrenching himself up.

The branch shifted under his weight, rustling the leaves. Tim jumped, scrambling to his feet from where he'd been sitting and looking around wildly. Krista had told him that the witches would be feeding a lot of their power into the ceremony. Even the guards who weren't part of the circle could offer up their power to Ava.

They wouldn't be using wards tonight to keep the lions out. It was a mistake of epic proportions. Witches didn't know how to set a perimeter without magic, they were blinder than humans and more vulnerable.

Luke held himself absolutely still until Tim relaxed. And once that witch was convinced that it was only the wind, Luke moved, vaulting himself across three trees and tackling Tim from above, his claws dug into the witch's neck, drawing blood.

Tim tried to speak, but Luke squeezed harder, feeling something pop under his weight. The witch clawed at the ground, trying to find a weapon or to use his hands to summon magic. But Luke had him completely pinned, completely under his control. There was nothing for the witch to do but die.

Bob approached, as silent as a mouse. What kind of magic user could walk as quietly as a shapeshifter? If they survived the night, Luke would ask him.

The black man knelt beside them, he rolled up Tim's sleeves and examined his arms. Finding them free of any jewelry, Bob pulled down the man's collar. His throat was bare.

"It's not him," he said and faded back into the night to let Luke finish him.

But Luke wouldn't just leave it at that. "Who hexed my sister?" he demanded.

Tim sputtered, unable to speak over the weight on his throat.

Luke let up, giving him just enough air to speak.

When Tim spoke his words were nonsense. Luke gave him even more room and leaned forward.

Tim spoke again, his words louder now, but still complete gibberish. He sounded similar to when Krista had performed her spells to help Cassie. He was doing magic.

Luke lunged forward to slit his throat, but a tree branch caught him off guard, swiping at him and sending him tumbling from on top of the witch.

Tim didn't waste time trying to fight. Instead, he took off, heading further south towards where they knew the witches were gathered.

Luke took off after him, easily closing the distance between himself and the injured man. Tim rolled as they went down, tossing dirt into Luke's face. With a word, it caught fire, singeing Luke and blinding him for a moment.

But Tim was injured and in unfamiliar territory. He didn't have a chance.

Luke kept coming at him, deflecting the magic as it was thrown. Tim was backing away, trying to keep his eyes on Luke, but it meant he moved slowly. Finally, he mis-stepped, tripping over a log and tumbling backwards.

In a second, Luke was on him, digging his fingers

into the witch's throat and letting the blood run. He didn't even have a moment to struggle.

Luke stood up, leaving him there. They would worry about the bodies tomorrow; tonight they fought the witches.

The witches were not alone. After he and his group left Tim lying in the dirt, they made it another quarter of a mile before scenting anyone else. And then the sickly-sweet smell of a vampire assaulted Luke, nearly stopping him in his tracks.

Maya took this one, slinking ahead of them. It took her seconds to subdue the vamp, her growl the only sign he had that death was at his door.

The path grew narrow as they moved away from the river and they were forced to walk in single file. Luke didn't like it, the skin at the back of his neck prickled with awareness. They were moving too slowly, the witches were going to hear them coming and they'd all be as dead as the vampire that Maya killed.

But then the trail widened again and Luke could smell gasoline. They were closer to the road, but this wasn't coming from there. No, this was the smell of a vehicle.

They were close.

He felt two arms clamp around his shoulders and stiffened, ready to fight off his attacker. But it was only

Cassie. She leaned in close, burying her head against his neck. "I love you, big bro," she said, before letting go and stepping back with Bob and Krista.

Luke turned around and smiled at her. He felt the same way and couldn't wait until she was better, until the futile sadness in her eyes faded.

The sounds of fighting drew them in. The other members of his pack had joined the fray and the witches and their vampire guards fought for their lives. Maya took off, bounding forward to join the fray. Luke looked at Krista and Bob, and he pointed to Krista, "You, come with me. We're bringing this damned witch."

Krista stepped forward and they were off.

The brunt of the shapeshifters were aiming for the group of witches gathered in the clearing in front of the burned out house. It was chaos. The shifters kept bouncing off an invisible wall, all the while fighting the vampires and witches who weren't within the protective boundary.

"I thought you said that they wouldn't have wards," said Luke.

Krista looked over at the witches. "They're using a lot of their power to keep that ward up. It will weaken once they begin the spell. Soon your lions will be able to overwhelm them." She flinched when one of his lions, he couldn't tell who from the distance, launched himself at the ward and bounced off, flying back ten feet. He was immediately set upon by two vampires.

This was different than fighting in the dense woods. The house here was a historical relic and during the summer tour groups would hike through the woods to have lunch in this spot. It was just far enough into the woods to let unexperienced hikers feel accomplished for making the two-mile trek.

The forest had been cleared around the house and the forestry service maintained it. They had a hundred feet of open space to fight in, the only cover a few fallen logs and a half dozen picnic tables.

Ava's witches were circled together beside the house and the air shimmered around them, protecting them with a ward. Vampires and the witches not involved in the ceremony were trying to fight off the angry lions who were hell bent on disrupting the ritual.

Already there were casualties, vampires and witches lay on the ground, some lifeless, others near death. While he could see that some of his shifters were injured, he didn't see that any had fallen. He only hoped that the luck held.

"Stay close to me," he told Krista.

There was no cover except for the burned out house and the witches quickly spotted them. Luke dived forward as a bolt of magic zeroed in on them, but Krista threw up a hand, shielding the two of them. The bolt dissolved as the air shimmered in front of her.

She offered him a hand, but Luke got up on his own. He still had his claws out and didn't want to hurt her.

More magic shot towards them, streaks of colored lightning. But it didn't seem to be coming from the main battle. A rain of hellfire momentarily blinded him, but they weren't hit.

"Can you protect everyone with that?" he asked.

Krista shook her head. "It's basically an invisible concrete wall. I'll need to drop it if we're going to fight."

He couldn't see where the magic attack was coming from, but that answered his question. "They're in the house."

They sprinted, Krista's protection saving them from a wave of magic blasts that assaulted them as they ran. The ruin was only two walls, more hole than solid. Two witches were hunkered down, a man and a woman. Luke recognized neither of them.

But what he did see was a large metal bracelet on the woman's arm covered with blonde hair. Cassie's hair. This was the witch holding the hex.

He wanted to tear her to shreds, but he kept that instinct in check.

Krista dropped the magic protection and Luke

launched himself at the man, swiping his claws across his throat and rolling away. The man was dead before he hit the floor.

The witch tried to scramble away, but she butted into the other wall and stumbled, giving Luke time to get to her. He put a knee on her stomach and gathered both of her hands in one hand, the claws of his other hand dug into her throat.

"Get them," Luke commanded, the sound guttural.

"I signaled them," Krista responded. She kept her eyes on him and the witch as if she didn't trust him to leave the woman alive.

Shock reverberated through the ruin, knocking a loose piece of wood to the ground.

"That's the ward," said Krista. "You need to go help them."

Luke was torn, he needed to see to Cassie, but there was nothing more that he could do to help her. "Keep her safe," Luke demanded.

Krista nodded. "You have my word."

Luke took off, running straight toward the battle and into hell.

12

M el knew there was no turning back once she and Brynne crossed the bridge. But she didn't expect the moment to fly by so quickly. They were beyond the bridge, sure of its relative safety in a matter of minutes after leaving Eagle Creek. The rest of the lions weren't far behind, and they'd rally to Mel and Brynne shortly.

Then it was through the forest, taking out the witches and vampires as they passed. She was confident that the town was relatively safe for the moment. There were too many people in the woods for there to be a great force fighting in the town.

She didn't know the names of these lions, not all of them. She'd barely known this pack for a few weeks.

But if she died tonight, she would be glad to do it at their side.

Not that she planned to die.

Battle raged around her. Mel lost track of time once they made it to the burned out house. There were only the witches and the vampires and the fight. She couldn't see the ward that protected Ava and her cronies, but she could almost feel it. It was like bugs rubbing their wings against her.

She threw herself at the ward with the rest of the lions, fighting off the magic and the vampires as they came. The only thing that could defeat this ward was physical strength. They would pound at it just like it was a brick wall. And like a brick wall it would fall.

Twelve witches surrounded a blonde woman. Mel only caught fleeting glimpses of her. The rage in her belly was confirmation enough. Ava was in the circle, summoning the magic to destroy Luke and his pack. If there had been a doubt in her mind, it was all washed away now.

Mel redoubled her efforts, scraping her hands bloody. Though the ward was nearly invisible, hardly more than a wisp of air, it burned to the touch, an unseen fire trying to protect the women and men behind it from the consequences of their actions. But fires could be quenched, smothered.

The snarl grew from the back of her throat, gaining power and becoming a fully bellowed roar. She didn't sound like one of the lions, but she didn't need to. All of the cats were together in this mission. Today they were one pack.

The ground gave way, first an inch and then two more. For a moment everything held still, and then she felt a blast in the gut, the air whooshing out as the ward fell in front of them with a shuddering silence.

Those witches outside of the ward realized before those within. She heard a shrill voice call, "Protect the coven!" But it was too late. She was already diving in, her claws springing out of her hands, ready to reap her vengeance.

She pushed a tall man out of her way. He wasn't the one she wanted.

No, this was between her and Ava.

But she couldn't get to her. The coven was bound together in a circle of twelve around Ava. They all fed their power to her, their voices raised in a chant. Mel had no idea how long they'd been performing the ritual. Their volume didn't change as the lions descended upon them.

First a short woman fell, tackled to the ground by a lioness in full animal form. She barely screamed before she bled out.

Mel swiped her claws against the back of another tall man. He fell in place, but still chanted. She leaned over him, but as her eyes met his bright blue ones, she saw the pain and fear within. He was terrified of what she would do to him.

He stopped chanting long enough to beg, "Please, don't kill me." Despite his height, his voice was high, as if he were still a young man. He was maybe twenty.

And in that moment Mel remembered that she had never killed anyone. She was a criminal, an unrepentant one at that, but violence was not her game.

The young man took advantage of her hesitation.

He flung his hand up toward her and a bolt of energy rushed her way. It would have hit her square in the face if a different large man hadn't tackled her out of the way in time.

Luke.

She found herself under him, his hand accidentally resting on her throat.

Mel smiled up at him, glad that he'd found her, that he was safe for the moment. "I think we've been here before."

He flattened himself, nearly crushing her with his weight. A moment later Mel felt the heat of magic rush over them. Luke winced, but kissed her cheek after taking a deep breath. "No, this time's much better," he breathed.

They rolled apart, unable to steal more than a moment in the midst of battle.

The young man had crawled back to the circle. He was on all fours with the wounds on his back pouring out trails of blood. If the ritual didn't end soon, he'd die of blood loss anyway. But Mel wouldn't give him the chance.

Her moment with Luke was enough to remind her why she was here, why she needed to take these lives. It wasn't only to take vengeance for the family that had been stolen from her. It was to protect the man that she had chosen and the family that she would build with him.

He was her mate, damn it, and it was time for her to protect him.

She didn't give the young man with the fearful blue eyes a chance to defend himself, instead reaching around and digging her hands into his throat. Her approach was silence in the midst of the fight. He didn't know that she was behind her until he was dead.

At least two down. They needed four more.

But the witches had recovered. Those who'd been in the coven circled close to Ava. They stood within a large ring of stones and out of each of the stones rose a shimmering red fire. Mel tried to count them. There were at least seven witches inside, including Ava. The stones blocked her view, but she didn't think there were more.

Still, it was enough to finish the ritual.

She looked over at Luke, hoping that he had any idea of how to get through the ward. But he glanced at her at that same moment, his eyes just as hopeless.

Mel didn't know how to give up. This was too important to lose. She wasn't going to let Ava take everything away from her again. She reached down and scooped up a stick that had fallen from one of the trees. It was insubstantial, hardly more than a twig. If she used it to whack someone, the stick would splinter without leaving a bruise. But she had fists for hitting. She reared her arm back and tossed the stick towards the newly erected ward.

The wood hit up against and invisible wall and fell to the ground.

There was no using physical force to take down this ward. At best, they'd be too injured to fight by the time they got through. At worst, the entire pack would be dead long before Ava took in the power of the Well.

Mel watched the witches circle behind the flames, their images hazy. She couldn't hear their chanting. Even though the fighting had dwindled, most of the other witches and vampires either dead, injured, or fleeing, the forest was still too loud to pick up whatever sound the magic didn't block.

Luke made his way over to her, stepping over the fallen body of a nameless witch.

"Do we run?" he asked. He didn't sound defeated, but his shoulders sagged just a little.

"There's not enough time." They were well into the seven minutes it would take to complete the ritual. Even with shifter speed, they'd only clear a few miles. Ava would obliterate them before dawn with her newfound power. She turned to Luke and waited until he looked down at her. "I love you, you know," she confessed.

The corner of Luke's mouth pulled up in a grin, "Tell me that tomorrow."

"Okay." It wasn't the first promise that she'd made that she couldn't keep.

"Krista said they'd lower the ward," Luke turned his attention back to the circle as Maya sidled up beside them in her lioness form. "Any idea when that's going to happen?"

Mel shook her head, "We won't have a lot of time to act."

"It will be enough." There was something different about his voice. He wasn't just reassuring her, he was giving her the promise of an alpha.

Time crawled forward as they waited for the witches to drop the ward. Each second seemed to take five minutes and Mel could feel the urge to pace growing.

Krista ran over to them, her shirt covered in drying blood. "Why—"

"Is Cassie alright?" Luke didn't let her finish.

Krista didn't answer immediately, finally saying, "The hex is gone." She gestured at the coven, "But why are you all just standing here?"

Mel looked between the flaming ward and Krista. "The flames?"

Krista slammed her palm against her forehead and groaned. The action might have been funny if she hadn't left a giant streak of blood over her left eyebrow. "It's a freaking glamor. It'll be a little hot, but it shouldn't stop you."

Mel grabbed Krista by the shoulders, "You're sure? This is Ava."

Krista nodded. "They're channeling so much power into the spell that the glamor is barely stable. Until they finish the ritual, they don't have enough juice to throw anything at you."

Mel turned to Luke. "Now or never."

He was already running, gathering up his cats to

flank the witches. Mel set off to run with them, but Krista put a hand on her shoulder.

"We go in from behind. While the cats are taking out her witches, you know that Ava will try to escape. She's not going to let some measly lion pack kill her." Krista's hand on her arm was tight, as if she thought that Mel would try to run towards the main fight.

But she knew that Krista was right. No way in hell would Ava let herself be taken, and if she got away today, she'd be back in greater force sometime soon. This time she'd murder all of Luke's people with extreme prejudice before even attempting to seize the Well.

So she and Krista took off, away from the main fighting and into the woods back towards the road, back towards the small parking lot that served the picnic area.

Mel helped Krista up into a tree and then climbed over to another branch. Staying in the trees kept them hidden, but it didn't allow for mobility. Still, this was the path Ava would take, it was the fastest way away from the cabin and she knew that she could not outrun lions in their own forest.

Minutes passed. Mel could hear the clash of fighting, the screams as witches died and lions were wounded. Finally, lightning struck, making the forest shine white for a second and blinding Mel.

"They stopped it," said Krista. "She's going to run."

Despite the vision impairment, Mel crouched on her branch, ready to tackle the witch.

"Be quick," Krista warned. "Most of her magic will have drained out of her during the ritual, but she'll gain enough back to do major damage quickly. I'll give you magic support if you need it. Now that the ritual isn't happening my spells should be on target."

Mel was glad that Krista was here. She'd never have known the nuances of magic without her guidance. No matter how much she could study of Ava's tactics - and from her personal experience - nothing beat having a witch by her side.

But Mel didn't have time to say that all, not yet. She could hear branches snapping and heavy breathing as someone ran through the woods, fleeing the fight. She was downwind, but Mel caught a glimpse of white-blonde hair.

Ava.

Mel took a final deep breath and waited until just the right moment. Ava was nearly to Mel's tree when Mel jumped. She only glanced the witch, but it was enough to make her stumble to one knee. Mel pressed the advantage, not giving Ava a chance to take advantage of Mel's mistake.

It was a quick scuffle, but Ava wasn't a fighter. Not a physical one, anyway. If she had even a fraction of her power available to her at the moment, Mel would be a burnt outline on one of the nearby trees. But in this one moment, Mel had the advantage.

"You dumb animal," Ava spat. "If you think that this means anything besides your doom, you have less intelligence than a gnat."

She didn't recognize Mel. After all of these years, the nightmares, the plans to take her down, the relentless determination to be prepared for this very moment, and Mel's foe didn't have the decency to know who she was. It shouldn't have come as a surprise. Ava hadn't seen her since she was twelve years old, half-feral, her hair a knotted mess and her skin constantly bruised. She'd barely looked human.

There had been a speech she'd planned to give in this moment. She'd mentally planned it out in a fit of maudlin sentimentality when she was twenty-one. But even that was too much for this sad excuse for a human being.

And so, without ceremony, Mel swiped her claws against Ava's throat, severing the jugular and watching the blood spurt out.

She had no regrets.

It was a massacre. With their magic protections gone, the witches seemed to freeze. They had no spells to throw at the lions, and they had erected no wards. The bloodbath was over quickly. Luke saw one or two witches flee into the woods, but it didn't matter. Ava and her coven were defeated, the Well would not be emptied of power, and his pack was safe.

He didn't see Ava. Between one breath and the next, she'd stepped out of sight. Luke tried to catch her scent. She was the one witch that needed to die. The mastermind of his sister's hex, the butcher who'd slaughtered Mel's family, the asshole who'd tried to hand his territory over to bloodsuckers. The charges against her were too many for mercy.

Most of all, if he didn't kill her now, she would be back.

Luke gathered half a dozen of his lions to him and sent them out to search for Ava. He had the sinking feeling that they wouldn't find her. He didn't know how to tell Mel that she got away, but Mel was off somewhere else, they'd split up just before the final assault.

He could feel it in his heart that she was okay. He would find her soon.

But at the moment, he needed to find Cassie. He'd been suppressing the urge to look for her and get her out of here for too long. He'd hoped that once the hex was broken that she would stay safe, out of the fighting. But the fact that he hadn't seen her since he left Krista and Bob worried him.

He'd seen Krista, but Bob must have stayed by Cassie. He'd seen no sign of the other man since then.

Luke made his way back to the burned out ruined house where he'd left Cassie.

All thoughts of the fight fled his mind when he rounded the corner and spotted his sister. She clutched her hands to a wound in her side, but it seeped thick, dark blood out between her fingers. Bob was gaunt beside her, a wisp of saliva cracked beside his mouth, his eyes glassy and his skin a sickly greenish-brown. A bloody knife lay beside Cassie's hand. It looked as if she had dropped it. The body of the witch who'd hexed her lay limp in the dust on the floor, a pool of blood from a wound identical to Cassie's in her stomach.

Luke rushed to her side, fear a thousand pound weight in his chest. He placed his hand on top of hers and found them cold. But her eyes flickered open and he saw pain, but he also saw hope.

"The hex is gone," it was barely a whisper.

"Good," he leaned forward and placed a kiss on her forehead before turning his attention to the injured man beside his sister. "Thank you."

Bob nodded, "She's strong."

Cassie started coughing and Luke called out for a healer.

Everything after that went quickly. A few lions bundled her up, bandaging her wound as best they could.

The rest of the night passed in a blur. The wounded and dead needed to be tended to, and they needed to dispose of the fallen witches and vampires. Luke put a call in to Peklo, the vampire leader, but he wasn't surprised when the number was disconnected. He couldn't be sure that Peklo was in on Ava's scheme, but even if he could contact the vampire, he knew that the man would deny all knowledge.

Luke would deal with him later. Even if Peklo had agreed to move against him, he would not attack now that the witches were defeated. Luke had counted at least twenty dead vampires – the loss was too high to mount an immediate attack if those had indeed been his men.

As for Luke's lions, they'd lost two in the battle and

another three were seriously injured. But beyond that, his lions were hurt, but the rest would recover.

By the time the sun began to peek over the horizon, Luke was ready to collapse with exhaustion. He'd settled so much, worked so tirelessly, that he didn't realize that he hadn't seen Mel since the battle.

He knew she had to be around. She wouldn't just confess her love and run off.

At least, he didn't think she would.

Luke would find her after he caught a couple of hours of sleep.

That sleep passed in a blink, and the next thing he knew he was awake as the noonday sun streamed into his room. He wouldn't have woken if not for Maya banging on his door. Luke pulled on a t-shirt and opened it, running a hand through his hair to tame it.

"What?" he demanded.

Maya looked as if she hadn't slept at all. But she held herself straight and didn't let the fatigue stop her. "Everyone made it through the night. Murphy says that he thinks everyone will pull through."

Luke nodded, relieved.

"And Cassie wants to talk to you."

"I'll be right there."

Maya nodded and retreated, speaking as she turned away. "I'm going to catch some shut eye."

Luke was about to let her go, but asked, "Any sign of Mel?" at the last minute.

Maya shook her head and kept walking.

Cassie was back in the room she'd been shackled in throughout the course of the hex. She was no longer handcuffed and needed no guard. But Bob was still beside her. They both looked recovered. He'd gained his color back and her face was peaceful.

She opened her eyes and smiled when Luke shut the door quietly behind himself. "How are you doing?" he asked.

Bob stood and greeted Luke before excusing himself to give them time alone.

"I feel like I've been stabbed in the gut, but other than that I'm good." She sounded tired, but it was a good kind of tired. She no longer sounded defeated and on the edge of death.

"What happened out there?" He'd seen the knife, and it hadn't looked like the witch stabbed Cassie.

Cassie took a deep breath and grimaced. "Well, we needed to kill the witch to break the hex."

Luke nodded, he'd known that.

"And she ended up using some magic that meant I couldn't get through her spell." Cassie was stalling, he'd known her long enough to know her tells.

"And...?"

"I want you to remember that I'm alive and that I'm going to heal. Dr. Murphy said I'll be okay." Now this was the little sister he remembered. Trying to keep herself out of trouble, no matter what she'd done. Luke could feel frustration mounting. Cassie continued before he could prod her. "Bob's link to keep me alive was what saved me. Krista told me that I was linked to the witch through the hex. And that hexes are really dangerous. So I took a shot in the dark and stabbed myself."

Blood pounded in Luke's ears and he had to take a deep breath to keep from doing anything drastic - like ringing his sister's neck. She was alive, that was what mattered.

"So what do we do now?" Cassie asked after Luke was quiet for too long.

"I was going to ask you the same thing." He couldn't make Cassie's decisions for her. She'd made mistakes - horrible, catastrophic mistakes - but the last few weeks had opened his eyes to the fact that his sister was growing up. "You know that you can't keep this from Mom or Scott."

Cassie groaned, her face scrunching up from a pain that had nothing to do with her wound. "They're going to kill me. And then lock me up for a hundred years. And then kill me again just to teach me a lesson."

Luke laughed, the sound pure, something he'd forgotten how to do in the chaos. "I'll take you home. They won't kill you when I'm there."

"Maybe Bob could hide me in the forest?" She brightened.

Luke raised an eyebrow, "Why would he be able to do that? What forest?"

Cassie rolled her eyes, "You know, the forest where he's a freaking elven prince? How have none of you figured that out?"

Luke tried to recall anything that would suggest that Bob was an elf, let alone a royal one. But Luke had never met an elf before, he hadn't quite believed they were real. "How do you know what he is?"

"That life-bond thing. I picked up a few things he might not have meant to share." She smiled and leaned in two inches before wincing, the wound in her gut making itself known. "Maybe just keep this between the two of us? I don't think he'd like it if I told you."

Luke nodded, "Of course."

"And what about Mel?" asked Cassie.

Luke wanted to know the same thing.

13

Burning the body took longer than Mel expected. Even worse than that was the matter of scattering the ashes. She and Krista agreed that separate batches of ash needed to be spread far apart, just in case. Neither of them really believed that Ava could come back after her corpse was burnt to a crisp, but there was no reason not to be careful.

Mel meant to say something to Luke before disappearing, but after a night of rest she realized it wouldn't be a good idea. He'd insist on going with her. Then Maya would throw a fit and convince him to take an escort. Then there would be negotiations on who would go and when and where. And after all that, they'd need to negotiate safe passage through the territories they traveled in.

It would be so much less of a headache if she just went alone.

Sometime between Mexico and the night of the battle her phone had been destroyed, so she couldn't even give Luke a call. And if she did, she was afraid that he'd come after her before she was done.

Mel was so busy for the week that it took to scatter Ava's ashes that she only missed Luke when she had time to stay still. Unfortunately, the amount of traveling she did in that week mean that she was still for a lot longer than usual. It was an ache inside of her to be away from him. And as she scattered the last of Ava over an isolated cliff in the Smokey Mountains, there was nothing she wanted to do more than to go back to Colorado and snuggle up close to her alpha.

But there was still one thing to do, and it's why she'd saved the trip to Tennessee to the end.

It was time to go home for the first time in twenty-three years.

Mel was just outside of her family's old territory. It had seemed treasonous to scatter their murderer's ashes in the place where they'd once lived. But she hoped that she was close enough to settle their ghosts.

Mel hiked through the forest for hours, trying to find the house that she had once called home. It was more difficult to find than expected. No one lived in these woods, and everything was different than when she'd been a child. When Ava opened the Well, a wild-fire had blazed for days, taking out hundreds of acres of forest. The house was only saved because of favorable winds.

It was those old trees and new saplings that finally brought Mel to the valley where she'd grown up. The house which had seemed like a mansion to her child's eye was now merely big, and in a sad state of disrepair.

All but one of the windows were cracked or completely broken, the blue paint had chipped and rotted. The roof on the north side of the house had collapsed completely.

The only thing left of her family was a ruin.

But the veranda looked sturdy enough and Mel decided to take her chances. She'd risked more for less.

She sat on the splintered wood and drew her legs in close, resting her cheek against her knee. Sitting like this on the porch, she expected the weight of the past quarter century to lift. She thought that she would be relieved that she'd wrought her vengeance, she'd hoped that the hole in her chest would be filled.

Instead she felt a little peace and an irresistible urge to cry. And she gave in. Mel let the tears run down, and when the hiccups came, she hiccupped and sniffed until her head hurt and her eyes burned. She was a mess, but there was no one in the forest to see it.

But the tears subsided and Mel wiped her eyes with the back of her hand. She stood up from the porch and stretched. And then she walked away, not looking back at the house.

This wasn't her place anymore. The territory should have been hers, but life had a way of screwing all of that up. She was a thief, she was loved, and she had done right by her family by destroying the woman that had destroyed them. But she wasn't going to live in a moldy house in rural Tennessee. She wasn't going to hide away in these woods now that her mission was complete.

She had a flight to catch.

Luke's mom insisted on driving him back to the airport after he brought Cassie home. As his sister predicted, her parents were not happy, but a lot of the anger had fallen onto him. After all, he'd chosen not to contact them when she was near death.

Luke almost felt bad for leaving Cassie with them, but she'd survived the hex. He doubted that his mom and stepdad could do any worse.

"Cassie told me you met a girl," his mom said as she pulled into the parking lot at the airport.

Thirty-one years old, alpha of his own pack, and he still blushed when his mom asked him about girls. Luke wanted to groan, but then the thought of the shit Mel would give him if she could see him know and grinned.

"Ah, now I know you have," his mother's smile could have lit up the sun.

If only Luke knew where the hell Mel had gone. Who confessed love in the midst of battle and then ran off without saying goodbye? He and his thief needed to have a talk about communication.

"She stole the Scarlet Emerald from me." They'd recovered it in the aftermath of battle, but Luke was ready to rid himself of the gaudy red stone. He didn't want to risk another theft, especially now that he knew the stone could be used to tap into the Well.

"Try not to sound so proud of larceny," his mother was bemused.

"She's my mate," pride, satisfaction, and love laced his words. Luke wasn't a cat burglar, he didn't approve of theft, but knowing that his woman was one of the best somehow surmounted his moral qualms.

That was enough for his mother. She walked him inside the airport and left him with a hug and a big kiss on the cheek. Luke made it through security and to his gate with time to spare.

Even better, before he boarded the plane, a flight attendant called him to the desk and let him know that his ticket had been upgraded to first class. They didn't explain why, but Luke didn't turn it down. He wasn't that big of a fool.

As he waited for the flight to board he sent off several emails and texts, but something on the edge of his consciousness kept distracting him. It wasn't quite a sound or a scent, and he couldn't put his finger on it.

After half an hour, the flight boarded and Luke got on first, sliding into his aisle seat and making himself comfortable. He stretched out his legs as far as he could and his knees didn't even come close to the seat in front of him.

Heaven.

Or as close as he could get on a domestic flight.

The passengers filed in and stowed their packages as the minutes ticked by. Luke was ready to be off, but still they loaded. After what seemed like a small eternity, the sounds of people getting situated quieted.

They were ready to go.

The window seat beside him was empty and he assumed that he'd have no neighbor for the rest of the flight. That was until a woman approached his row and stood just beside him. As her scent washed over him, Luke grinned.

He looked up to see Mel in her outrageous red wig, a purse in hand. She wore huge black sunglasses and a yellow dress.

"I think that's my seat," she pointed to the window, her voice nearly an octave higher than normal.

"By all means." Luke stood to let her in, but Mel took her time, letting their bodies brush together. Luke's hands drifted to her hips, sliding over them before she sat down.

"So," Mel said once she'd put her purse down in front of her. "Come here often?"

Luke grabbed her hand and laced her fingers with his. "Did you upgrade my flight? How did you know that I'd be on this one?"

Mel raised his hand to her lips and kissed it. "A thief never tells her secrets."

He wanted to kiss her. He wanted to do much naughtier things, but the lack of privacy put a damper on his ardor. But his happiness and relief at seeing Mel didn't change the fact that she'd left without a word.

He took a deep breath to get it all out, but she beat him to the punch, speaking before he could interrogate her.

"I'm sorry I took off. Krista and I took care of Ava,

and then we needed to make sure that she couldn't come back." Luke could only imagine what that meant. Dead was dead. Most of the time. Mel continued. "And then I needed to take care of some stuff before I could come see you."

"See me?" Thoughts of stolen moments as she traipsed the world, stealing, getting into danger, meeting other men danced across his mind. "I'm not a paramour."

She bit her lip and looked so damned cute that Luke couldn't stop himself from leaning forward and capturing her lips. She wrapped her arms around him and in that moment he would have taken any promise she would give if only it meant that he would have another minute kissing her.

A flight attendant brushed by him as she walked by and it was enough to remind Luke that he and Mel were in public. He pulled back, but not far.

"How does mate sound?" Mel asked. "I thought that had a nice ring to it."

Luke's thumb brushed softly against her cheek. "Mate is more what I'm looking for."

"You're not going to do anything crazy, right?" She pulled back just enough to give him space to breathe.

Luke didn't want the space. "Crazy?"

"You know, ask me to quit my day job? Something

like that?" The fact that she was here meant that she knew him better than that. But Luke also realized that she was terrified. Happy, ready, but absolutely unsure of what this would mean.

He held up a finger, "One request. For now." He added the last bit as a precaution.

"What?"

"Don't steal from my allies. No matter what they have." Taking a thief as his mate would complicate things, but he didn't care.

Mel rubbed her cheek against his shoulder, cuddling up beside him and resting there. "I think I can manage that."

As the flight took off, Luke could see the days and years spread out before him with Mel by his side. They'd probably drive each other crazy a hundred times over. But they would love and laugh, fight and make love for hours. They would face their enemies and stand side by side as the alphas of his pack. There would be complications, hardships. But Mel was the woman for him. He loved her, she was his mate, and his equal.

As their flight flew west, the future stretched out before them. There wasn't anyone else that he'd rather be sitting beside, ready to face it together.

MEL & LUKE AT THE MUSEUM

A BONUS STORY

1

"You're taking a thief to a museum?" Maya looked at Luke like he'd grown a second head. He and Mel had been together for more than two years by now, but his second in command was still slow to trust.

"I'm taking my *mate* to the museum," Luke corrected. Calmly. He knew why Maya didn't trust her. Mel had nearly destroyed the pack and she'd found flaws in Maya's security that no one had thought were there. But it had been two years. Maya had to get over it sometime. "You could see if the witch is busy while we're out."

That got Maya to look away, her cheeks turning pink. She'd been dancing around the witch for years at this point and a part of Luke wanted to lock the two women in a room and wait until *something* happened. Mel said that would only lead to bloodshed, but maybe that was what they needed. "We're staying the night in the city."

"So she'll have enough time to meet with her fence?" Maya shot back, but some of the distrust had faded and now she was just teasing.

Luke shooed her away and finished sorting the last of his work for the week. An alpha's work was never done, but he hoped he could steal away a single day every now and then. And being mated to a thief certainly helped with that.

A knock at the door to his office made him look up and his heart lifted as a smile bloomed on his face. Mel. Shifter. Thief. Love of his life. And the sexiest woman he'd ever known. Her own smile matched his as she sauntered into the room and hitched a hip onto his desk. "Is the warden letting you out?" she asked.

"With much objection." He leaned in and kissed her, savoring the taste.

Her hand went to the back of his neck as her fingers curled, holding him tight. She kissed him like she still didn't believe they were forever, like they'd have a lifetime of kisses to come. Luke hoped that one day the desperation might fade away, even though he knew they'd never lose their passion.

She pulled back with a smile, one he'd seen when he caught her stealing and she thought she'd get away with it. Mel had been raised a thief and she didn't know anything else. Luke didn't want to take that away from her, and they'd found ways to... accommodate her skills that ended up helping the pack more than he'd realized was possible. Having a mate with moral flexibility had its own particular challenges, but he knew her, knew what she would and wouldn't do, and he was certain that she'd never betray him. That was all that mattered.

"Cassie called. School is boring, the pack there sucks, there's a boy frustrating her to no end, and she wants to come home," Mel relayed the message with the breathless delivery his little sister liked to employee. It was a little scary how well Mel could mimic people.

"So no changes there," he responded. "At least she's going to classes." Getting Cassie to agree to college had taken a lot of doing, especially with everything that had gone down with Ava, but now she was nearing the end and Luke had promised her she could officially join his pack when she was done, if that was what she wanted. She'd been adamant that it was, but something made him think she would change her mind.

"I'm all packed," Mel said. "A night in the city will be a nice break. "And I've been wanting new jewelry."

"You're not stealing from the museum."

Mel rolled her eyes and pecked him on the cheek. "You're adorable, honey. Let's get out of here."

2

The Denver Art Museum was absolutely fine. Mel had walked through countless museums in her life and she didn't have anything more to complain about here than she had anywhere else. And this museum had the added benefit of a tense alpha at her side, clenching his jaw every time she stepped up to a piece and made appreciative noises.

He knew she was just teasing. Or, at least, she thought he knew she was just teasing. She hadn't exactly gone straight in the years since they'd been mated, but she'd become much more selective about her jobs, and a good portion of those jobs ended up having some tangential benefit for Luke's pack.

Mel's pack, too, but that was still kind of weird to think about.

It hadn't been a smooth adjustment. Mel couldn't remember much of her life before she'd fallen into Ava's hands, and in the coven she'd been the lowest of the low. In the years after that, her pack had just been her, Krista, and Bob until things went south. And now she was mated to the alpha of a huge lion pack and in charge of their safety and well-being.

Things like thinking about how her jobs would impact the pack or even just being unable to go for a drive without letting someone know she'd be gone had rankled at first. But at night she went to bed with Luke and the feel of his arms around her was enough to make her remember why it was worth it to do something so strange.

That didn't mean she wasn't going to play with him.

She pulled a small notebook out of her pocket and made a show of measuring the size of one of the more ostentatious paintings in the museum. It wouldn't be *that* difficult to purloin if she wanted to put in the effort, but she didn't have a fence set up and she wasn't about to pull a job so close to home.

Luke put a hand on her wrist and snatched the

notebook. "Really?" he asked, his lips pressing together tight as if he couldn't quite suppress his smile.

"What?" Mel asked innocently, eyes wide and blinking quickly.

Luke shook his head and gave her a searing kiss before sticking the notebook in his pocket and guiding her towards the next exhibit. Mel didn't bother to try and stop her own grin. "Can't I have any..." something moved in the corner of her eye and Mel turned to follow the sight.

"Any what?" Luke asked, oblivious to the distraction.

"Did you see that?" She took a step towards the wall and almost tripped over a wet floor sign. The room didn't smell like cleaning products and the floor was bone dry.

"See what?"

Mel looked around the room again, this time actually observing instead of playing, and what she saw made her curse. "Someone's trying to rob the museum."

3

Luke might have been skeptical, might have assumed his mate was playing some kind of joke on him, but her face got just as serious as it did when things got tense at pack meetings. She tugged on his hand and led him to a bench in front of an impressionist painting, looking around as if she didn't have a care in the world. But he could feel the tension thrumming just under her skin.

"Camera in the corner," she whispered to him. "The angle is wrong."

Luke looked, but to him, the swiveling camera looked just as it should. But Mel was the professional and he'd take her word for it. "Anything else?"

"Wet floor sign in front of the security panel. And the men's bathroom was closed when we walked by it.

Little things add up." She stood and nodded towards the exit of the exhibit. "Let's get out of here. No use getting our picture taken if we're not doing anything wrong."

"Let's get out of here and warn security, that's what you mean, right?" Mel's penchant for larceny and her moral flexibility normally didn't bother him, not anymore. But sometimes his sense of right and wrong conflicted with his mate's and Luke had to remind himself that she'd been raised to be a thief.

Mel scrunched up her face and tilted her head to the side. "That seems a bit rude. How would you feel if some stranger came in and interrupted your job? It's not any of our business."

He really shouldn't smile. "It's standard procedure to report a crime when you see it."

"What crime? All I see is a wet floor sign." She smiled brightly and Luke gave up fighting his smile.

"We're reporting this. If you think someone's going to rob the place, then it's definitely happening. And are you really going to let other thieves operate in our territory?" Denver didn't *quite* fall within pack territory, but as Luke's lions were the closest shifters to the city, he considered himself responsible.

"Art thieves don't care so much about territory. And if we talk to the guards it's going to raise some uncomfortable questions. We should just go." All playfulness had fallen from her face and she was anxious to leave.

And she had a point. He believed her without doubt, but a security guard wasn't going to take a wet floor sign and a closed bathroom as proof of a crime in progress. Besides, this wasn't a shifter problem. The chances of the thieves being shifters was low which meant this fell completely under human jurisdiction.

But Luke couldn't do nothing.

"We're calling in an anonymous tip. But then I'll drop it."

"It feels wrong to mess with someone's livelihood like that."

"And the fact that someone is messing with the livelihoods of museum employees?" Really, their differences were never more apparent than when talking about crime.

"My dear mate, that's what insurance is for. But if it will make you feel better, we can call it in."

It would. They'd made it to the entrance when another person crossed their path. Mel was a step in front of Luke and froze in place. Slowly her head turned and Luke followed her gaze to see another man looking right at her.

"Mel?" the man asked.

"Fuck," his mate whispered.

4

Mel's gaze snapped forward and she tugged on Luke's arm until they were through the doors and out in the bright Denver sun. She couldn't believe it, but her nose and eyes didn't lie. Her skin itched and she wanted to run, wanted to get as far away from the museum as she could and never come back.

"What was that about?" Luke asked. He seemed to sense her urge to run and held onto both of her shoulders, keeping her in place and offering her comfort. Only he could hold her like that and not make her feel trapped.

A few people rushed towards the museum doors as if they were racing to get inside, but otherwise the place was quiet. Still, Mel didn't want to talk in such an open space. She tugged out of Luke's hold and walked towards the parking lot, her mate following right behind. Once they were safely sitting in the vehicle she took a deep breath and stared out of the window. "Did I ever tell you about Belgrade?"

"With the jet-skis?"

"That was Barcelona."

"Then no." He reached out and laced their fingers together, grounding Mel in the present even as a ghost from her past tried to drag her away.

Her insides were shaking, even if she looked steady on the outside. She had too much discipline to give her nerves away, even to Luke. "I almost died in Belgrade and over a job that barely paid the rent." Okay, that might have been an exaggeration. The job could have bought her a modest house in a decent neighborhood, but it wasn't worth the blood she'd spilled. "The gallery I was hitting blew up. Killed a guard and two tourists and damn near took my leg off." If she closed her eyes she could still see the smoke, still smell it in the air trying to suffocate her. "Back then a new player got introduced at the last minute. And he just walked into that museum."

5

Luke could feel his mate's distress and he wanted to leap out of their vehicle and run after the person causing it, to show him that no one was allowed to hurt Mel. But she placed a hand on his arm to keep him in place. "We have to warn the museum," she said. "I know I was against it earlier, but it's one thing to steal and something completely different to kill."

On that they agreed. Luke pulled out his phone and looked up the number for the museum. When he dialed he wanted to growl in frustration as the number went directly to a voicemail account.

"Cops?" he suggested, following their earlier plan. If there was a possibility of a bomb, he wanted his mate far away and the museum visitors evacuated.

Mel shook her head. "That's where it went wrong last time. He blew it the second he heard sirens." She looked straight ahead and breathed deep several times before turning her gaze on him. "If we get the cops involved and Belgrade gets spooked, we're dooming whoever's left in the museum."

"Belgrade?"

"I never caught his name." Her fingers tapped against the door as if she were desperate to get out of the car.

"Is he a shifter?" Luke hadn't caught the scent, but Mel had been closer and she had the history with the thief.

She jerked her head from side to side. "Can't say for certain that he's human, but he's not one of us."

"Good." A hum of danger lit a spark in his veins and Luke wanted to run toward it. Things had been peaceful in the pack for the last two years and he wouldn't want anything else, but the lion in him was looking for a fight, and fighting a person who threatened his mate was just the kind of satisfaction he needed.

Mel's own lips curled up into a matching smile. She leaned over and kissed him, quick, harsh, and leaving him wanting more. She jerked back before he could grab on and deepen the kiss, but given the dark heat in her eyes it was clear she wanted more. "We have to be good," she said, her voice pure seduction. "Things are getting dangerous."

"Then let's show him what shifters are made of."

6

As they walked back into the museum Mel could feel herself slipping into her old role like she'd never left it. Before she'd only noticed the obvious flaws with the museum's security but now she was looking and she spotted three points of entry and four camera blind spots. She could clean this place out in a matter of minutes if she had the crew set up, but when Luke crossed into her line of sight she was reminded why she was there, and who she was now.

Sure, she still stole stuff from time to time, but she was no longer the unrepentant thief she'd once been. So she turned her mind from the weaknesses in the museum to the mission at hand, determining whether there was a bomb and getting rid of it before someone got hurt.

She pulled in a deep breath, but the scent of the visitors and cleaning products overwhelmed her and kept her from scenting anything that might have been explosive. She saw Luke's lungs fill, but he shook his head after a moment, encountering the same problem.

"He wouldn't want to cut off his escape," she said, voice low. "And he'd want something more showy than destructive."

"What does that mean?" Luke asked.

"He probably doesn't care about getting a huge body count. This is theft, not murder." She hoped. Belgrade had already shown he was willing to kill, she only hoped he considered the deaths collateral damage rather than the goal.

"So this is Die Hard?" her mate grinned at her and stepped close as a museum visitor passed them by. "Which one of us is Bruce Willis?"

"Yipee-ki-yay," Mel grinned back.

They sobered when a child's cry cut through their banter. At the other end of the gallery a young father was holding up a stuffed animal and trying to get the toddler to calm down. If Mel and Luke failed, the father and his child would have much greater worries and she didn't want to risk it.

"We can cover more ground if we split up. I'll take the lower level and any restricted areas. You take upstairs. We don't have a lot of time."

Mel had begun to turn away when Luke placed a hand on her arm. "I love you," he said, stealing a kiss.

"I love you, too," she kissed him back and hoped it wasn't a goodbye.

7

L uke watched Mel depart and his lion roared. He wanted to chase after her, to keep her safe from would be bombers and all the dangers of the world. But she wasn't a woman made to be protected. She was his partner in all things and capable of facing any challenge. Still, that didn't make her fire proof, which meant he had to act quickly and thoroughly to see this mission completed before it was too late.

He passed by the elevator without pausing and headed for the stairs that led to the upper level of the museum. His lion scratched inside his skin to get out but Luke kept it caged. Now was no time to shift, not unless he was going to take down his prey. There was no reason to alarm the patrons or bring down the guards.

Not yet.

He breathed in deep, trying to sort through the scents all around him and find something out of place. If it hadn't been for Mel's tip, he wouldn't have thought to look. Everything looked normal. When he saw a family with small children studying a painting by one of the masters he wanted to warn them to get out, but causing a panic would only make things worse, and Luke wasn't willing to do that.

He almost passed by a sign that said the west gallery was closed for maintenance work before tilting his head and *listening*. He and Mel had passed by earlier and there hadn't been a sign. No sounds came from the gallery and that only made him more suspicious. Maintenance work was never quiet.

He ducked under the sign and headed down the hall on silent feet, alert and ready to spring at any threat. The first two rooms off the gallery were empty, but Luke could hear the tiniest hints of activity coming from the third. He paused and took a deep breath, readying himself for the attack.

Luke stepped into the room and watched as the man from Belgrade confidently stripped a centuries old painting from its frame and rolled it up with the efficient moves of a professional.

"It wouldn't be wise to alert security," the man said without turning. "Really, no one's been hurt and I'm nearly finished." Belgrade had the faintest British accent that fit his thief persona perfectly. He fit the rolled painting into a tube and slung it over his back before turning around. He looked Luke up and down. "I can't say that you're the one I expected."

Luke shrugged. "And yet here I am. Now put the painting down and we can both walk away." Not that he cared *that* much about the painting, but Mel was looking for the bomb and she needed as much time as he could give her.

The thief rolled his eyes. "Not going to happen. Step aside."

Luke didn't move.

Belgrade heaved a put upon sigh and pulled his phone out of his pocket. His fingers flicked over the screen until he pressed something decisively and then flashed it towards Luke. "I'm not here to fight you. And if you want to get out with all your bits attached I'd suggest you move." He tossed the phone at Luke and grinned when Luke caught it.

Luke didn't want to take his eyes off the thief, but he spared a glance at the phone and saw a timer counting down from three minutes. "A bomb?" it came out more growl than words.

"A distraction. Now, shall we go?"

Luke's heart kicked into high gear. Three minutes was no time at all, but he wasn't letting this thief escape.

He let go of the phone and pounced.

8

Mel heard the beeping before she found the bomb and she knew something had gone wrong. She had to believe Luke was okay or she was never going to get this thing done. She followed the sound of the beeping and found a small device wedged behind a trash can. Was it the only one? No clue, and she didn't have time to look for more.

How exactly did one dispose of a bomb?

And how long until it went off?

She could have really used Krista at a time like this. A little magic would have gone a long way.

When in doubt, she did the one thing she'd always known how to do. She ran.

Shifter speed had her out of the building, device in hand, in a handful of seconds, she was across the parking lot in a blink after that. A large lot stood just far enough away from anything that she knew it would have to do. She gently set the device off and ran back, covering as much distance and hoping it did the trick. She couldn't hear the beeping anymore and she didn't know how much time had past. But a wave of heat licked at her heels and the sound of a blast made her ears popped. Mel didn't stop running. There could be a fireball chasing after her. She didn't exactly know how these things worked, but she'd seen enough movies.

But no fireball appeared and by the time she got back to the museum Luke was standing at the entrance, hair mussed and a bruise blooming under his left eye.

"I'm going to kill him for touching you," Mel vowed.

Her mate grinned, then he sniffed the air and his expression tightened. "Why were you outside the building? And why do you smell like smoke?"

She shrugged. "The bomb started beeping. Had to get rid of it."

His eyes went wide and she waited for him to detonate, his explosion sure to be much more impressive than anything Belgrade had managed to pull off. But he took a deep breath and pulled the rage back in. "He's tied up inside with all of his gear piled on top of him. I think security can deal with him at this point."

"So you're saying he'll take the blame for anything that goes missing?" Mel's eyes lit up at the possibility.

"No stealing!" Luke hissed. They began moving towards the parking lot as a police cruiser pulled in front of the building. They kept their heads down and moved quickly, not wanting to be drawn into the fray.

Once they were inside their vehicle and driving down a nearby street Mel couldn't stop laugher bubbling up from inside of her. "What are we doing for our next relaxing vacation?"

Luke held it in for a minute before his own laugh joined hers. "Never a dull moment with you, mate."

They shared a grin as he sped off towards their hotel. They'd survived. It was time to celebrate.

WHAT TO READ NEXT:
HUNTING SEASON

This werewolf will protect his mate.

Owen has one job: keep Stasia from being abducted. Easier said than done when his fiercely independent client tries to fire him the moment they meet. His werewolf senses howl to life and he's certain of one thing: Stasia is his.

She's sick of cocky men.

When her wealthy father hires a bodyguard, Stasia says no. Not exactly a smart move after someone tried to nab her off the street. But she doesn't need a babysitter. Especially not a cheerfully overbearing bodyguard who makes her heart pound and her fantasies run wild.

When Stasia is yanked out of her glittering world and into Owen's she'll need to grapple with an impossible new reality that includes werewolves, silver bullets, and fated mates. Is she ready to embrace her new world?

Or will she run back to a universe of glittering high rises and leave her destiny behind? Step into the world of Guarded by the Shifter where a team of ex-military bodyguards are also werewolves and fated mates are just one job away.

Check it out!

ALSO BY KATE RUDOLPH

Dragon Brides
Dragon Princes. Fierce Women. Love.
Fated mates, fierce women, and dragon princes are
ready to find their mates.

Crux

Ranger

Saber

Cipher

Storm

Drake

Asher

Knox

Flint

Pine

Guarded by the Shifter

Werewolf. Bodyguard. Mate.
The origins of these shifters are shrouded in mystery, but they're determined to protect their mates from any harm that comes their way.
Also available in audio!
Hunting Season
On the Prowl
Stalking Magic
Hungry for the Wolf
Wolf Cursed (novella)
Wolf's Temptation

Alien Mates: Planet Exile

Guerran is no place for pretty human women. But these alien heroes will protect their mates!
Also available in audio!

Exile's Hunter
Exile's Adored

Zulir Warrior Mates

Kidnapped humans. Alien Warriors. Electric wings.

The Zulir Warrior Mates series brings you human heroines and heroes abducted from Earth who find love – and wings! – with the alien warriors who rescue them.

Also available in audio!

Synnr's Saint

Synnr's Hope

Synnr's Spark

Synnr's Kiss

Synnr's Ride

Mated to the Alien

Fated Mate Alien Romance

Detyens are doomed to die young if they don't find their fated mates.

Follow along as these mated pairs fight off aliens, corrupt dictators, prejudiced humans, pirates, and more! The books can be read or listened to in any order, though some characters show up in multiple stories.

Select books available in audio.

Pick a book and jump into the action today!

Ruwen

Tyral

Stoan

Cyborg

Krayter

Kayleb

Shayn

Braxtyn

Doryan

Dekon

Detyen Warriors

Detya was destroyed a hundred years ago. These doomed warriors are out to find justice... and their mates.

The Detyen Warriors series brings you kick butt heroines, alpha alien heroes, fated mates, and relationships strong enough to span the galaxy!

The entire series is also available in audio!

Soulless

Ruthless

Heartless

Faultless

Endless

Alien Holiday Romance

Christmas... in space????
These alien holiday romances look beyond Earth's winter holidays and ring in the season across the galaxy!
Select titles available in audio.
Snowed in with the Alien Beast
The Alien's Winter Gift
The Alien Reindeer's Wild Ride
Trapped with her Alien Mate

Alien Outlaws

Outlaws, schemes, and love... it's all there in the Alien Outlaws series...

Andie Munster is sick of life on Ixilta, the planet she got dumped on after being abducted from Earth six years ago. And when the mysterious and dangerous Xandr shows up looking for a way off the planet, she's half-prisoner, half-co-conspirator in a wild rush to escape.

Rogue Alien's Escape

Rogue Alien's Woman

Rogue Alien's Secret

Rogue Alien's Legacy

Find more by Kate Rudolph at www.katerudolph.net

ABOUT KATE RUDOLPH

Kate Rudolph is a paranormal and sci-fi romance writer who lives in Indiana. She loves writing about kick butt heroines and the steamy heroes who love them. She's been devouring romance novels since she was too young to be reading them and had to hide her books so no one would take them away. She couldn't imagine a better job in this world than writing romances and sharing them with her fellow readers.

If you enjoyed this story, please consider leaving a review.